He needed her love...

but would a haunted past keep them apart?

To Clary,

Awakening Heart

When I read
the back of this book,
I thought it would be
one you would enjoy!

Love
Rhonda

Awakening Heart

MELODY CARLSON

BETHANY HOUSE PUBLISHERS
MINNEAPOLIS, MINNESOTA 55438

Awakening Heart
Copyright © 1998
Melody Carlson

Cover illustration by William Graf
Cover design by the Lookout Design Group

Published by Bethany House Publishers
A Ministry of Bethany Fellowship International
11300 Hampshire Avenue South
Minneapolis, Minnesota 55438

Printed in the United States of America by
Bethany Press International, Minneapolis, Minnesota 55438

Library of Congress Cataloging-in-Publication Data

Carlson, Melody.
    Awakening heart / by Melody Carlson.
        p. cm. — (Portraits)
      ISBN 1-55661-998-7 (pbk.)
      I. Title. II. Series: Portraits (Minneapolis, Minn.)
PS3553.A73257A9   1998
813'.54—dc21   97-45445
                                              CIP

With heartfelt gratitude to my "old" critique group:

Heather Harpham-Kopp, Linda Shands,
Linda Clair, Michele Wilson, Tonya Johnson

Thanks for your encouragement—
and for believing in Emma

Portraits

MELODY CARLSON's talent is reflected in her award-winning career as an author of nearly twenty books, most of them for children and young adults, including *Jessica*, a SPRINGSONG BOOK, *Benjamin's Box*, *Tupsu*, and THE ALLISON CHRONICLES series. Melody resides with her husband and two teenage sons in Oregon.

Monday's child is full of grace.
Tuesday's child is fair of face.
Wednesday's child is full of woe.
Thursday's child has far to go.
Friday's child is loving and giving.
Saturday's child works hard for a living.
Sunday's child is blithe and gay, and good and
kind in every way.

One

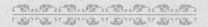

*E*mma poured her second cup of coffee and turned the page of the *Des Moines Morning Herald.* Saturday was the only day she took time to read the news, and then only briefly. Headlines depressed her—always someone else's heartache or shame plastered across the front page in unfeeling black and white. Even when she washed the newsprint from her fingers, the stories remained indelibly pressed in her mind.

"Emma Jane," complained Grandma from the tiny front room. "What's that yappy dog barking about next door? She's been at it all morning." The worn Naugahyde recliner squeaked as Grandma shifted her bulky frame, her groans in accompaniment to the chair. Emma sighed. These familiar sounds were more aggravating than usual today. She folded her paper, and walked into the living room. *Living* room—what a contradiction in terms.

"What's the matter with that animal?" Grandma scowled as if the annoyance were all Emma's fault.

Emma avoided the penetrating gaze, instead moving her eyes to her grandmother's swollen feet. They seemed to ooze right out of her threadbare corduroy slippers.

"I don't know, Grandma," answered Emma, supressing the urge to throw something. "Maybe Miss Finley hasn't let her out yet. You know how Bitsy gets herself all worked up." Emma sipped her now lukewarm coffee, hoping her answer would pacify the old woman.

"Don't I know it! And here I sit, day in, day out, subjected to that dreadful noise. Why anyone in their right mind keeps a snippy little mutt like that is beyond me!" Grandma's voice grew loud and grating. Emma wondered if poor Miss Finley could hear her ranting through the thin wall that separated their apartments.

Emma never looked forward to weekends the way most people did. Not that she particularly liked her job that much, but Saturdays with Grandma always stretched her endurance to the limit. It was on weekends that she longed for her own home—to do nothing, to sing out loud, or even to walk around in her underwear, if she wanted to.

"Run over and see what's up, Emma," ordered Grandma. "Maybe you can shut that stupid dog up!"

To argue would be pointless, and to pretend she hadn't heard would only increase the volume of the demand. Besides, Emma hadn't visited with Miss Finley since Christmas. Surely even her questionable company would be preferable to Grandma's right now.

Bitsy barked madly as Emma rang the bell. Miss Finley's door, like theirs, needed painting again. She rang once more, then walked over to the front window. Year-round, Miss Finley kept faded plastic flowers poked into the window box. Sometimes, especially in the cold of winter, Emma longed to rip out those vulgar-looking blooms and toss them into the trash bin. Now she leaned over and peeked inside. She spotted Bitsy leaping about, yipping and jumping like an overwound mechanical toy.

Then Emma noticed a pair of fluffy pink slippers and a flowery bathrobe on the living room floor. She peered more closely. It was Miss Finley! Her pale face was motionless, and her mouth gaped open. Emma beat on the window until she feared the glass might shatter, and Bitsy flew into an even wilder frenzy. But Miss Finley didn't budge.

Emma raced back to Grandma's and grabbed the phone. Her hands were shaking, and her fingers fumbled with the number—was it 1-1-9 or 9-1-1?

"What in the world is going on, Emma?"

Over Grandma's raspy squawk, Emma was finally able to dial

the correct digits for the emergency dispatch operator and told the calm woman on the other end to send help. As instructed, Emma called the apartment manager and asked for a key.

Before long, the sounds of sirens screamed down the avenue, and an emergency vehicle pulled into the parking lot. Emma leaned over the balcony, waving her arms to signal the paramedics. Uniformed technicians bounded up the stairs just as the manager unlocked Miss Finley's door. Bitsy's startled yelps added to the chaos, and Emma scooped up the poor little dog and tossed her into her grandmother's apartment, ignoring Grandma's protests as she closed the door firmly behind her.

The paramedics were crouched around Miss Finley, equipment in hand, poking, prodding, examining. One by one, they all stood.

"We're too late," said the tallest one in a matter-of-fact tone. "She's been dead two, maybe three hours max. Looks like cardiac arrest." They packed up their gear, then turned to the apartment manager. "We'll notify the coroner, but this is Saturday, you know. It might take a while for him to get here. You might want to make other arrangements."

The balding manager threw up his hands, "I dunno nothing about this kinda thing. Never had a tenant die on me before. I didn't hardly know her. Can't you just take her?"

"Nope, it's against regs. Might be quicker to have the funeral home come out, but you have to sign an agreement."

"Not me," protested the manager.

"Well, you better call someone then."

The manager frowned. "I thought you guys knew what to do. . . ."

Emma wanted to scream. How dare they stand around arguing about what to do with poor Miss Finley as if she weren't a real person—or had been until very recently. For the second time that morning, Emma felt capable of violence—she really thought she might punch Mr. Potts in the face.

She stared at Miss Finley's lime green sponge-curlers, still tightly wound in the mousy gray hair, and Emma felt her knees begin to wobble, and she clutched the door frame for support. "You can't just leave her lying there," she said weakly.

The three paramedics turned and studied her, as if they hadn't noticed her before. "You know this lady? You a relative?" asked one of the uniformed men.

"I'm her neighbor—and friend, Emma Davis."

"Well, maybe you can take care of this, then." He pulled a dog-eared business card from his pocket. "Here you go. My uncle runs this joint. He's a decent guy. I can call him for you on the cellular phone, if you like."

She stared at the flowery lettering—Eternal Rest Mortuary Services. She nodded mutely, signed a paper, and they were gone.

Emma stood alone on the balcony, unwilling to go back inside and submit to Grandma's inquisition. Yet she felt even more uneasy about being alone in Miss Finley's apartment. Emma knew Grandma would probably say Miss Finley was in heaven now and that was only her shell on the floor. After all, Miss Finley was a religious woman. Still, somehow Emma couldn't picture Miss Finley with wings and a harp, perched on a cloud. To her, Miss Finley appeared just plain dead.

Emma stared blankly out on the gray morning and shivered in the cold. Everything seemed surreal. One moment a person is alive, and the next, she is gone.

Finally, a long, slate-colored hearse slid to a stop in the apartment complex parking lot. A stoop-shouldered man in a dark suit emerged and quickly approached, followed by a lanky, younger guy. He murmured something that sounded sympathetic, then handed her a form. She signed without reading the fine print, eager for them to take Miss Finley away.

After the hearse left, Emma stood on the balcony wondering what to do next.

Seeing the door to Miss Finley's apartment still ajar, she stepped inside. She should probably notify someone about Miss Finley's death. As she looked for an address book, she noticed a little red light glowed in the kitchenette, signaling that the electric teapot was still on. She unplugged it and poured the steaming contents down the sink. It left an ugly brown streak across the scrubbed white porcelain. She turned on the tap and watched as the water ran, finally erasing the last traces of Miss Finley's morning tea.

Emma had known Miss Finley for almost twenty-five years—ever since Emma and her sister, Fran, had come to live with Grandma. Could it have been that long? She remembered the first time Miss Finley had invited Emma for tea. That had been on a Saturday, too. Six-year-old Emma had been sitting outside on the cold cement steps, leaning into the wrought-iron handrail, and wishing she could disappear—the same way her parents had disappeared from her life after their terrible accident.

That day, Miss Finley had been on her way upstairs with a grocery bag in her arms. Emma remembered how pretty the woman had looked in her floral print sundress. Of course, Miss Finley had been much younger back then. Actually, about the age Emma was now. How very odd.

"Hello, love," Miss Finley had said brightly. She called everyone "love." It had something to do with her being British. "Care to come in for a spot of tea? I just bought some yummy-looking biscuits—or, rather, cookies, as you Yanks call them."

Being six and fond of cookies, Emma had accepted. Miss Finley's apartment had intrigued her with its vibrant colors and modern furnishings. Now the colors seemed garish, and the furniture, with its peeling vinyl edges, tasteless and tired.

A small pink address book lay next to the phone. Emma thumbed through its nearly empty pages until she found a Finley—in Liverpool, England.

"Hello? Is this a relative of Maggie Finley?"

"Maggie? Why yes . . . I'm Maggie's aunt."

"I'm Emma Davis, Maggie Finley's neighbor . . . and I'm sorry to be the one to tell you . . . but—well, unfortunately, your niece was found dead this morning. A heart attack, I think. . . ."

There was a long silence. "Oh my—poor little Maggie." The aunt was sobbing now.

She gave Emma the number of an uncle in Los Angeles who could help out, and Emma gave him a call. He offered to cover the expenses if Emma could handle the arrangements. She agreed.

"Just what is going on around here?" demanded Grandma

when Emma returned to their apartment. Bitsy quivered in a corner with a pathetic look in her eyes, as if she'd lost her only friend in the world. Emma supposed it was true. "And why in heaven's name did you dump Miss Finley's dog in here?" The old woman's tone softened. "Is Maggie okay, Emma? I heard sirens. I just know something's wrong."

"Yes, Grandma, something's very wrong. Miss Finley is dead. Probably had a heart attack early this morning."

"Dear me! So that's why the dog was barking her head off. I just *knew* something was amiss as soon as I got up this morning. I always sense these things, you know. And when this dog wouldn't stop barking—"

Emma interrupted the monologue. "Grandma, I've got lots to do. I agreed to handle the funeral details for Miss Finley."

అ   అ   అ   అ

By noon, Emma had completed much of the arrangements by phone. Oddly enough, the procedure seemed almost familiar—selecting flowers, music, the casket.

Then, at the funeral director's request, she returned to Miss Finley's apartment to search for some appropriate burial clothing. She tried to imagine what the woman might choose. What does one wear to one's own funeral? After thumbing through the sparse but orderly selection of office wear, she discovered a garment bag stashed way in the back. Zipped inside was a lovely cream-colored, street-length dress. It looked to be about twenty years old, trimmed in lace, with a yellowed price tag still hanging from the sleeve. It hadn't come cheap, not even way back in those days—which was odd, since Miss Finley was a fanatical bargain shopper. It had to have been a wedding gown, although Emma had never heard her neighbor mention any romantic interest. She wondered what had happened, why the wedding had never taken place. Surely Miss Finley would want to wear her dress this once—even if it was for a funeral rather than a wedding.

After delivering the garment, Emma walked sadly back to the apartment, contemplating Miss Finley's unfulfilled and insignificant little life. Who was her mystery lover? What had gone wrong? Maybe he'd died in Vietnam. A wartime romance.

Or maybe it was more like Emma's own story. Even after almost seven years, it still hurt. But then perhaps today was as good a day as any to mourn lost love. So for the first time in years, she allowed his face to force its way back into her consciousness.

She'd been sure that he'd loved her, and almost as sure that she loved him. But he knew about her fears, and still he insisted she come to France that summer. He knew she was afraid to fly, afraid to visit strange countries, afraid of so many things. Yet he would not take no for an answer. He went to Paris without her.

And that was the end of it. She shook her head as the apartment building came into sight. The memory wasn't painful anymore. It was almost a disappointment—she'd expected to cry.

Two

*E*mma pushed open the heavy, carved door of the funeral parlor. Walls, chairs, carpet—all were a nauseating shade of mauve. Why in the world would anyone purposely choose such a depressing color for a mortuary?

She recognized the man who'd helped her earlier with the arrangements. Today he wore a shiny black suit, complete with coordinating mauve tie. He smiled, in a funereal sort of way, and shook her hand. His grasp was smooth and almost slippery, and Emma suppressed the desire to run into the bathroom and wash her hands. Instead, she shoved them into her pockets and took a seat in the second row of padded chairs.

She had decided Saturday that the main chapel would be too large, but now, as Emma looked about this empty room, she wondered if a service would be necessary at all. She'd notified Miss Finley's employer. Surely, some of her fellow workers would show. Perhaps even the uncle who'd footed the bill.

She wished she hadn't come. She hadn't been to a funeral since her parents—

"This must be it, Gladys," whispered a voice from behind Emma.

"Poor Margaret," said the other. "I never even knew she had a weak heart."

"Actually, I didn't know her that well. But I assumed by her accent she'd come from England, though I never asked."

"It sure was nice of the boss to give the morning off to those who wanted to attend her service. Maybe if it's not too long, we can stop by Lucky's for pie afterward."

The funeral director stepped up to the podium and cleared his throat. Maggie's pastor was attending a seminar this week, and the funeral director had offered to do the eulogy. She heard his voice, but the words were lost as she stared blankly at the roses in front of the pale blue casket. Soon the roses blurred, and instead of one casket, there were two. Two blue caskets in a stuffy, crowded room. Fran sat on one side of her, Grandma on the other. Mournful organ music filled the air, accompanied by much sniffling and nose-blowing. The three of them were smothered afterward by people who looked down from their lofty height. They seemed all hands. Emma didn't want them to touch her. She didn't even know them—

Suddenly, a hand patted her shoulder, and she started. "Are you all right, miss?" asked the funeral director. The room was empty.

"I'm fine—thank you." She felt as if she couldn't breathe. The air in the parlor tasted old and stale and tainted with death, and she bolted for the door.

As soon as she was outside the door, she sucked in the cool air. Even the acrid smell of diesel fumes was an improvement.

The bus stop was right across the street, but Emma decided to walk. She never drove. She wouldn't admit it to anyone, but this, too, was due to fear. Fear that her car, like her parents', would sail off some unknown cliff and plunge her to certain death. She knew it was ridiculous, but she was resigned to the fact that this cloying fear was a part of her. And so each year she purchased a bus pass. It pretty much took her wherever she wanted to go, which usually wasn't far. She never went far from home.

Thursday's child has far to go. The cadence of the old rhyme reverberated through her mind, mocking her. She remembered the first time her mother had read that rhyme in the big picture book, pointing out that Emma had been born on a Thursday. But as Emma studied the sweet pictures of childish faces, she secretly wished she'd been born on Sunday, instead. Sunday's child seemed to make out the best of all of them. In fact, once, when she was older, she'd actually double-checked her baby book to make certain of her birthday. Of course, it was true. Yet here she was—at thirty-one—and she'd never gone anywhere. She should have been Wednesday's child—"Full of woe." She'd had her share of *that*.

"Silly old rhyme," she muttered as she hurried across the street.

A horn blasted, and tires skidded to a stop. She looked up in shock to see a shiny red hood just inches from her elbow. Inside, a group of teenagers laughed loudly, teasing their careless driver.

"Hey, watch where you're going!" yelled the pock-faced youth from behind the wheel.

"Aw, lighten up," said the stringy blonde next to him. "Can't you see it's just an old lady?"

The girl's words hit hard. *Old lady?* Emma scurried to the safety of the sidewalk and caught a glimpse of herself in Franklin's Department Store window as the car screeched off again. Her shoulders were slumped, and her long, lifeless hair was pulled back in a barrette on the nape of her neck in her usual style. Her face was pale and devoid of makeup, and her heavy tweed overcoat seemed to swallow her. She did look like an elderly woman; if she'd been pushing a rusty shopping cart, she might have even passed for a bag lady.

Beyond her sad image she noticed the rigid mannequins with flowing hair flaunted the latest spring fashions. They hinted of fun and sun, and a life someone else lived—not her. She turned away and continued down the street.

Emma paused in front of the travel agency. Each evening after work, she waited for the bus here in front of this little office. Inside, a pretty woman sometimes waved at Emma. Today, she waved again. Emma smiled and returned the anonymous greeting. She didn't even know the woman's name, yet she was part of Emma's daily routine.

In the window hung the same travel poster that had been there forever. The sun had faded the once-warm colors to tones of blues and purples, but the tropical oasis still looked tempting—with a magenta-colored girl in a bikini stretched out on the sun-drenched beach. A faint longing stirred within Emma—the longing to break free, to escape.

In the past she had secretly harbored that idea, playing it out step by step in her mind. It was like an invisible security blanket—something she could cling to. Like a promise of what could be. Over the years, she had saved a fair amount of money—"for a rainy day," though she used to think of it as her "run-away" money. Now she rarely thought of it at all.

She crossed the next street and entered Lou's Coffee Shop. It was one place she almost felt comfortable, and the friendly waitress, Marie, was almost like family. The aroma of fresh coffee and pastry wafted through the air in a familiar welcome.

"Hi, Emma," called Marie, from behind the counter, tucking a pencil behind one ear. "You're a little early today. What's the occasion?"

"Oh, I went to a funeral this morning and wasn't going in to work until noon. Coffee and a cinnamon roll, please."

Marie set the pastry before Emma and frowned. "I'm sorry, honey. Was it someone close?" she asked as she poured the coffee.

"Not really. A neighbor."

"Funerals are so depressing." Marie let out a big sigh. "When I die, I just want to be cremated. And then my folks can throw a big party or something." Marie laughed her big, hearty laugh and Emma smiled. The woman had a way of making people feel better. "Did I tell you, my daughter out in California just had a baby girl? I'm a grandma now—can you believe it?"

"You're kidding, Marie. You don't look old enough to be a grandma."

Marie patted her tinted curls and stood a little straighter. "Why, thanks, Emma. Well, I got an early start. Not like you kids nowadays. Seems everyone waits until they're thirty-something before they even think about marriage, let alone babies. How 'bout you, Emma? You ever think about settling down, raising a family?"

Emma looked down at her coffee and tried to come up with a glib answer, but none came.

"Sorry 'bout that, honey. It's none of my business, but you know me—just an old busybody. Really, Emma, you're not getting any younger, and you're still nice looking, if you'd just fix yourself up a little." Marie turned and preened in the foggy mirror behind the counter.

Emma forced a laugh. "You may be right. Some kids almost ran me down this morning, but the worst of it was when they called me an *old lady*!"

Marie chuckled. "Well, you're no old lady, Emma. But sometimes you act like one. You need to live a little—have some fun. Maybe a vacation or something—"

"Oh, I have my grandma. I couldn't leave her—"

"Well, let the old ball 'n chain hire a gal to come in and stay with her. You need to quit making excuses, Emma. Life's too short."

Emma glanced up at the clock behind the counter. It wasn't time to go to work yet, but this conversation was hitting a nerve. "Thanks, Marie." She wiped her mouth and laid a tip on the counter. "I'll think about your suggestion."

Emma strolled along the sidewalk, hoping everyone else would be out to lunch by now.

A man in paint-splotched coveralls was carefully repainting the lettering of the sign by the front entrance: "Smith and Grant, Certified Public Accountants." She remembered when that sign had gone up—almost a dozen years ago. She'd been so thrilled to be hired by this impressive new accounting firm. Rick Grant had struck her as a fine young man. Now she could barely tolerate him.

She went upstairs and hung up her coat. The office was empty except for Bea, the front receptionist, and she nodded at Emma, then turned back to her crossword puzzle magazine.

Emma had picked up the pile of papers on her desk and started on the first account. Some papers were missing, and Rick would be at lunch now, so she could retrieve them without having to speak to him. She slipped into his dark office and pulled open the lower drawer of a file cabinet.

Just as she closed the drawer something squeaked, and Emma turned to see Rick Grant swiveling around in the chair behind his desk. His eyes reminded her of a pig—small and bright and stuck in his face like raisins in a pork roast.

"Well, well, Emma," he began in that condescending tone she detested. "Heard you were at a funeral this morning—so sorry. Anything I can do to help?" He walked toward her, and she rose to her full height, holding the file in front of her like a shield.

"I was just getting the Yates file, sir." She glanced over her shoulder toward the open door. "Sorry to disturb you. I thought you were at lunch."

He smiled and leaned against the doorjamb, loosely folding his arms against his chest. "We haven't really talked in quite a while. I almost get the impression you've been avoiding me. Now, you wouldn't be avoiding me, would you, Emma?" He reached over and touched her arm. Even in the dim light, the large gold band on his finger glinted, even though everyone knew his wedding ring meant nothing to him.

She pulled away. "Excuse me, Mr. Grant. I have work to do." She moved toward the door, but he blocked her way. She looked over her shoulder, hoping for a witness, but Bea's desk was empty now. Emma tried to mask her frustration, knowing her face was like an open book. She told herself that she could handle this. After all, she was a grown woman. She squared her shoulders and moved purposely toward the door.

"Come on, Emma, don't be such a stick. Don't you ever want to have any fun?" He reached for her. But when she jerked away, the contents of the file flew out of her hands and lay in a jumbled pile all over the floor. She looked down at the papers, face burning in humiliation. More than anything she wanted to stand up to him, to tell him off, once and for all. Instead, she stumbled past him, angry tears burning in her eyes. The sound of his mocking laughter echoed through the deserted hallway. Why did she let him treat her like this?

She didn't return until the lunch hour ended. Everyone was at work—business as usual. The Yates file lay on her desk in a conspicuous heap. She worked in quiet humiliation. Did they all know what a fool Rick had made of her today? She tried not to look at the clock as the afternoon crawled along.

Just before five her phone rang. "Hi, sis, how ya doing?" asked Fran brightly, in her I-need-a-favor voice.

"I'm okay, Fran. I thought you were coming to Miss Finley's funeral today—"

"Oh, was that today? Well, it figures, since I'm in a fine mess right now. I totally forgot that Roger's boss wants us to go to his cabin this weekend for a management retreat. I really need someone to watch the kids. I already talked to Grandma, and she said you guys could come over. But I wanted to make sure it was okay with you first. You're not busy, are you, Emma?"

"No," said Emma, dismissing her earlier reservation. "I'm not busy—as usual. When are you leaving?"

"Friday afternoon. But I'll ask my neighbor to come over until you get off work."

Emma agreed and hung up. A weekend with a husband by a lake sounded like heaven to her. No matter how much Fran complained about Roger or the kids, her sister's life was a dream.

At last Emma turned off the computer and went outside to wait for her bus. She stared at the taunting travel poster. How she hated the magenta girl! The little clock on the door sign said the office was open until six. Emma glanced at her watch. Half past five. She looked at the poster again, and for the first time in conscious memory, she did something completely unplanned and totally impulsive. She didn't stop to think, to weigh, to measure, to rationalize, to reason, or to deliberate. Instead, she stepped away from the bus stop, pushed open the door, and walked in.

The pretty woman who had waved to Emma was seated behind the desk, studying the computer screen. Up close, she actually looked older than Emma. Perhaps it was the way she dressed and her hairstyle that suggested youth.

Hearing the door open, the woman looked up. "Hello. May I help you?"

Well, yes, I—uh—I don't have an appointment, but I wanted to inquire—"

"Linda," called someone from the back room, "I need you for a minute."

The woman named Linda gestured toward a chair. "Why don't you have a seat, and I'll be right back."

Emma considered slipping out, but she didn't want to offend this nice woman. Instead, she walked over and examined a large globe. She slowly turned it and watched as patches of green and gold and blue whirled past—so many places she'd never seen. She compared her bleak life to the magenta girl in the poster—even a faded cardboard character had more fun than Emma Davis! And in that same instant, she knew. Maybe it was Miss Finley's funeral, or that jerk, Rick Grant. Or maybe the globe was just making her dizzy. But somehow she knew she had to go—somewhere. Anywhere. She had to do something before she ended up like Miss Finley.

She spun the globe hard, and for a moment she watched the continents merge in a colorful kaleidoscope. She closed her eyes and stopped the spinning motion with one finger. It was a little game she and Fran had played at the public library. Usually, though, Emma's finger landed in the middle of the ocean, and she'd "drowned" and lost her turn.

She was afraid to look, thinking her finger was in the ocean somewhere. But when she did, she found her fingertip planted in the South Pacific. She peeled it off to reveal a good-sized island. She leaned over and peered at the globe. Such small writing. "Papua New Guinea," she said out loud. She'd never even heard of the place.

"Sorry about the wait," said the agent. "My name is Linda."

"I'm Emma Davis," she said, hoping to sound confident. "I'd like to find out about going to Papua New Guinea."

The next few minutes passed in a blur. Emma was handed a brochure picturing a beautiful tropical bird on the cover. Inside were photos of sandy beaches, towering palm trees, exotic flowers. She was sold. The paper work was begun for a cruise departing San Francisco in just ten days. Only an inside cabin was available on such short notice. No windows. Fortunately, Emma wasn't claustrophobic.

"And exactly where in New Guinea will you be heading?"

Emma studied the little map on the back of the brochure. "Lae," she announced with false confidence, reading the name of the centrally located coastal town.

Linda made some entries on her computer and then requested a fairly large deposit. Emma wrote out the check without blinking.

"You'll have to fill out these passport and visa papers tonight." Linda handed her a stack of forms. "I'll fax them tomorrow. And you'll need to get a passport photo taken first thing in the morning. Then all that's left is packing and tying up loose ends. That should keep you busy enough. Stop by tomorrow and I'll give you the details and an exact total cost for the trip."

Linda put out her hand. "It's nice to meet you finally, Emma. If there's anything else I can do to make your trip more pleasant, just let me know."

Emma thanked her and left. She felt partly numbed, partly frightened. But best of all, she felt alive. She pulled out her bus pass, wondering how in the world she could pull this trip off.

Three

"How was the funeral?" yelled Grandma over the blaring TV. "Okay, I guess." Emma closed the door and glanced around the messy apartment. Newspapers and magazines littered the floor, and a tray of dirty dishes balanced precariously on the arm of the chair at Grandma's elbow. Emma picked up the food tray, scooted the walker out of the way with her foot, and turned down the TV on her way to the kitchen.

"My legs are feeling better. Maybe I should have gone, after all. You know, I always liked to go to funerals," said Grandma in her philosophical tone. "Oh, I know it sounds morbid—and it's not that I haven't had my share of suffering, you know—but there's something about a good funeral that's always fascinated me—"

Emma turned on the garbage disposal and drowned out her grandmother's latest discourse. She fed the gurgling disposal the leftovers of Grandma's lunch—the same meal Emma had left in the refrigerator this morning, now reduced to mush. Then she opened a can of soup, sliced some cheddar cheese, and threw together a green salad. These she arranged on a clean tray with crackers and a cup of Sanka.

"—Yes, as I always say, I'd rather be a guest at a funeral than the main attraction." Grandma continued without missing a beat. "Did Frannie call you today? She wants us to come watch Shane and Rosie for the weekend. I told her we would. Change of scenery'll do me good. I get so blessed tired of staring at these four walls all day, and you know Frannie has cable TV."

Emma placed the dinner tray before her and wondered why Grandma said "we" when it was Emma who would do all the work. Not that she didn't love her niece and nephew. They were nice kids, even if they were a little spoiled. But she couldn't help resenting the way her sister and grandmother always assumed she had nothing better to do than to baby-sit. Well, that would soon change.

"Canned soup again?" croaked Grandma. "Emma, can't you rustle up something else for a change? You know I hate canned soup. I don't think there's any nutritional value in it at all. And I read in the paper about a lady who found a severed fingertip in her can of lima bean soup—"

"Sorry, Grandma. I've got paper work to do tonight, so canned soup will have to do. Besides, this isn't lima bean—it's chicken gumbo."

The old woman jerked up her head and squinted at Emma, probably surprised that she would use such a sharp tone with her. But Emma picked up her things and headed for her room. Sighing, she laid the travel-agency folder across the tidy surface of her student-sized desk—the same desk that she'd had since fourth grade. Her room still smelled of Bitsy, along with the faint aroma of lavender. Grandma had insisted she get rid of the little dog, and fortunately a neighbor downstairs had offered to take her just this morning.

She paced back and forth across the matted brown carpet. One moment, she felt like a bird ready to test her wings; the next, like a caged animal who had lost the will to live. Guilt weighed on her like a bag of bricks. Grandma needed her—Fran needed her. . . .

Suddenly Emma envisioned Miss Finley, laid out in her coffin—the sad remnant of a life that had never been fully lived. Only instead of Miss Finley's face, she saw her own. The vision chilled her, and for the first time in ages, she prayed. It was a wordless prayer—perhaps just a desperate cry from the depth of her heart—but it was genuine.

She filled out the papers, going over each item with meticulous care, as if for one of Rick Grant's most valuable clients. Tomorrow she'd give her notice. She wouldn't state the reason she was leaving. Maybe he'd get the picture—would even fear sexual harassment charges. But she doubted it. People like Rick weren't afraid of anything.

❧ ❧ ❧ ❧

Emma rode the bus to work with a sense of anticipation. She'd called ahead about the passport photo, and the photographer was able to fit her in before eight. It took less than five minutes for him to take the shots and another ten to develop the film.

She studied the pale, sober-looking face in the picture as she rode the bus on into town. Was it really her? The wide, hazel eyes and thin nose hadn't changed much since childhood, but the person in the photo seemed like a stranger just the same. Her even features weren't unattractive, but something about her face reminded her of a tightly closed rosebud. When the bus reached her stop, Emma strode into the travel agency and handed Linda the papers and photos with a sigh of relief. She wanted this trip confirmed, written in stone, and the sooner the better—before she changed her mind or lost her nerve.

Linda was pleased. "Great! I'll fax these right away. Fortunately, I know someone who can fast-track this stuff. Any questions before I send them off?"

"I'm sure it's all there. I went over everything very carefully."

"Well, Emma, I think you're in for a real treat. In fact, I envy you. I'd simply love to be able to just take off like that."

"Really? I figured a glamorous job like yours would take you just about anywhere you wanted to go."

"Most of my travel has been limited to the States—though I did get to Europe during my college days, and to Hawaii on my honeymoon."

"Then you're way ahead of me." Emma confessed. "I've never taken a trip like this in my life!"

"Emma," Linda seemed to study Emma's heavy coat. "You'll need some light, summery clothes for the tropics."

Emma frowned. She hadn't even thought about clothing.

For that matter, she only owned one small suitcase. It used to belong to her mother. Of course, money was no problem right now, but how would she explain her purchases to Grandma? She'd already decided to keep her secret until she was safely gone. If she told Grandma now, she'd be sure to talk her out of it. And if that failed, Grandma could be counted on to resort to guilt. Guilt trips were her specialty. Still, Emma had no plans to take one of *those* anytime soon.

"Did you hear me, Emma?"

Emma came to with a start, realizing she'd been lost in her own thoughts. "Sorry. What were you saying?"

Linda gently smiled. "Are you sure you're up to this? I mean, your trip sounds fabulous, but it's a big step if you've never traveled much—"

Before she knew it, Emma had launched into the whole dreary story—Grandma, Miss Finley, even her horrible boss. "But I don't want to upset my grandmother," she added miserably.

"Oh, Emma," began Linda soothingly, as she handed her a tissue. "I understand. Of course, you *must* go, but are you sure you want to stick with this destination after all?"

Emma nodded and blew her nose. One place was the same as another to her—just as long as it was far from Iowa. She glanced at her watch. It was almost time for work.

"Then let me help, Emma. We could shop for your trip together. Then we could stow your things in the storage room here until you're ready to tell your grandmother."

Emma stared at her in disbelief, but Linda looked sincere. It was agreed they would meet at the mall Thursday night.

Emma floated out of the travel agency and into her office, her letter of resignation securely tucked in her purse. It wasn't a full two weeks' notice, but it would have to do. On the way to her desk, she handed the letter to Mr. Smith's secretary. She wished she'd been more specific about Rick's behavior, but hopefully she'd said enough to plant some doubts in Mr. Smith's mind.

During lunch break, Emma tied up some financial matters at the bank, then stopped by the employment agency to inquire about a live-in for Grandma. She would carefully cover all bases before she left. The last thing she wanted was to be haunted by unwarranted guilt. The other kind she would deal with later.

᪥ᷢ   ᪥ᷢ   ᪥ᷢ   ᪥ᷢ

On Thursday night, Emma served Grandma another make-shift dinner, ignoring the loud complaints as she hurried off to change for her much anticipated shopping spree.

"Where you going, Emma?" grumbled Grandma, looking up from her microwaved meal as Emma pulled on her coat. "I don't know what's come over you lately, but it smells like trouble to me. Shouldn't you be home getting ready to go to Frannie's tomorrow? Have you packed our things—cleaned out the fridge—?"

"Yes, yes. I'll be home late, so don't wait up—"

"Emma Jane! Who'll put me to bed?"

"Well, you can either do it yourself, or you can sleep in your recliner until I get back." Emma closed the door with an emphatic bang, vowing not to be manipulated tonight. Besides, Grandma usually slept in her chair until the late news anyway.

Still, Emma felt a hot poker of guilt as she waited at the bus stop. *Get over it*, she chastised herself. Times like this would only make the break easier on Grandma in the long run. At least, she hoped.

Emma never rode the bus after dark, but this was the time to buck up and be brave. She needed the practice. She slid into a front seat near the driver and kept her eyes straight ahead.

When they reached the mall, Emma bolted out the door and toward the warmth and light of the shops. To her immense relief, Linda was waiting in front of Klopenstein's Department Store.

"Hi, Emma! Ready to shop till we drop? I brought a list—just some suggestions. A formula I learned at a travel seminar seems to work well. My clients swear by it." She handed Emma a list.

Emma studied the list. "Is that enough for the whole trip?"

Linda nodded. "Well, I find that most people overpack. But

then again I'm not sure how long you plan to stay, since you booked an undated return. Of course, you can always pick up extra things once you get there. Why don't you check off the items you already have—and we'll go from there."

Emma checked off only a couple of things. "I'll also need some luggage. But we don't have to get everything tonight."

"The mall is only open until nine, you know," Linda quipped. She located a designer rack and held up a jacket, skirt, and pants in a soft shade of mossy-green with abalone buttons. The next thing Emma knew, she was in the dressing room. She fingered the smooth fabric as she slipped the skirt over her hips. She would never have chosen it for herself, but she loved the feel as she slid her hands in the roomy side pockets. The jacket could be used to mix and match, and the pants fit comfortably.

"Emma, you're too easy to shop for—a perfect size eight." Linda sighed. "I should be so lucky. Here, try these with the suit." She handed her some bright-colored shells. "With these few items alone, you can make lots of outfits." Linda slanted her an appraising look as Emma slipped on a sleeveless apricot shell. "See what I mean? And that top brings out the highlights in your hair."

"Really?" Emma peered in the mirror. "I always think of my hair as mouse-brown."

"Then you've just been wearing the wrong colors. You should stick to warm tones. And if you don't mind my saying so, you could do with a good haircut and a perm. It would be handy for the trip."

Emma considered the suggestion while Linda hauled in more and more clothes, and soon the "keep" pile grew nearly as large as the discard.

"Try this dress, Emma. I think the melon color will be nice on you. . . . Now wrap this scarf around your waist like a belt."

Emma followed orders, then gazed in fascination at the stranger in the mirror. The fabric skimmed her body, and the belted scarf added an almost gypsy-like look.

"I can just see you with soft curls and some dangly gold earrings! Add a pair of strappy high-heeled sandals—and wow! What a knock-out!"

"What are you—my fairy godmother or something? I feel like Cinderella." Emma giggled, trying to remember when she'd last felt like giggling.

Linda laughed and glanced at her watch. "Hey, it's almost nine, and the store's going to close. You'd better hurry before you turn back into a pumpkin. While you're changing, I'll take these out and have the cashier start ringing them up. We made a pretty good dent on this list tonight, but we'll have to do the rest later—how about this weekend?"

Emma thought of her babysitting commitment. Shane and Rosie would be okay with Grandma for a few hours. Fran wouldn't mind. "Sure—you name the time, Linda. I really do appreciate your help."

Linda offered Emma a ride home, and together they hauled the parcels out to Linda's little white sports car. Emma liked the rustling sound the bags made as they were tossed into the trunk. It sounded important—like a new chapter in her life was about to be written. She leaned her head back into the leather seat and sighed, willing her fears of being in a car to disappear. She felt like someone else—someone besides drab Emma Davis—and she liked the feeling.

"Have time for a cup of coffee?" Linda asked. "I know this funky place over on Forty-third where they have scrumptious pie."

"Sure, that'd be nice."

Linda pulled into the fifties-style restaurant. The interior was done authentically with aqua blue booths trimmed in shiny chrome. James Dean posters lined the walls, and a lighted juke-box played an old Patsy Cline tune.

"I like coming here—it reminds me of when I was a little kid," said Linda. "And their blueberry pie is to die for."

"Yeah, I like this era, too, even though I wasn't around in the fifties," confessed Emma.

Linda chuckled. "Well, I just left myself wide open for that one, didn't I? But age never bothers me. I always figure you're as young as you feel."

Emma nodded. "Do you have children?"

The bright smile faded a bit. "No." She sipped her coffee.

"I always wanted children, but several years after I was married, I had to have a complete hysterectomy—" Emma's fork clanged against her plate as she stared at Linda in surprise.

"I used to chastise myself for not getting pregnant early in my marriage—you know, have kids while I could, but Ted wanted to wait." An expression of pain crossed Linda's even features. "Then he left me about six months after the operation. He married within the year." She paused, then looked up, her customary sparkle intact. "I don't know why I'm telling you all this, because I'm really quite happy. God has been so good to me. I belong to a fantastic church, and I've been dating a wonderful man. I hope you don't think I wanted you to feel sorry for me."

"I'm the one who should apologize." Emma began uncomfortably. "I didn't mean to overreact when you mentioned your hysterectomy. But it's just so odd. You see, I had the same operation about seven years ago. I can't have children, either." Emma looked down at her plate. Her untouched ice cream had melted and swirled among the blueberries, creating a soft shade of periwinkle. She wished she knew how to act at such awkward moments.

"Oh, Emma, that's so amazing! All these years I've waved at you out at the bus stop and wondered what you were like."

"Thanks, Linda. You'll probably never know how much that means to me right now." They talked on and on, until Emma realized the late-night news was long over. She could only imagine what Grandma would say.

"Still want me to keep these things at the agency for you?" asked Linda as she dropped Emma off at the apartment.

"If you wouldn't mind. It'll save lots of explaining, and I'm not very good at lying. Thanks again—for everything."

Emma let herself in silently. The lights were still on, but Grandma's chair was vacant. Emma paused by Grandma's bedroom. The walker was parked next to the bed, and loud, even snores floated into the hallway.

She closed the door and began to straighten the little apartment. So many years of her life had been spent here, doing the same things over and over, day after day. How many times had she dusted these veneer end tables, or vacuumed this matted-down carpet? Sure, it had been a place to call home after her parents' death, and she'd always appreciated the way Grandma had taken them in as little girls.

But Emma should have moved on long ago. She had allowed this apartment to become her prison. But she wouldn't allow it to become her tomb. And before long, it would only be a memory.

Four

*S*eat belt buckled, tray table in locked, upright position, Emma closed her eyes and gritted her teeth as the jet lifted from the runway. The weight of her body pressed against the back of the seat, and the meaning of "white-knuckle" flight dawned on her with absolute clarity. It wasn't the gravitational force that paralyzed her; it was fear. Only when she imagined the crew having to carry her off the plane bodily and ship her back to Iowa did she begin to snap out of it.

When Linda had dropped her off at the airport, she'd left her with another tip: "Dramamine will help with certain aspects of air travel," she said, "but whenever you're afraid, there's nothing like prayer." Emma tried it now.

When she opened her eyes, she took a moment to orient herself in the cabin. Having no desire to look out the window, she'd purposely requested an aisle seat.

She admired the graceful flow of the skirt Linda had found for her on their second shopping trip. Reaching up, she pushed a stray curl away from her forehead. She'd gotten the recommended cut and perm, and Linda had been right. Her red highlights showed up more that ever as her hair curled loosely onto her shoulders. Grandma had even commented on how much younger she looked.

This morning Emma had left the apartment at her usual time. Only today, everything in her room was neatly packed into boxes and stacked in her closet. Her farewell letter to Grandma was safe in Linda's keeping, to be hand-delivered at noon.

She'd spent a week interviewing potential caregivers—everyone from a chain-smoking teen to a woman who looked like a middle-aged Barbie doll. She'd finally settled on Bernice Fontaine, a church friend of Linda's. Bernice was a little younger than Grandma, but appeared to be patient and kind, and her interests were similar to Grandma's.

This morning, Emma had kissed Grandma good-bye. She'd never done that before—not even when she was little. Grandma had looked up with wide eyes tinged with suspicion—almost as if she somehow knew what her granddaughter was up to. That Emma had also seen a trace of understanding might have been wishful thinking. But it helped.

Later, head held high, Emma had walked right past her old workplace without even looking. She tried to suppress a smug smile as she recalled her last day of work. Rick had cornered her by the water cooler, admiring her new hairstyle. But when he reached out to fondle a curl, she'd let him know—loudly and in no uncertain terms—just what she thought of his advances over the past twelve years. To her surprise, senior partner Gordon Smith had happened around the corner just then, and Rick's face had turned three shades of crimson. Emma could think of no better way to say good-bye.

"Magazine?" offered the young male flight attendant. "We'll serve lunch in about half an hour." Emma thanked him, and the man next to her looked up from his paper. He was dressed in a navy suit, with blue eyes, blond hair, and a neatly trimmed mustache.

"Now, there's one thing I could live without," he said, leaning over to speak in a confidential tone. "Airline food—it all tastes like cardboard. But it does help to break up a long flight. Sorry, I should have introduced myself. I'm Stan Jones. You headed to San Francisco on business or pleasure?"

"Just passing through, actually."

"I'm traveling on business," he continued, apparently oblivious to her growing discomfort. "But San Francisco is one of my favorite cities, and I never pass up a chance to take in some of the great night spots in the Bay area—if I'm lucky enough to have some company, that is."

Was he asking what she thought he was asking? She looked up, and his eyes met hers. She blushed, telling herself she was probably imagining things and wondering if her ex-boss had warped her for life.

"I won't be staying in San Francisco," she answered smoothly, observing his tanned hands refolding his paper. On the ring finger of his left hand was a shiny gold band. She stared for a moment longer, then shook her head. Men could be such jerks.

"Too bad. It's really quite a town." He reopened his paper and didn't disturb her again.

After lunch, Emma pulled out the thick English novel Linda had given her at the airport. She soon became absorbed in the affairs of a young heiress in turn-of-the-century Scotland.

25 25 25 25

Despite a blanket of fog, the jet found San Francisco, and Emma exited the plane victorious. Emma's heart was still pounding as she collected her baggage in the busy terminal. She took deep breaths, as Linda had recommended, and fought her fear as she waved for a cab. In no time, she was heading toward the wharf, clutching her purse strap in tightly clenched fists, breathing deeply, and wondering if this was how it felt to hyperventilate.

Despite her constant worries and imagined fears, everything continued like clockwork. On the wharf, a uniformed man rolled up with a large flat cart already loaded with luggage. He opened the door of her cab, tagged her bags, and tossed them on top. Another uniformed official escorted her and an older couple through a large, dark building that led to the pier. It was comforting to hear the couple chattering away about what fun lay ahead. She could use that kind of confidence about now.

When they stepped out of the darkness of the building she saw it. There, docked majestically before them and reminding Emma of a queen donning her glittering diamond tiara, was a huge white ship, trimmed in colorful flags and strings of lights just beginning to twinkle on.

"Dinner is now being served,"the steward informed her as they approached the long, narrow gangplank.

Emma hesitated before taking the step that would separate her from American soil. "I—uh—I need to make a phone call first—"

"Don't worry, there are phones on board. While in port, you can place a call anywhere you want. At sea, there are radio phones for the use of our passengers."

They seemed to have thought of everything. She couldn't put it off any longer. Emma walked slowly up the gangway, as if in a trance. Was this all just a dream? People milled about, stylishly dressed for dinner, chatting, laughing, strolling the decks. They appeared to be completely at ease, as if they knew who they were and that they belonged here. She wasn't so sure.

After she checked in at the registrar's desk, the cabin steward politely introduced himself and offered to escort her to her room. She'd never been treated like this before, as if she were royalty. Feeling like an impostor, Emma followed him down several steep flights of narrow stairs. Down, down until she felt she was being swallowed by a gigantic whale.

They stopped on the E deck, and the steward unlocked the door to an inside berth. As Linda had warned, there was no window. The tiny cubicle became even more crowded as her luggage was stacked by the closet. But it was the best that could be found on such late notice. And it was all hers. She sighed and closed the door.

After checking and rechecking tickets, traveler's checks, passport, and visa, she hid them in the bottom of her suitcase. Then she took a deep breath and surveyed her cabin—home for the next few weeks. Linda had explained that this was a refurbished older ship from a British line. It seemed to be sturdily built, but one never knew. . . .

Pushing images of the *Titanic* from her mind, she ran her hand across the polished dark mahogany panels that lined the walls. Shiny brass fittings added to its nautical charm, and she wondered how many lonely travelers this room had harbored during its many years of service. She stared into the small round mirror above the miniature sink. Did that face belong to her?

Was she really doing this? She felt her heart lightly pulsing—like a butterfly trapped in a jar. She drew in a deep breath, stepped out into the narrow hallway, and locked the door behind her.

The steward showed her to a phone, and she quickly dialed Fran's number, hoping desperately that she could leave a message on the machine.

"Hello?" Fran's voice was wound tight.

"Hi, Fran." Emma closed her eyes and composed herself, ready to do battle.

"Emma Jane! Is that you? Where are you? What's going on—"

"Calm down, Fran. Let me explain—"

"You better!"

Emma spoke slowly, deliberately, as if addressing a small child. "I just wanted to let you know that I'm okay. I'm on a ship, and I'm taking a trip." Unsure of her sister's reaction, Emma hadn't decided how much to tell her. Fran might try to stop her, might even threaten to have her locked in a padded cell. But there was dead silence on the line.

"Fran, I would've told you, but I couldn't—" Emma's voice broke slightly.

"Emma, I'm your sister—your own flesh and blood, for pete's sake—and you couldn't tell *me*?"

"I was too scared, Fran. Can't you see? This is the hardest thing I've ever done. But I had to do it . . . or else—" She let the thought dangle. No sense worrying them unnecessarily.

"Yeah, okay, Emma." Fran sounded incredibly sad.

"Is Grandma all right?"

"She'll get over it. Besides, it's given her something new to complain about—she's already called me about twenty times this afternoon. Think I'll put the answering machine on now that I've heard from you—" A pause. "I went over there and met Bernice. She seems nice enough."

Emma sighed. "Frannie—believe me, I would've told you—"

"It's okay, Em. I think I understand—" Now Fran choked, and she broke into quiet sobs. Emma's tough older sister wasn't one to cry, and this was the most disturbing of all.

"I'm so sorry, I really am. I know it sounds stupid, but I have to find myself. I don't even know who I am anymore—can't you see that?"

Fran sniffed loudly. "Sure, Em, it's okay. Maybe I'm just jealous."

Emma laughed now. "Oh, Frannie, you? You've got Roger and the kids and a home—you have a life!"

"It's a pretty boring life, if you ask me."

"You don't even know the meaning of boring."

"Yeah, Em, I s'pose you're right. When will you be back?"

"I haven't decided." Emma bit her lip.

"Hmm . . ." Her sister sighed loudly.

"I better go now, Fran. Take care. Hug the kids . . . and Grandma." She started to give her a message for their grandmother, then thought better of it.

"Hey, have fun, sis! And don't forget to write." Another pause. "And Em," said Fran in a barely audible voice, "I do admire you for having the guts to do this."

Five

A tuxedoed host ushered Emma to an unoccupied table for four near the kitchen door, explaining that this would be her assigned seat for the duration of the cruise. As soon as she was seated, the waiter stepped up and brushed bread crumbs off the white cloth with a little whisk broom, then expertly flipped a crisp linen napkin into Emma's lap and filled her goblet with water—all in one swift motion, it seemed.

"Care for a drink, miss? We have champagne tonight, compliments of the Captain."

Emma had never tasted champagne, or any other strong drink, for that matter. Grandma had always frowned on "Imbibing."

"Yes, thank you," Emma heard herself saying, and the waiter smiled and left to get her order.

She wondered if it was wrong to have a drink, and imagined Grandma waving her Bible in Emma's face, then shrugged off the notion. Maybe it wouldn't hurt—just this once. Besides, hadn't Jesus provided wine for a wedding reception?

Emma looked around for her dinner companions, but seeing no one making their way to her table, she didn't mind dining alone. She was ravenous, and everything tasted delicious. Her Greek waiter spoke very little English, she discovered, but he made up for it in fine service and frequent toothy smiles. She remembered not to tip him after the meal, but would wait until the end of the trip, per Linda's instructions. Instead, she thanked him and stood to leave.

The dining room was nearly deserted now. Only a group of elderly people sipping coffee remained, along with a couple in a corner, hunched head-to-head in a romantic interlude, completely oblivious to their surroundings. Probably honeymooners, Emma thought with unwanted interest. A ship seemed such a romantic place. Feelings of loneliness welled up in her, but she shoved them down like a cork in a bottle, determined not to succumb to selfpity. This was her time to break free of all entanglements—romantic ones included.

The ship wouldn't leave port until midnight, she'd been informed. She decided to step out on the promenade deck and have a last look at San Francisco. At home, she didn't venture out much at night. But somehow, here on this ship, she felt safe.

It took a moment for her eyes to adjust to the darkness before she could take in the beauty of the Bay. The city lights were veiled in wispy tendrils of fog—like a woman's hair trailing over her shoulders—and reflected off the water in a luminous glow. The scene reminded her of a Van Gogh—his *Starry Night*. She stared in wonder for a long time at the bridges, silhouetted against the darkening sky. It was as if the city were wrapped in a giant veil of pale blue tissue paper. Delicate and beautiful.

The soulful cry of a saxophone drifted through the air, teasing her ears with its piercing notes. She'd rediscovered jazz in her late twenties and often tuned her radio to a jazz and blues station. Remembering how much her parents had enjoyed the musical style somehow linked her to them—even now. They'd kept an old stack of 78s in a wooden apple crate, but somewhere down the line, the records had all disappeared—just like everything else.

She followed the sound to a smoky room filled with blue haze, the sound of tinkling glasses, and the rich tones of the alto sax. She slipped into a straight-backed chair in the far corner, hoping to blend into the walls and absorb the music and atmosphere without notice. Emma watched in fascination as men and women mingled and socialized. The glittering sequins and low-cut gowns made her feel conspicuously underdressed in her simple skirt and jacket.

"What will you have?" asked a cocktail waitress, wearing a

snug-fitting red number and too much mascara.

"Do you have something . . . light?"

The waitress shrugged impatiently and looked her over. "You mean, like a Shirley Temple?"

Emma's face burned with embarrassment. "I'll have a club soda."

The waitress disappeared for a while, and Emma hoped she'd forgotten. But eventually she returned and flopped down a coaster and a tumbler of bubbly liquid.

Emma fumbled in her purse and handed her several crumpled bills.

"Soft drinks are free," the waitress said loudly.

"Oh," said Emma, feeling stupid. She sipped her drink and tried to relax, but she felt someone watching her. She looked up to see a man just a few tables away. Dark, penetrating eyes bored into her, and his full beard distinguished him from every other man in the room. At least, as far as she could make out in the dim lighting.

She picked up the tumbler and took a sip. Her eyes burned from the smoke, but she was determined to stay long enough to enjoy the music.

Cautiously she peered through the haze. Since the man wasn't looking in her direction, she took some time to examine him. He was dressed entirely in black—black jacket, shirt, tie. It made for an almost sinister look—not unattractive. Seated beside him was a beautiful woman with long, blond hair. Emma wondered how she could have missed seeing her before. This woman had the kind of look one doesn't forget, and she wasn't wearing sequins. Just a simple white dress with a touch of gold jewelry. Classic. Elegant. They made a striking pair—his dark, sultry looks. Her blond beauty. Then without warning, the woman smiled at Emma.

Truly self-conscious now, Emma turned her full attention to the little stage in front and focused on the band, hoping to lose herself in the sophisticated melody.

"Hey, folks, we're leaving!" called out a tall young man, sliding from his stool and staggering out the door.

Sure enough, the ship was moving, though Emma wondered

how the inebriated fellow had been able to tell. She slipped out behind him, wanting to catch a last glimpse of her homeland.

The fog had cleared, leaving behind the Bay, shimmering like a giant star sapphire. She breathed in the fresh air and shook her head. Here she was—little Emma Davis. She still couldn't believe she was doing this.

One by one or in pairs, the other passengers disappeared, and only she remained on deck. The city lights grew smaller and dimmer as the ship steadily churned along, plowing the vast black ocean. She'd never felt so completely alone, so cut off from all she'd ever known. Soon she glimpsed a few stars in the midnight sky, and a brisk sea breeze blew up. She shivered, prayed a wordless prayer . . . and hoped that God had heard.

Six

*E*mma awoke to thick, heavy darkness. Where was she? Holding her breath, she listened to the steady hum of the ship's engines and remembered. She snuggled back into the cozy berth and contemplated this strange adventure before her. Here she lay, down in the belly of a giant ship, out in the middle of the ocean. Virtually no one on board knew her. If she were to fall overboard, unobserved, quite possibly no one would even notice she was gone. It was an eerie feeling, almost like being nonexistent.

She flicked on the bedside reading lamp and checked her watch; she was still on central time, and it was too early to get up. Last night she'd adjusted her watch to "ship time," which would advance one hour each day as they journeyed farther out to sea. She stretched, telling herself she'd better enjoy this unaccustomed treat, but she couldn't stay in bed a moment longer.

After a quick shower, she slowly unpacked and hung up all her new travel clothes. She would write Linda a postcard today, thanking her again.

The windowless cabin offered no clue as to the weather outside, but surely at the pace they were sailing, they hadn't yet reached the tropical zone. So she pulled on khaki pants and a T-shirt topped with a pretty hand-knit cotton cardigan. After tying a paisley silk scarf as a headband around her head, the way Linda had shown her, Emma fluffed out her hair and added a touch of lipstick. She still found it hard to believe that the reflection in the mirror belonged to her.

A predawn light spilled across the decks, but the sun hadn't risen yet. Neither had the other passengers. A couple of crew members nodded as they passed by. Today she welcomed the solitude, strolling the well-polished wooden deck from lee to port and back again.

Finally she settled into a wooden deck chair facing east to witness her first sunrise at sea. She felt as giddy as a child as she pulled a scratchy woolen deck blanket over her legs and peered off into the dusky horizon. The cool air tasted fresh and clean, and for the first time since her exodus had begun, she felt absolutely certain that she had done the right thing.

Slowly at first, the slate sky lightened, and a soft glow washed the horizon. Then, as if painted by sweeping brushstrokes from an artist's hand, the eastern sky shone with a warm radiance. She watched in fascination, as if it were a part of her.

"Lovely, isn't it?" A deep masculine voice startled her from her thoughts, and she glanced over to see a man who had taken a seat next to her. He wore a faded denim jacket that seemed to match his eyes. To her astonishment, she recognized him as the man in black from last night, looking nothing like the villain she'd imagined him to be.

"I've been on board since Vancouver, and I haven't missed a sunrise yet." He spoke as if he'd known her for years. "Of course, that's only been four days now." He chuckled. "Could I get you a cup of coffee? It's still too early for breakfast service, but I happen to have connections."

Still speechless, she nodded mutely. When he disappeared, she didn't really expect him to return, though the fact that she hoped he would bothered her a little. Then suddenly the image of the beautiful blonde snapped her back to reality. Who was that woman? His wife? His girlfriend?

"Here you go." He extended a steaming mug of coffee. "I hope you take yours black." She accepted and nodded again, bobbing her head like a mindless robot.

"I should introduce myself. I'm Aaron Fitzpatrick." He held out a strong hand, and she awkwardly extended her free one, which happened to be her left. He grasped it graciously and held it a moment longer than necessary. But in that split second, their eyes locked and she felt her breath catch.

She really should tell him her name, but her tongue felt like a sausage. "I'm Emma," she managed in a hoarse whisper. She cleared her throat and tried again. "Emma Davis."

He smiled and released her hand. "Did you board in San Francisco, Emma?"

She nodded again. If he wanted to talk, the conversation would be up to him. At least until she could compose herself and stop acting like a tongue-tied adolescent.

"A cruise is the most relaxing way to travel, and mornings are best of all. Funny thing—no one else seems to have discovered that. It's always deserted up here until after nine, and then only a few devout walkers and joggers show up, faithfully doing their laps, but neglecting to enjoy the view. It's funny how we take such good care of our bodies and so sadly neglect our souls." He paused and looked out across the ocean. "And where are you bound, Emma?"

She took a deep breath. "New Guinea." This time the words came out more easily.

He quirked a brow. "And what takes you to such an out-of-the-way spot, Emma?" The way he spoke her name sent tingles down her spine.

"I . . . uh . . . I needed to get away, and one place was as good as another."

He smiled again. "You must have an adventurous soul, Emma."

The laughter that rumbled from deep within surprised her. "I seriously doubt that."

"And what will you do in New Guinea?"

Now that was a hard question. For some reason, though, it seemed important to be honest with him. "I'm not really sure. I guess I'll know when I get there."

"Will anyone be meeting you?"

So many questions. She really didn't know this man. And what about the suspicious character he appeared to be last night? Would she be telling *him* the details of her trip? Better to be safe than sorry. "My travel agent has taken care of that."

"Well, it was nice to meet you, Emma." Abruptly he stood

and left—just like that. She leaned back in her chair. She couldn't begin to make sense of the feelings tumbling inside. Maybe he had been a mirage, after all. She shook off the perplexing incident and headed for the dining room, hoping another cup of strong coffee would help to clear her head.

Only a few early risers were seated for breakfast. But as she was escorted to her table, she noticed it was occupied. An older couple and a teenaged boy were already eating their meal. Unwilling to break in on the family group, she looked for another table. But this was her assigned seat, and before she knew it, the friendly Greek waiter had snapped a napkin into her lap.

"Good morning," the woman greeted her warmly. "We're the Millers. I'm Charlene, this is my husband, Fred, and our son Tim." Fred looked up with a smile. Tim remained slumped in his chair without looking up.

"I'm Emma Davis, and I feel like I'm intruding on your family breakfast. With so many empty tables—"

"Oh, don't give it a second thought, Emma. You know those seating charts. Besides, we're ready for some fresh company." Charlene glanced at her son. "The conversation drags around here sometimes."

"Where are you folks headed?" inquired Emma, deciding to jump the gun before they asked her.

"Probably no place you've ever heard of," Fred said. "Papua New Guinea. You know, the land of headhunters and cannibals."

Emma felt her eyes bulge. "Cannibals? You're kidding, right?"

Fred laughed, and Tim actually cracked a faint smile. "Well, none have been reported lately," Fred confessed, "though I've known a few in my day."

"Yeah, remember old Komiko, Dad? He used to brag about how many people he'd tasted."

"Well, Komiko was given to exaggeration," his mother corrected. "Are you interested in New Guinea, Emma? We have pictures."

"Actually, I'm very interested. That's where I'm going, too."

"Well, what do you know!" exclaimed Fred. "If I were a bettin' man, I'd wager no one else on this ship has ever even heard of Papua."

Emma grimaced. "You make it sound like no one would want to."

"Honey!" Charlene jabbed Fred with her elbow. "Don't scare the poor girl off."

"Oh, no problem, Emma. It's just that most folks don't know what they're missing. We've lived there almost twenty years and can't wait to get back." Even Tim nodded. That was pretty convincing.

"What do you do there?"

"We're translators," Charlene explained. "There are over seven hundred different tribal languages in New Guinea."

"Really? How do the people ever learn to communicate with each other?"

"They use a trade language—Pidgen—but it's very limited. What we're working on now is teaching our villagers to read in their mother tongue." Fred spoke with enthusiasm, then leaned closer and said in a confidential tone. "But our main goal has been to complete the translation of the New Testament. We expect to send it to the printer within the year."

So these people were *Bible* translators. Grandma would definitely approve. Emma looked at Tim. "Have you lived there all your life?"

He nodded. "Yep, 'cept for when we have to come back to the States on furlough." He hunched again over his Belgian waffle.

Charlene smiled apologetically. "It's pretty tough on the kids, leaving their friends in New Guinea. But this time going back is harder than ever, because we had to leave Tim's older brother, Brad, in the States. He just started college last fall."

"And what will *you* be doing in New Guinea?" asked Fred, quickly changing what appeared to be a touchy subject. Emma gave a quick explanation and then plied them with questions about the strange-sounding tropical island she would be visiting.

After breakfast, Charlene gave Emma a short tour of the

ship, while Fred and Tim went up to play shuffleboard. Emma looked longingly at the glistening blue pool as they passed. With the air warming steadily and the brilliant sun beating down on their heads, she could tell they were nearing the tropics.

"Well, this is it, Charlene," said Emma as they stopped in front of her cabin. "Thanks for the tour. I had no idea the ship was so big—shops, theaters, salons—it's like a little town. I can't wait to try out that swimming pool."

"And I can't wait to do some reading I never have time to do. See you at lunch." With a little wave, she was off.

Emma closed her door and changed into her new swimsuit. Opening the narrow closet door, she peered into the full-length mirror and scrutinized her slim body in the sleek, one-piece teal suit. She frowned, realizing she wouldn't be winning any swimsuit competitions.

The pool was deserted except for a single swimmer doing laps. Emma dropped her things on a lounge chair and executed a neat dive into the sparkling water. It was shockingly cold, and surprisingly, tasted salty. But what stunned her even more was Aaron's grinning face, only inches from her own.

"Why, Emma, we seem to travel in the same orbit."

Amazingly enough, she was able to utter a coherent reply this time. "Oh, hi, Aaron, I didn't realize that was you. I couldn't resist a swim before a crowd gathers." She treaded water with ease and watched as a couple of bikini-clad women scooted lounge chairs into sunny spots. "And I'd better get at it before I freeze."

"They filled the pool early this morning. They say it'll take a day or two to warm up." He swam alongside her with slow, easy strokes, but after a few laps, returned to his own slightly faster pace.

She watched him from the corner of her eye. His lithe, muscled torso sliced through the water with barely a ripple. She tried to guess his age—thirty-something—and wondered about his marital status and the identity of the beautiful blonde she'd seen him with on the first night out.

When Emma tired, she was reluctant to climb out and expose her scrawny, pale body to the cruel glare of the sun. But somehow, when her back was turned, Aaron had disappeared, and she scampered out and draped herself in a huge white pool towel.

After a shower and shampoo, she peeked out of the poolside dressing room to see if she could spot him. By now the area around the pool was thick with sun worshipers. And the water churned with children, splashing each other and creating general bedlam.

Failing to find Aaron's among the well-oiled bodies—in various stages of burning and broiling—Emma settled into a lounge chair and began to rub suntan lotion on her legs.

"Need some help with that?" A shadow loomed over her, and she recognized Aaron's voice. He handed her a pink drink with a skinny straw. "Here, something to refresh you after your workout." He took the lotion from her, squirted some on her shoulders, and began rubbing before she could object.

She took a sip. "Thanks, this is good."

"Great. Now lean forward, and I'll do your back. You don't want to burn, you know. This tropical sun is strong, and your skin's as smooth and white as porcelain."

A warm feeling—unassisted by the sun—swept over her. *Porcelain!*

Seven

*A*fter lunch, Emma begged out of a card game with the Millers in the hope of bumping into Aaron. She scoured the ship without success. Instead, she discovered an old Humphrey Bogart classic playing in the theater and slipped into a back-row seat shortly after it began.

She was soon immersed in the mysterious war romance, and when the houselights came on she self-consciously wiped a tear and glanced around. There, at the opposite end of the same aisle, he stood looking her way. Goosebumps prickled down the back of her neck as their eyes met and locked, and she wondered if life might be even more exciting than the movies.

"Well, hello again, Emma. Are you a Bogie fan?"

"I am now," she replied, just a trifle breathless.

They stepped outside together, and Emma inhaled the fresh sea air—would she ever get used to it? Overhead a cloudless sky stretched boundlessly over the ocean, only a little bluer than the heavens. The water sparkled like diamond chips where the long afternoon sun rays bounced off the faceted surface. Emma leaned against the railing, peering down the side of the ship as it split the sea, leaving in its wake frothy, white foam. The sheer force of the vessel amazed her as it effortlessly thrust aside tons of water and propelled itself gracefully along.

"Have you seen the engine room?" asked Aaron, following her line of vision. "You really should have a tour. I'll arrange to take you down tomorrow." He seemed to like calling the shots, and Emma wondered if he always got his way.

"I'd like that."

"Tell me about yourself, Emma. Who are you and what are you running from?" He looked deep into her eyes, as if trying to see into her soul. To her surprise, she didn't mind.

"Oh, I'm pretty ordinary, and I'm not really running *from* anything. I guess I'm running *to* something—trying to live my life before it's too late. Something like an early mid-life crisis." She laughed, then told him about Grandma and Miss Finley and how her death had caused Emma to stop and take stock.

He listened, nodding with empathy. "And do you have other family, Emma—aside from your grandmother?"

She found it easy to talk to him. "Just an older sister. Both our parents were killed in a car wreck when I was six. My dad has family somewhere back East, but they pretty much cut him off when he married my mom."

"Cut him off?"

"Well, I heard his family had money, and they didn't like my mom. I don't even think they came to the wedding—or the funeral. People can be horrible."

He nodded again. He was truly sensitive, she decided. A sensitive, caring man. "People can be horribly unforgiving, but they hurt themselves most in the end—don't you think?"

"I suppose . . ." The dinner bell rang, scattering her thoughts across the horizon.

"Do you dance, Emma?" She glanced at him, listening for the double entendre.

"There's a disco downstairs," he explained. "It doesn't kick in until after ten, but it's rather amusing. I'd like you to come tonight."

"Sounds like fun." She wasn't sure if this was an invitation or merely a suggestion, but felt embarrassed to ask. They walked in silence to the dining room, parting at the door. He continued to the far side of the room and melted into the crowd.

"Emma, you're looking well," Charlene observed when Emma sat down. "The sea air must agree with you. Or could it be that handsome man we've seen you with?"

Emma felt her cheeks heat. "Oh, that's Aaron Fitzpatrick. We always seem to be running into each other."

The Millers were beginning to feel like family, and she enjoyed the security of sitting with them at mealtimes—something like an anchor. They were comfortable to be around and appeared genuinely interested in her. Though they weren't old enough to be her parents, she found herself wishing she had a family like theirs. After dinner, they lingered over coffee.

"Emma." Charlene touched her arm hesitantly. "I don't mean to interfere, but do be careful, dear. You know, some people may not be all they appear to be."

"Oh, Charlene," moaned Fred, "you sound like a mother hen. Emma's a grown woman. You don't need to worry about her. Come on. We have some galleys to read."

Charlene gently squeezed Emma's hand and rose to leave. Still, she appreciated the woman's concern and once again thought of her mother. The memory stung a little—not because it was particularly unpleasant, but because it was so intangible.

She was like a hungry child, haunted by the faint memory of an untasted meal. She knew her mother had loved her, but she recalled no closeness, no warmth or intimacy. Her mother had an artistic temperament and had spent many hours in her workshop, painting and sculpting. Emma remembered watching, hiding unobserved in a corner as she watched her work on a large painting, full of splashy color and bold streaks. What had become of that piece? Likely lost, along with all other traces of Emma's earlier life. Sometimes she wondered if her few childhood memories were authentic or simply fabrications of a fertile imagination. As she lay across her bunk, she tried to recall her mother's face. But, lulled by the rhythm of the ship, she fell asleep.

🙚 🙚 🙚 🙚

She awoke with a start, her heart beating furiously. It was the same nightmare that had tormented her as a child. The dream was generally brief, and some of the details varied from one night to the next. But it always ended the same way—with the family car careening over the edge of the cliff and plunging, slow motion, into the rocky ravine below. But she always awoke before it crashed. She'd heard that if you ever hit bottom in a nightmare, you'd die. She didn't believe that anymore.

Emma freshened up in the tiny sink, pushed these memories from her mind, focusing instead on the evening before her. With trembling anticipation, she pulled on a silky dress, wrapping the colorful scarf around her waist. The gypsy-style ensemble filled her with a feeling of carefree abandon as she fastened golden hoops into her earlobes and slipped into strappy, high-heeled sandals. This was a dancing outfit. And though she hadn't danced in years, somehow she knew she would tonight. She fluffed her hair, applied a little more makeup than usual, then stared with wonder into the porthole-shaped mirror. Was this really her? She blew herself a kiss and popped her key into her compact evening bag, locking the door behind her.

Since it wasn't yet ten, she stopped by the jazz bar to get into the night-life mood and hopefully find Aaron. Tonight the cheeky waitress was wearing a shiny purple jumpsuit when she bounced up to take Emma's order, but Emma stuck with club soda with lime. She took a sip and glanced around, but Aaron wasn't there. She did, however, notice the beautiful blonde visiting with a lively bunch. Once again, the attractive woman seemed to be smiling in her direction. Emma returned the smile uneasily. To her surprise, the woman walked over.

"Hi, I see you're alone tonight. I'm Angeline Thomas." The young woman extended a smooth, beautifully manicured hand. "Want to meet the gang?" Emma didn't know how to respond to the unexpected friendliness, but she introduced herself and followed Angeline back to the noisy group at the table. A tall, redheaded fellow leaped up and offered her his chair.

"This is Emma." Most of the names were lost on Emma, except for Betsy, a petite dark-haired woman who reminded her of her old Betsy McCall doll.

"I guess we've formed a club," said Angeline. "The twenty-thirty-something-gang. In case you haven't noticed, most of the passengers are a little on the elderly side."

"Yeah," chimed in a nameless female. "We gotta stick together, or the Geritol crowd will take over, and before long, all we'll hear will be Lawrence Welk tunes." There was a round of laughter, and Emma smiled and tried to fit in. They seemed to accept her right away. Amazing! They all looked so self-assured and sophisticated. If they only knew what a wallflower she'd been up till now.

"Emma," began Angeline quietly as the rest of the crowd turned to accept the tray of appetizers brought by a waitress. "I noticed you've already met Aaron."

"Aaron Fitzpatrick?" answered Emma guardedly.

Angeline nodded and sipped her soda. "I know it's none of my business, Emma, but I thought you might want to know— Aaron is a little strange."

Emma regarded her with suspicion. "What do you mean?"

"Oh, don't look so worried. It's probably nothing. Just my overactive imagination. Now, tell me, Emma, where are you going? Australia?"

"For a few days, then on to New Guinea."

She glanced up from her soda with interest. "Vacation?"

Emma tried to explain, simultaneously weighing what Angeline had said about Aaron along with the fact that the woman was apparently not involved with him.

"We're heading down to the disco now," announced Mark. "You two coming?"

Emma and Angeline followed at a more sedate pace as the rowdy bunch trooped down the stairs, whooping and laughing like kids no older than Tim Miller, or maybe even Shane, her little nephew back home. Mark actually slid down the banister. Emma found herself entering into the relaxed mood, shedding some of her stuffiness in the process.

In the seventies-style disco, lights flashed and music roared. Emma danced with several of the fellows, glancing at the door every few minutes in hopes that Aaron would soon show up. But when the disc jockey played the last tune, Emma realized he wasn't coming. Why had Aaron mentioned dancing tonight if he hadn't planned to show up himself? Still, she'd had fun. In fact, she couldn't remember when she'd ever had a better time.

As the group left the disco, Emma noticed a solitary figure in the shadowy walkway. Aaron! But he simply turned and walked away. Emma felt confused and torn. Part of her wanted to run after him. Another part of her was furious with him for standing her up.

"Don't worry about him, Emma," whispered Angeline. "You're better off without him."

❧ ❧ ❧ ❧

Emma lay alone in her cabin, unable to get his face out of her mind. The hurt look in his eyes burned into her soul and smoldered there. She had no relationship with the man really. Nothing to lose. So why did she feel that she had failed . . . again?

Eight

The next morning Emma joined Angeline for a lecture and
film on the history of Hawaii. Once again, she searched the
crowded theater for Aaron, but saw mostly gray and balding
heads. She and Angeline were definitely the youngsters in this
group.

After the lecture, Angeline was full of suggestions. "Why
don't we rent a car in Hawaii? We get only one day there, and
we'll want to get in as much sightseeing as possible. I heard you
can circle Oahu in a single day and still see a lot along the way."

"I'd love to." Emma could hardly believe her luck. She had
expected to be stuck in Waikiki for the entire day. She admired
Angeline's take-charge attitude, wishing at the same time she
could be more like her.

"Good. We'll start out early. I already have a map, and we
can arrange for the rental car from the ship."

They headed to the lunch buffet, where Angeline picked up
a plate and turned to Emma with a smile. "I'm having a great
time. I haven't had a vacation in two years. I worked for a law
firm that bribed me with all kinds of incentives to give up my
vacation time. You'd think being engaged to one of the asso-
ciates would have helped some."

"You're engaged?"

"Not anymore." Angeline paused at the seafood section and
lowered her voice in a conspiratorial tone. "I broke my engagement to my fiancé, Emma. Practically left him at the altar, I'm
ashamed to say."

"You're kidding?" Emma spooned some crabmeat onto her plate, then stared at the woman, hoping she'd explain.

Angeline popped a bay shrimp into her mouth. "He was wealthy, successful, good-looking, and he treated me like a queen. But when I left, I forfeited my job, too." They sat at a table in the middle of the room as Angeline continued her tale. "We'd been engaged for a year."

"Why did you give it all up?"

"Well, as I've told you, things are not always what they seem. Apparently, Bill, who traveled for the company, had an 'Angeline' in every port, so to speak. I doubt if he'd have gone through with the wedding, but I didn't stay around to find out." Emma nodded, wondering why she wasn't absolutely crushed. "Anyway, my uncle—he's a movie producer in Australia—has invited me to come work for him."

"So you're going to be an actress."

Angeline laughed, showing two even rows of white teeth. "No, silly, I'll just help out until Uncle Jake decides what to do with me. Besides, he only produces documentaries."

That afternoon they sunned and swam. Angeline, as usual, did most of the talking, but Emma enjoyed listening. It was an education of sorts. Social Skills 101. Throughout the afternoon and dinner hour, Emma kept a secret vigil for Aaron. He seemed to have evaporated into the sea air.

The gang planned to meet again after dinner, and Angeline, the undesignated but accepted leader, made sure Emma came along. This time, the smoke and the noise got to her earlier than usual, and she slipped away, unnoticed, from the rest of the crowd.

The warmth of the tropical evening caught her by surprise, and she strolled toward the bow of the ship, pausing on an upper deck where a gentle ocean breeze drifted across her face. Slowly her eyes adjusted to the darkness, and after a bit, she noticed someone standing nearby. The presence of another person slightly spoiled her pleasure, but she was not going to relinquish this delicious spot.

"Emma?"

Aaron! Hearing his voice emerge out of the night was like a

match being struck. A flame ignited in her heart and sizzled there. She turned and looked at him.

"I thought I recognized you, Emma. How have you been?" He leaned against the rail, then continued without waiting for her reply. "You seem to be quite the party girl—somehow I hadn't quite pictured you like that—" It was the way his voice trailed off—leaving room for doubt and shame—that reminded her of her grandmother.

"Actually, Aaron, it was *you* who mentioned the disco in the first place." She hadn't intended to sound quite so defensive.

He nodded in understanding and looked up at the sky. She followed his gaze, feeling her irritation fade in the brilliance of a million stars winking back at her.

"Beautiful, isn't it?" He spoke quietly, soothingly. "I'm sorry, Emma—about the other night. I got caught up in this remarkable discussion with an elderly gentleman, actually a retired dean from a theological seminary." He chuckled. "We didn't agree on much, but the old chap was quite a conversationalist. I peeked into the disco, but it was just closing."

"I see . . . thanks for telling me. It *had* bothered me a little. . . ." The breeze was cooler now, and she shivered beneath her thin cotton blouse.

"Come with me," he said, and she obeyed without question. Her heart thumped loudly, and she wondered if she were being foolish for blindly following a man she barely knew. But to her relief, they wound up in the ship's cozy library, and she sighed and sank into a deep leather armchair.

"This is one of my favorite haunts," he said as he sat across from her. "It's usually deserted in the evening, and I've found it to be a peaceful refuge."

Emma glanced around with approval. She felt at peace in a library. It was one of the few safe places back home where she had been able to escape from her grandmother periodically. This one was furnished with floor-to-ceiling bookcases, partially filled with dignified volumes, a comfortable sofa, and a leather reading desk and chairs that lent the small room an air of dignified elegance. On the floor was what had to be an authentic Oriental rug.

Aaron stretched out his long frame and rested the heels of his loafers on the coffee table. "Rooms like these make me long for a pipe. I'd probably be a smoker, were it not for cancer. A good pipe has such a nice look and feel to it, don't you think?"

Emma nodded, wanting to know more about this mystery man. "Where are you going, Aaron?"

"I plan to circle the globe, Emma. Take in places like Bangkok, Nepal, maybe even New Guinea." He dangled the last revelation like a baited hook. She didn't bite.

"It's my belief that people are books." He gestured toward the shelves. "Books just waiting to be read and understood." He swung his feet to the floor and leaned forward, bracing his elbows on his knees. "What's *your* story, Emma?"

She shook her head and laughed nervously. "Oh, I've already told you pretty much everything there is to know about me. I suppose I'm just one of those boring short stories."

"I very much doubt that." The intensity of his gaze took her breath away. "I suspect the best part is yet to be written. Recalling the past is a good way to get in touch with your present—and your future. Tell me about your parents, Emma—your earliest memories—"

She looked up at the ceiling, avoiding his probing eyes. "I don't really have many memories. It's funny, I was just trying to recall my parents today, and that part of my life seemed so blank—"

"Do you remember what your father looked like?"

"Let's see, he was tall—but, of course, as a child I thought everyone was tall! He had hair about the color of mine—I've always called it 'mouse brown.' " At Aaron's frown, she dropped the self-deprecating humor. "He was an architect—"she brightened—"actually designed our house. It was a fantastic house—huge fireplace, lots of windows. But Mom didn't like it."

"Do you know why?"

Emma closed her eyes, straining to recall. "Money. Yes, I remember—the house cost too much, which meant Mom would have to get a job outside our home. But she was an artist and wanted to do her art."

"Hmm, and did she? Get a job—before the accident, that is."

"Yes, I'd just started first grade when Mom went to work in Dad's office." Emma shook her head, the foggy memories rolling in. But they weren't happy memories. And suddenly she wanted to tuck them safely away once more.

Aaron was relentless. "Were you sad because your mom was busy at work and didn't have time to spend with you?"

Emma swallowed the lump in her throat. "Oh, we were well cared for," she said, feeling fiercely loyal. "A nice neighbor lady baby-sat us after school." She took a deep breath, a particularly painful memory beginning to surface. "Mom and Dad fought a lot. Sometimes Dad got really angry, and it was scary—"

"Was he abusive?"

Emma squeezed her eyes shut and nodded. What good did it do to remember?

"Did he ever hurt you?"

She let herself go. The tears came, first in a trickle, then in a torrent as she remembered long-forgotten pain. Her father's rages, his drinking—

Fumbling for a tissue, she came up short. Aaron reached out, but instead of handing her a handkerchief, he pulled her over to the couch and into his arms. She didn't resist.

She allowed him to stroke her hair. He murmured soothing words in her ear, comforting her like a child, and suddenly she felt safe and protected. She clung to him and sobbed until there were no more tears.

Finally she sat up, feeling foolish and hoping he'd say something. She frantically dug through her purse again, as if her life depended on finding a tissue. He looked on, strangely silent. What must he be thinking?

Gathering her last shred of dignity, she rose and announced, "It's getting late, and I'm tired. Think I'll turn in now."

He stood beside her. "I'll see you to your cabin."

At her door, he held her again, tilting her chin toward his. "My poor, little Emma," he whispered, bending over to kiss her lips softly. He kissed her again, this time with more passion. After a moment, she pulled away. She wanted him to kiss her—

but not like this. Not after tonight's emotional outburst.

Right now, all she needed was a chance to make some sense of her painful memories and then, hopefully, to lock them away once and for all. "I'm sorry, Aaron. I can't do this," she said as she fumbled with her key.

"It's okay, Emma. I understand." He smiled, released her, and walked away.

Emma closed the door behind him and collapsed onto her bunk. Over the years, she and Fran had seldom spoken of their parents, and if they did, only of the superficial things—the beautiful home they missed, Mom's talent, Dad's design skills. Never any details. And never, ever any feelings.

The house and furnishings had been sold to cover her parents' unpaid bills. That was probably where their old jazz records had gone—

Emma sighed and got up to splash her face with cold water. She stared into the mirror. Just as she suspected. Her eyes were puffy and swollen now, and her skin was blotchy and red. She'd never looked worse. What a memory for Aaron!

How was it that what had happened so long ago still had the power to interfere with the present? It wasn't fair! Just when her opportunity for romance came along, her parents' problems had surfaced like some sea monster, its long tentacles choking the life out of her, stealing her special moment. Aaron probably thought she was emotionally disturbed, and now she'd be embarrassed to see him again.

Maybe it was hopeless. Maybe, no matter how hard she tried, she would never be able to run away from the past.

Nine

$\mathcal{E}$mma awoke early, though she'd hardly slept that night. Aaron would surely be out watching the sunrise, but she couldn't bring herself to face him. Instead, she ate her continental breakfast in her cabin, not even wanting to sit with the Millers. She knew Charlene would probably notice her red eyes and wonder what was wrong.

Donning dark sunglasses, she met Angeline as planned. The anticipation of seeing Hawaii somewhat lessened Emma's anxieties, and before long, Angeline's contagious zeal eclipsed Emma's gloom.

Angeline navigated their rental car through the busy streets of Honolulu until they reached a winding coastal road. At a viewpoint they pulled over to see Diamond Head protrude majestically from the sea. The water looked perfectly clear from their vantage, exposing the ocean floor in patches of varying shades of blue.

"It's fantastic!" breathed Emma. "I had no idea it would be so beautiful." She felt the world was at her feet. At the same moment, the frightening realization dawned on her that she could have been sitting at her computer back in Iowa, and she noted how fortunate she truly was.

They picked up some fruit and snacks and continued on their journey, stopping at Sunset Beach for a swim in the warm surf. Emma felt sure this was paradise as she admired the white, sandy shore bordered by tall palm trees. She smiled as she recalled the travel poster in Linda's office and then rubbed on another layer of sunscreen—determined not to end up like the magenta girl.

Even with Angeline's careful scheduling they began running short on time, but they still managed to squeeze in a whirlwind tour of the Polynesian Cultural Center. There Emma paused briefly at a bamboo kiosk to purchase a pair of beaded leather sandals for herself and some shell necklaces to send home. They feasted on a walking dinner of teriyaki skewers and pineapple slushes, then rushed back to the car.

The ship's whistle blew just as they dropped the car off at the wharf. Knowing the ship waited for no one, they linked arms and ran up the gangway, laughing breathlessly over their day's escapades. Emma felt like a naughty child as the crew sternly gated off the walkway behind them. It was then that she noticed Aaron leaning against the railing, looking their way. But when he saw her glance in his direction, he quickly turned and walked off without so much as a nod.

❧   ❧   ❧   ❧

The next few days passed in a continuous barrage of activity, orchestrated by Angeline. Almost every moment was filled. Emma felt as if she were riding a carrousel at high speed. But the busy schedule made it easier to bury those troublesome childhood memories that never should have been exhumed— and to stick to her resolution to forget all about Aaron, who remained conveniently out of sight.

On the morning they were to dock in Fiji, Emma rose early and went out to see the sunrise. The morning air was warm and humid, and clung to her like a damp sheet. He wasn't there. She settled into a deck chair and tried to convince herself she didn't care.

Leaning back in the chair, she stared out over the blue ocean that stretched as far as the eye could see. The sun emerged in a brilliant blaze, sending a blinding streak of light slicing through the water directly toward her—like a long, pure finger of white. It was almost as if God himself were reaching out.

"Coffee, Emma?" Aaron held a steaming cup before her.

"Thank you." She accepted the cup, and he took the chair

beside her. "Haven't seen much of you lately—" She purposely ended her sentence midway between question and statement.

He nodded, "But *I've* seen *you*."

She sipped her coffee, struggling with the confusion he always stirred in her. She couldn't deny the fact that her heart twisted ecstatically at the sound of his voice, and yet life was so much more peaceful when he wasn't around. If this were love, then she'd better change her definition. Still, he seemed so indifferent—

"I suppose you'll be joining your friends for the tour of Fiji—" He had such a strange way of asking a question, so aloof and noncommittal.

"Uh-huh." She didn't dare look at him, but pulled her knees toward her and gazed out across the water again, trying to focus. Trying to remain calm.

"Under the circumstances, I probably shouldn't ask, but I'd love to show you Fiji, Emma."

A little warning whistle went off in her heart, but she ignored it. "I suppose I could beg off," she heard herself saying. Suddenly Sam and Mark seemed like college boys next to this mature, seasoned man of the world. "I'm sure they'll understand." She wondered what Angeline would think. For some reason it was important to please her new friend. Still, her desire to be with Aaron was even stronger.

"Great!" His eyes actually twinkled, filling her with a rush of warmth. "Meet me by the gangplank after breakfast."

"Are you sure *you'll* be there?"

"I'll be there, Emma." His solemn gaze was both promise and premonition. A delicious shiver ran down her spine.

Emma spotted Angeline on her way to breakfast and explained the change of plans.

Disapproval showed on her pretty face. "Just be careful, Em," she warned. "He may be good-looking, but I get the distinct impression he could be . . . dangerous."

Emma laughed uneasily. "Don't worry, I can handle it. He's my friend, Angeline. It's not like he'd harm me or anything."

"Just the same—watch your step." She gave Emma's hand a squeeze and went to find her table.

The Millers, as usual, were already eating breakfast. Emma had felt a little guilty around them lately. It seemed they were always inviting her to join them for one thing or another, and most of the time she'd declined, opting for the livelier crowd. But she did enjoy their company at mealtimes.

"We'll be docking in Suva shortly," Charlene told her. "Will you be seeing Fiji with friends today, Emma?"

"Well—yes. Aaron Fitzpatrick has offered to show me around." Emma watched Charlene's brow lift slightly.

"Fiji might give you a little taste of what New Guinea is like," injected Fred, apparently not noticing his wife's subtle expression. "I haven't been there in years, but there are a few similarities."

Tim was more verbal than Emma had ever heard him. "I wonder if the Suva police still have a band to welcome the ships. They're a crack-up, Emma. They wear these funny outfits and play out of tune."

"There's lots to see in Fiji. Is your friend Aaron familiar with the area?" Charlene managed to bring the conversation back to him.

"He seems to be." Emma had barely touched her breakfast when she stood and excused herself. Food was out of the question with her stomach tied in knots. "You folks have a good day. I'll see you later."

She went to meet Aaron, wondering if it was a mistake. And why everyone was so concerned, especially when they didn't know him. But there he was, waiting for her, looking cool and casual in a white shirt and neatly pressed khaki pants. Reassured, she quickened her step.

"Ready?" he asked, taking her arm. "I ordered a car and a guide."

"Isn't that nice?" Just as Tim had described, the police band—in full regalia—was playing, off-key.

Aaron nodded and directed her toward a man waving a paper high in the air. Drawing nearer, she could make out the words "Feetspatrik Tour."

"You are Meester Feetzpatrik?" asked the small dark fellow, as he pumped Aaron's hand. "I am Shano, your personal tour guide for the day." He proudly led them to a beat-up Toyota, opening the door as graciously as if it were a limousine. The car's dusty interior reeked of stale cigarette smoke, and Emma cranked down the window as Aaron discussed the day's itinerary with the driver.

They drove just a few blocks before Shano stopped and parked the car. "Thees ees the market," he announced, opening the door again.

Palm-roofed shelters lined the street while dozens of people, toting baskets and bags, milled about. She and Aaron joined the shoppers, and Emma allowed him to guide her past the tables overflowing with goods. Women draped in layers of silk were selling textiles and household items. Fijians in brightly-printed cotton sold produce and hand-crafted goods. Everywhere she looked, there were dirty, ragged children, like a swarm of hungry mosquitoes, their little faces peering up with unmasked curiosity.

"What do they want?" whispered Emma to Aaron. A skinny boy with matted hair tugged on her skirt, looking up with pathetic dark eyes.

"They're begging," he replied in a matter-of-fact tone.

She unzipped her purse and the children immediately pressed closer. Aaron grabbed her hand. "No, don't do that!" he grated out. "That will only cause trouble and reinforce the behavior."

"I just wanted to give them a little—"

"Put it away, Emma," he ordered, his hand still on hers.

"Shoo, shoo!" hissed Shano, stomping his feet and waving his arms to frighten the children. The skinny boy gazed into Emma's eyes with a final, silent plea and she felt her heart splinter, but Shano's voice grew louder and more insistent, and in the next instant, the children had scattered.

They departed the busy marketplace—none too soon for Emma's peace of mind—and soon left the city behind. Shano drove down a narrow road entering what seemed a tropical garden of lush undergrowth, palm trees, and flowering plants.

They passed over a rickety bridge and stopped at an orchid farm run by Hindus, so Shano explained. He led them through the huge, open-framed buildings that housed thousands of orchid plants. The colors, ranging from the palest hint of pink to deep magenta, were magnificent, and the exotic fragrance was a pleasant relief from the rotting coconut husks. Emma was thrilled when Aaron picked a white orchid, after a nod from Shano, and tucked it behind her ear.

After leaving a hut where vanilla beans were processed into extract, Shano announced that it was time to move on. On the way to their next stop, Aaron shared some interesting tidbits about Fiji's history. But with so much to take in, Emma's mind was whirling, and she tuned him out. Was this what it would be like in New Guinea?

Shano took them to his village, where they would experience authentic Fijian culture and meet his family and friends. Apparently the villagers were celebrating some special occasion today, and she and Aaron were welcomed warmly. Before long they were pressed into a circle of people, watching a demonstration of spear-dancing staged by some older village men.

One event followed another in rapid succession, the motions and music growing louder and louder. At some point during the festivities, a large, rotund man picked up a gigantic knife and, with a loud whack, split a coconut into two neat halves. He then took a half and twisted it quickly on a carved, rounded point, protruding from a wooden bench. Fluffy, white flakes of coconut fell into a large wooden bowl, which was then presented to Aaron and Emma.

Imitating Aaron, she scooped up a handful, eating with her fingers. She'd never cared much for coconut, recalling how Grandma had spoiled many a perfectly good cake by covering it in the dried, shredded stuff. But this was something entirely different—moist and delicious, with a delicate flavor.

Aaron went over to a group of men and returned with two round cups made from coconut shells. Inside was some sort of concoction that tasted sweet but different. Wanting to be polite, she drank hers and watched as more musicians played.

More and more people joined the dance. The music swelled

and throbbed. Emma's head was whirling as she tried to con- centrate on the gyrating dancers, but the music faded in and out. She heard a strange buzzing sound that steadily increased in vol- ume until it felt as if her head would explode. She placed her hands over her ears in a futile attempt to shut out the horrible roar.

"Are you all right?" asked Aaron, his face swimming in front of her.

"I'm so dizzy—I feel sick—I need to get back to the ship." she murmured.

Aaron's next words were lost on her. She saw him saying something to Shano, but all she could hear was the frantic drum- ming in her head. She did not resist when the two men lifted her, carried her to a small hut on the edge of the village, and gently laid her on a floor mat.

She closed her eyes and took a deep breath. The buzzing in her ears had subsided, but she was still woozy. The repetitive beat of the drums permeated the walls of the woven grass hut, and Emma felt herself sinking into the earthen floor as the prim- itive tribal sounds consumed her. She gave herself up to the hyp- notic rhythm.

Before she dropped off into a stuporous sleep, she felt some- one stroking her hair, and she forced her eyes open. Aaron's face swam above her, mouthing smooth words. She felt him trace her profile with his fingertips and then move down her bare arm. What was he doing?

His breath was on her cheek now, his lips very close to hers. But she couldn't move. It was as if she were wrapped in a thick, soggy blanket. She felt helpless, completely immobilized. She wanted him to stop, but she couldn't utter a sound. Then, slowly, everything faded to a hazy tone of gray.

Ten

Eastern Highlands, Papua New Guinea

$\mathcal{M}$r. Daniels, I know I promised to finish out the school year, but I just can't take it no more. I'm awfully sorry. But I'm giving you my notice—"

"What do you mean?" Josh dropped the bag of coffee beans and stared incredulously at the woman fidgeting before him. She tugged at the stained apron tied too tightly across her bulging middle, then stared down at her dusty white anklets rolled neatly over the tops of her sturdy brown shoes. He had never seen her wear anything but those sturdy shoes. No sandals. No canvas shoes. Perhaps these were the only shoes she owned, or perhaps she had several identical pairs. He shook his head in dismay. She had seemed the type of governess who might stay on for a couple years or even longer, if he made it worth her while. And now she was leaving!

"You can't do this to me, Miss Grouse!" he exclaimed as he landed a solid kick on the bag of coffee beans, sending at least two pounds spewing into the dirt. "What are we supposed to do now? You know the children have been through too many governesses already. And you've been here less than six months. You gave me your word! You promised me at least a year! You can't just run out on me like this. I've paid you good money—"

"I know. I know," she interrupted. "And it's like I've already said, I'm sorry. I truly am. I just can't—"

"*Can't?* You mean *won't*! You led me to believe you really cared about the children. But obviously that isn't so, is it, Miss Grouse? You couldn't care less about what this will do to them!"

"Well, of course I'm frightfully sorry for the poor, motherless babes." She pulled a hanky from her pocket and dabbed at her eyes.

He let out a long sigh. "Miss Grouse, you must understand how difficult this is for young children to get to know someone and then—lose that person. Can't you at least stay on until I can replace you?"

"I would, I truly would—but I just can't. I'm horribly sorry. Believe me, I know better than anyone how bad they need a woman's touch—especially in this godforsaken country! But, please, Mr. Daniels, try to see how hard it is for me to live up here all alone—all isolated like this. Why I haven't seen another white face, outside of yours and the children's, for nearly a month. I'm just not cut out for this sort of outback life. I'm the sort of woman as needs a town nearby. I miss the shops and the races and Bingo."

Josh leaned his head back and looked up at the sky. It was, as usual, clear blue, untainted by smog or diesel fumes. He drew in a deep breath of fresh highland air, then decided to give it one more try. He'd been told he had charm. Of course, it hadn't been tested in—how long now? Well, for years.

"But, Miss Grouse, if you could just reconsider. The children have been through so much—and they genuinely like and respect you. Couldn't you just stay until—"

"Mr. Daniels, I reckon I've not been one to give out my opinion too free. But if you're thinkin' to make me feel guilty about your children, then maybe you'd better get ready to hear a piece of my mind. You ought to be ashamed of yourself. If *you* really cared about your children, you'd be takin' them out of here and back to civilization. This is no fit place to raise a proper family. The wee bairns should be in a real school with other children their ages. Even boardin' school would be better than living up here like hermits. You'll turn them into misfits, you will, Mr. Daniels, mark my words!"

She didn't pause for breath, but continued firing her volley of accusations. "And the idea of keepin' people like Tabo in the house! Why, that woman makes my skin crawl every time I look at her. And the children are scared to death of her. Take poor little Holly—why, I haven't been able to coax a single word out of her the entire time I've been here. And Sara is turning into a little old woman right before your eyes. And Matt, well, he might worship the ground you walk on, Mr. Daniels, but he won't do his lessons half the time—"

"You never mentioned Matt's lessons before, Miss Grouse. If you had told me, I could—"

"Aw, you're always so busy with your coffee trees, Mr. Daniels. Most of time, you don't hardly know whether your children are even here or not."

"It isn't easy running a plantation with three children and no—" He stopped himself short. Even after all these years, it was too painful to say the words out loud.

"You mean,'with no mother'? Why not just out and say it? The children have no mother. And that's another shame, Mr. Daniels. Because just look at you—fit and handsome, you are, and not getting any younger, if you don't mind me sayin' it. Any other self-respectin' bloke would've gotten himself a new wife and mother for his children long ago—"

He threw up his hands. "That's quite enough, Miss Grouse."

"Well, if you were smart, you'd—"

"When will you be leaving then, Miss Grouse?"

She looked back down at her shoes. "Well, I'll give you a fortnight. But not a single day more. I've already written my sister to expect me in Port Moresby by then."

"Fine," he said in a resigned tone, then turned on his heel and strode off toward the south grove. Batty old windbag. Perhaps they were better off without her. But a fortnight! He would never locate another governess in a fortnight! He thought of Miss Grouse's suggestion that he find a new wife. Ha! If only it were that simple.

At first, right after Lila left, he had fully expected to see her back in a week or two—if only for the sake of the children. He figured she'd cry and carry on, and then beg his forgiveness.

And for the sake of the children, he would have forgiven her, too.

But when she didn't return, didn't write, didn't even ring him on the phone, he'd tried to put her out of his mind. And after awhile, the children even quit asking about her. He reckoned it wasn't so much that they didn't think about her, but probably more the result of his irritation when they did ask. He felt sorry for them, but he didn't have a clue as to what to do for them. How does one explain, or make up for, a renegade mother?

So he'd turned more and more to the plantation, leaving the care and education of his children to the never-ending string of governesses that had passed through their home in the last three years. Fair or not, that's how things had been with them. So what good was it to cry over spilt milk? Maybe this was the life he deserved.

He remembered a time in university when he had expected more. It had been an era when he had trusted God to steer his life. And although brief, he remembered it as a good time, a time when he'd had hope. That was before Lila. Somehow once she came along, everything changed.

He'd kept thinking that one day he'd actually sit down and talk it over with God. But time had raced by, and he'd never gotten around to it. Now he was too ashamed to expect anything from God. After all the neglecting he'd done, wouldn't God, in all likelihood, want to neglect him, too? Couldn't blame Him.

Josh reached the edge of the coffee grove—the place where the land fell away into a steep, rugged valley with mountains rising on every side. He sat down on a flat rock and shook his head. What now? He looked out across the mountains that were deepening to purple in the rapidly changing light that happened just at sunset. Usually so quick that he forgot to pause and take notice. That's how it was living close to the equator. One moment it was day, and the next, night. Sort of like his life. Maybe it was time to stop and take notice.

He'd never questioned the existence of God. That was a given. His parents had raised him to believe. And the beauty of the mountains had been a geological testament to the majesty of a creative Maker. But just like the mountains far off on the horizon, Josh had kept his distance from God. Or so he'd thought. Maybe God was not so far away, after all.

Josh took a deep breath and closed his eyes. Now, if he could just remember how to pray. . . .

Eleven

Fiji Islands

$\mathcal{E}$mma looked around groggily. Long slits of late-afternoon sunlight slanted across the woven floor mat, and tribal drums beat in cadence to the pounding inside her head. Slowly it all came back. She sat up and rubbed her eyes. She remembered Aaron kissing her. But nothing more—

"Emma!" exclaimed Aaron, bursting into the hut. "You're awake. How are you feeling?" He knelt down and looked into her eyes. The shadowy hut darkened his bearded countenance, and his eyes no longer looked blue, but black. She looked away uncomfortably, not knowing what to say. More importantly, wondering what had happened. She was angry and embarrassed, and Aaron said nothing to enlighten her.

Emma didn't mind that Shano drove fast. She just leaned back against the dusty seat of the Toyota and closed her eyes. Hopefully, he would think she was asleep. In reality, her head was clearer than ever. She felt his every movement, heard each breath he took as he sat beside her, his hand resting lightly, possessively, on her shoulder.

Oh, come on, Emma, she berated herself. *You're just being paranoid!* Like back in Iowa. Maybe she hadn't learned as much as she'd thought. All she knew was that she wanted to be back on board ship and rid of Aaron Fitzpatrick. The sooner, the better!

She longed to part ways on the deck, but he insisted on

walking her down to her cabin. Neither of them said a word, and the only sound was their footsteps echoing in the narrow hallway. She stopped at her door and slipped in the key, turning to look at him, hoping that his expression might hold some clue to this strange and frustrating day. His countenance was dark and impossible to read. She turned back to the now-open door and started to go in, hoping he'd go away.

"I'm sorry you became ill, Emma. I hope you'll feel better soon. Can I call the ship's doctor, bring you something?"

She shook her head. A huge lump pushed up in her throat. He walked away and she closed the door and collapsed in frustrated tears. What was wrong with her? Or was it him? All she wanted to do was sleep—and never see Aaron Fitzpatrick again.

When Emma awoke, it was after nine, but she was wide awake now and tired of her stuffy cabin. She changed clothes and ran upstairs. Strains of music floated out from the disco, but she had no desire to carouse with the night crowd.

Hoping her friends wouldn't spot her, she wandered the deck for a while until the fresh sea air cleared her head. Eventually, she ended up in the library. Not so much because she wanted to see him again, but because she had to know. Just what exactly was he up to? Had he put something in her drink? Maybe it was risky coming here alone like this, but she had to find out. Then she would tell him to get out of her life and leave her alone.

She absently perused the shelves until she found a fat novel, then settled into a chair, curling her legs beneath her, and pretended to read. He'd come, she was positive. She glanced at her watch again and then over to the vacant chair across from her. The leather wingback triggered a reminder of the painful conversation they'd had on that other night. Until now, she had managed to push it into a secluded corner of her mind. Now it rushed back at her, full force.

She shut her eyes tight, willing it to go away. It didn't work this time. Instead, she saw her mother cowering behind the laundry room door as her father shoved against it, wildly swinging his belt and hurling profanities and accusations. He'd kicked the door so hard he'd left a hole the size of a large grapefruit. But by the next evening, the door had been neatly replaced with a new one, and her father arrived home with a large bouquet of red roses—

"Emma, are you asleep?" His voice jerked her back to the present, and she opened her eyes to see him looming above her like a dark shadow.

Aaron eased himself into the chair and leaned forward. "Are you all right?" He looked straight into her eyes, his gaze magnetic, almost hypnotic. Even if she wanted to, she couldn't take her eyes off him.

She shook her head. Trying to sort through the wide spectrum of emotions was like trying to collect the white feathers of a burst down pillow. Her parents, her past, Aaron—it was too much.

"You look like you're in another world."

"Maybe I am—"

"What is it? Tell me what could cause such suffering, my poor, little Emma?"

She felt confused and angry when he called her that. It was no longer tender and sweet, only demeaning. "Oh, nothing worth rehashing." She wrestled her gaze from his, hoping her casual remark would convey that the subject was dismissed. In fact, she found herself wishing that she had never come here to this isolated spot.

"Thinking of your father?" His question caught her off guard, and she gasped and looked at him again. Why couldn't he leave her past alone? What good was it to dig these things up?

"You know, Emma," he continued, reaching out to take her hands in his. "When women have hang-ups about men, it often stems from a dysfunctional father-daughter relationship."

She jerked her hands away. "I don't have hang-ups about men!" She stood and turned her back to him, tired of his emotional prying. Why did he seem so insistent upon tearing into her past, leaving her wounds raw and bleeding?

"Emma . . ." He came from behind and placed his hands on

her shoulders, slowly turning her to face him. "I only want to help you. Come on, sit down. I'm your friend."

Mechanically, she did as she was told, responding as if she had no will of her own. She felt worn down, confused, tired.

Aaron leaned forward, intent on studying her, it seemed. "You hated your father, didn't you?" His words were very persuasive. He was right, of course. But how did he know? She nodded sadly and felt a tear trickle down her cheek.

He continued in the same monotone, almost like a prosecution attorney in an old movie. "And when your father died, you felt it was your fault. Felt your hatred had caused his death."

She looked at him in amazement. This man was either a prophet or a demon, but she was too stunned to determine which. Feeling like a child who had just been caught red-handed, she stammered, "I—I wished he was dead. I wanted him to die. But I didn't want my—my mother to die. Yes, I did feel like the accident was my fault—I've always felt that way—" She burst into sobs and he took her in his arms, stroking her hair. But when he tilted her chin to kiss her, she pushed him away.

"Don't do that!" she cried in frustration.

His smile was sad. "You see, Emma, there you go again, superimposing memories of your father onto every man you get close to. Until you conquer that, you'll never be able to give yourself completely to a man." His words, like a jagged knife, left her hurting and hopeless. Yet he offered no comfort, no solace, no practical words of wisdom.

"I don't understand you, Aaron," she said as she backed toward the door. "You act like you want to help, but all you do is hurt me. I don't need this!"

She turned and dashed from the room, eager to escape his probing inquistions.

"Emma!" cried Angeline when they nearly collided. "We've been looking all over for you. Charlene said she hadn't seen you, and I was worried that you might have missed the departure. My goodness, you look awful—what in the world is wrong?"

Emma didn't want to talk to anyone—especially Angeline. "I—I'm not feeling well."

Angeline glanced past Emma's shoulder. "I think I under-stand. Now, don't argue. You're coming with me." She took Emma firmly by the arm and marched her down a flight of steps.

"You're spending the night in my cabin." Angeline un-locked her door and pointed to the extra berth.

Too tired to protest, Emma sat down on the narrow bed in humility and defeat. "Oh, Angeline, my life is such a disaster!"

"Nonsense, Emma. You're not a mess. I just think you let the wrong guy mess with your head and, if I'm not mistaken, your heart as well. Right?"

Emma nodded sadly.

"I don't like to say 'I told you so.' I tried to warn you about Aaron, but I guess I should have been a little more specific." Angeline sat on her berth across the narrow room. "He tried to pull his junior psychology routine on me that night just out of San Francisco. I must admit he was pretty convincing." Her blue eyes clouded over. "Remember Betsy Nelson?" Emma nodded, thinking of the petite brunette who'd gotten off in Ha-waii. "Betsy knew Aaron from the university. Seems he has quite a reputation for preying upon young women—in fact, he may be facing legal problems when he gets home. Apparently he really goes for the vulnerable types. Know what I mean?"

"Yes, and I feel like a fool." Emma stared at the floor. "It figures. I'm absolutely hopeless."

"You're not a fool, Emma Davis. You're just pretty and in-nocent—and quite a find for Aaron. But now that you know what he's about, are you . . . okay? Did he break your heart?"

The hesitancy in Angeline's voice and her careful phrasing of the question were laughable. Emma did just that—at least a little bleat that passed for a laugh. "No, Angeline, not broken-hearted, just confused. I mean, I haven't dated much and—" Emma stopped, unsure of how to continue.

"Go on, Emma. I may not have a degree in psychology, but I know a thing or two about men."

"Well, judging from the way I feel when Aaron kisses me, I might be in love, yet I feel so uncomfortable with him. I can't explain how awful it is. What I've been feeling for Aaron couldn't be love, could it?"

Angeline grinned. "I think what you're feeling is called passion, Emma. Pure and simple—passion. Actually without love, it's not so pure—or simple. It can be lethal."

Emma nodded. "I think I understand, but don't the two ever go hand in hand?"

"Sure they do. I've even seen it in my own home. My parents have that kind of relationship—even after thirty-five years. It's what gives me hope. Well, that—and something else—"

"What's that?"

"I don't like to sound preachy, but I firmly believe God has someone special for me. You see, before I broke up with Kevin, I wasn't really happy, but I couldn't put my finger on the reason. Then one night I attended an evangelistic crusade with my little sister. I tried to cancel out, but I'd promised her." Angeline rose to pace the small cabin, and Emma could see her face reflected in the dark porthole. "It may sound strange to you, and I don't really understand it completely myself, but I felt I heard God speak that night. Oh, not out loud, but here"—she pointed to her chest—"in my heart.

"I gave my life to the Lord—like the evangelist explained— and soon after that, I knew I was supposed to break off with Kevin. At the time, it was the scariest thing I've ever done." She sat down on the berth beside Emma. "The funny thing is, I've never looked back. And the very next week, this job with my uncle came through. So—here I am." Angeline's radiant smile spoke volumes.

"So . . . you really believe God has a special man for you?"

"Maybe. But I'm not on a manhunt. I think God will work out the details." She rose, opened her suitcase, and handed Emma a blue nightgown. "Do you mind sharing a cabin with a religious fanatic?"

That night Emma lay in the small bunk, pondering her friend's words. When her thoughts drifted to Aaron, it was with a sense of finality. She sighed in relief. She hadn't really been in love, but the feelings he'd stirred in her were frightening, and, she had to admit, some of his observations had hit uncomfortably close to home.

She longed for the experience that Angeline had described. To confidently know that God was leading her life, that perhaps He even had someone out there for her.

Here's my heart, God, she prayed silently. *I can't trust it with anyone—not even myself. But I believe I can trust you. Show me how.*

Twelve

*T*he ship docked for a day in New Zealand. And although it was April, they were informed that this was actually autumn in the southern hemisphere. Strange, to see fall foliage this time of year.

By taking up permanent residence in Angeline's cabin, Emma had successfully avoided Aaron for the past few days. It was fun having a roommate, and her energetic friend kept them occupied almost around the clock.

"Look," whispered Angeline as they strolled through the bustling seaport town of Auckland. Following her gaze, Emma spotted Aaron with one arm draped around a redhead as he opened the door of a waiting cab. She was infinitely thankful that she was not the unsuspecting female getting into the cab with him.

They covered a lot of ground in one day—museums, botanical gardens, the shopping district, a Maori exhibit, finally boarding a tiny ferryboat bound for Devonport.

There, they enjoyed high tea in true English fashion, and later explored the quaint, old-fashioned neighborhood until dusk. This time of evening always moved Emma in a way she could never explain. Something about seeing people coming home from work left her with a sense of isolation and loneliness. Still early enough for the drapes to be open, the houses looked warm and inviting inside. She noticed a particularly sweet cottage and wondered who might live there. Some lucky family, complete with children and pets, no doubt. The homey scene filled her with a dull ache. Someone else's life—not hers.

"Emma, aren't you feeling well?" asked Charlene at dinner. "You've hardly touched your steak."

"It's funny," she confessed, picking at her salad. "I think I'm homesick. Not that I want to go back—not yet, anyway."

"Well, we'll be in New Guinea before you know it," Fred put in, lifting a forkful of prime rib. "What will you do when you get there?"

"I don't really know," she answered honestly.

"You can come live with us," offered Tim. "I'll even introduce you to a real cannibal."

Emma smiled in spite of her increasing nostalgia. The boy had really warmed up to her since the beginning of the trip. She'd begun to treat him like a kid brother, and he played right along. She rolled her eyes. "Thanks just the same, Tim, but I'll pass."

"Well, I'm working up a list of names—contacts, you know—with guesthouse addresses and phone numbers. You can't be too careful," said Charlene. "I used to feel so safe in New Guinea, but in the last ten years, we've seen a sharp rise in the crime rate. You can't trust everyone you meet."

"Now, don't go scaring her, Charlene," Fred interrupted. "New Guinea is a terrific place—nothing like it on earth." He launched into another exciting adventure story about the time they'd once discovered an old, undetonated bomb left over from the War. Emma, glassy-eyed, plastered a smile on her face, prepared to wait out a replay of World War II.

She awoke to a violent rocking motion that nearly threw her out of bed.

"Hey, this must be the bad weather the Captain was expecting in the Tasmanian Strait." Angeline pulled on her jeans, nearly toppling over as the floor moved beneath her. "Want to check it out?"

They dressed awkwardly and scurried out, struggling up the steps against the erratic movement of the ship. They both held on to the banister to keep from falling. Outside on the deserted decks, the storm raged with a vengeance, driving the vessel violently up and down as it cut across gigantic waves. The huge ship seemed small by comparison, at the mercy of the wild seas. They clung to the brass rail, watching in fascination as the huge, white-capped waves and massive, dark swells pounded the ship.

Their hair whipped into tangles by the wind, Emma and Angeline sought the shelter of the dining room and found Fred and Tim among the few braving breakfast. The tables were set with a minimum of cutlery, and tin cups instead of glasses.

"Charlene isn't feeling well," explained Fred. "Maybe Angeline would like to join us."

"Thanks," said Angeline. As they sat down, Emma caught a salt shaker before it slid off the table.

"Yep, it's usually like this," said Tim, sounding like an old salt. "Everybody gets sick and holes up in their cabins. Pretty soon it smells so rotten down there you don't wanna go down unless you can hold your breath for a long time. Mom always gets sick on this part of the trip."

"Does she need anything?" asked Emma.

"Privacy," replied Fred matter-of-factly. "She just has to sleep it off. She took some pretty potent seasick pills, and I expect she'll be out for the duration."

The four played cards in the game room, taking occasional breaks to monitor the storm until they got cold and wet, then returning to warm up with mugs of hot cocoa.

Angeline asked Fred about his work and appeared genuinely interested in learning about Bible translating. Emma still marveled at her attractive friend, so seemingly unaffected by her own good looks, her savvy, yet so intrigued with everyone else around her. Angeline was anything but the stereotypical dumb blonde.

But there was something else—something elusive, some inner strength that drove her, made her fearless. Maybe it had come from that encounter with God Angeline had mentioned earlier. . . .

"Hey, Em," whispered Tim as Fred and Angeline engaged in a discussion of the phonetic mysteries of the Taumani vernacular. "Wanna see something really cool?" Emma nodded and followed him.

They stepped out into the storm again, this time descending some steps to a lower front deck. Tim cut beneath a roped-off area that Emma was pretty sure was off limits. Against her better judgment, she went along, streaking through the rain after him until they reached the bow of the ship.

Here, the waves seemed very close—too close for comfort. The roaring of the wind drowned out her shouted warning as she joined Tim on the narrow ledge of the bow. He was peering over the edge, motioning for her to look. She knelt beside him and looked down. With each swell, the ship's bow rose high out of the water, revealing the curvature of the ship's bottom beneath. Clinging to the railing, coated with its slippery layers of paint, she watched in horror. The dark, frothy sea lurked below them like an open grave.

Suddenly the ship began to drop, like an elevator plummeting out of control. She struggled to hold on to the slick surface of the rail. The sea seemed to swallow them as a bulky wave washed over the bow, and they sprawled helplessly. She wasn't sure if she was still on board or actually lost in the sea. In that split second, Emma cried out to God and grabbed for Tim's pant leg, peeling his paralyzed hands from the railing just as he was about to go overboard. Seeing the terror in his eyes, she wrestled him from the bow.

Still gasping from exertion, they gathered their wits and dashed back across the deck. Spotting some crew members pouring down the port-side steps, waving their arms and screaming like madmen, Emma shoved Tim ahead of her. They sprinted up the stairs, not waiting to hear what the outraged crew had to say about this little escapade. Then, entering a dark corridor, they kept running until they were safely out of sight.

When they paused for breath, Emma grabbed Tim by the arm. "Tim Miller, are you crazy? What in the world were you thinking? We could have been drowned out there!"

The boy was still shaking, and his face pasty white. Regretting her hasty words, Emma gave him a playful punch, then wiped her nose on a soggy sleeve. The angry red faces of the crew flashed through her mind, and she began to laugh. Tim started to giggle, and soon they were both laughing hysterically as she continued to drag him down the hallway.

"We'd better go change," gasped Emma between fits of laughter. "These wet clothes are a dead giveaway. The captain might have us flogged."

"Or make us walk the plank," Tim snorted.

"Or throw us in the brig—with nothing but bread and water to eat."

Tim groaned dramatically at this dire speculation. Then, suddenly serious, he threw her a skeptical glance. "You gonna tell my parents, Emma?"

Emma pondered, considering her responsibility. "I don't see why they should know—it's over now, and we're okay." She fixed him with a stern look. "But I'm sure you won't pull that stunt again."

She left him at his cabin door with a hug, then headed for Angeline's cabin.

As she peeled off her soggy clothes, Emma realized she and Tim could have been shark food by now. Then she remembered crying out to God so naturally. And He had answered—miraculously saving them both. She whispered a heartfelt thanks.

Thirteen

The next morning Emma awoke early, shaking with fright. Another nightmare. She took a deep breath and waited for the terror to drain away, like the remnants of a flash flood. Angeline was still asleep.

The blue circle of dusky light drew Emma's eyes to the porthole, and she decided to slip out early to greet yet another sunrise. The thought of meeting Aaron on deck no longer filled her with anxiety. Nevertheless, she was relieved when he didn't show up.

She watched the leftover storm clouds on the horizon begin to blush with the awakening dawn. She pulled the woolly blanket around her and shivered, not so much from the cool morning air as from the knowledge that God was alive. She could *see* His hand at work.

The dining room was busier this morning, but many passengers still looked pale and wobbly. Once again Charlene was missing at breakfast, along with Fred.

After breakfast, she and Angeline reported to the fitness room for their regular workout. Emma could keep up with Angeline now, quite a contrast from her former computer-bound self. For the first time since high school Emma felt she was in top form.

"I'm sure ready to end this trip," commented Angeline as she adjusted the pressure on the Exercycle. "It's been fun, but

I'm beginning to get claustrophobia. Give me some solid ground."

Emma climbed onto the stepper beside her. "But we're going to keep in touch, right?"

"I plan to come visit you in New Guinea first chance I get," Angeline assured her, pedaling away. "It's not all that far from Australia."

"No," said Emma, wondering how she'd fend for herself in a strange country without her good friend. The prospect loomed before her like a black hole.

The rest of the morning was spent sorting and packing. At lunch, assigned seats were abandoned and the gang sat together, laughing and joking—only this time there was an underlying element of sadness. Like the last day of school, tomorrow they'd all go their separate ways. There was great anticipation, laced with the regret of saying good-bye.

After lunch, Emma slipped down to the Miller cabin to see Charlene. She lifted her hand to knock and, hearing an unusual sound coming from inside, she stopped, hand poised in midair.

"I can't take it anymore!" Charlene's shrill voice came through the door. "I don't want to go back, Fred! This is all your fault, and I'm sick—sick to death of it! I've given up my firstborn son, and I just can't give any more!"

Emma backed away, but not in time to avoid hearing Fred chastising Charlene for her childishness. Emma whirled and walked away, shocked and disappointed. She'd always thought of the Millers as an ideal family, the kind of people she'd have chosen for her own.

She wound up in the library, sinking into a leather chair, the winged back wrapping around her like a pair of arms. *Maybe that's just the way it is with most marriages*, she mused, Angeline's parents being the rare exception. After all, her own parents' marriage had been less than perfect—at least what she could remember of it.

She dug deeper, hoping to uncover just one happy memory to cling to, to take with her on the rest of her journey. There must have been some lighthearted moments. . . .

Christmas . . . The pungent smell of an evergreen tree—her artistic mother insisted on real trees. The year Daddy, grinning boyishly, had brought home an artificial tree. The argument that followed. Mom's sneer. Dad's slap—leaving a dark red welt on the smooth cheek. . . .

Emma couldn't really determine now who had been most to blame. At the time she and Frannie had been angry with Mom for spoiling their fun. But after the blow, Emma's allegiance had shifted. The fighting and arguing had gone on all night, with Fran smuggling in a box of graham crackers and a carton of milk to make up for the dinner that was never served.

Later that evening, Daddy, his speech slurred from drinking, had slipped into their room and tearfully begged forgiveness, though Emma had pretended to be asleep. "Daddy loves his little girls," he'd said. "If Mommy and I don't stay together, I want you girls to come live with me. Okay?"

"Don't worry, Daddy," Fran had readily agreed. "We'll come." Emma, eyes squeezed tight, had wanted to scream, "No!" Instead, she'd clenched her teeth and hated her father for making them choose. Hated Fran for speaking for her. After that, everything was a blur. She leaned back against the chair, her head spinning with fresh anguish as the memories played in her mind. . . .

A New Year's Eve party . . . The fragrance of Arpège cologne. A gold locket around her mother's slender white neck. Daddy—insisting she hurry before they were late. . . .

And then—Emma's mind regurgitated the whole ugly scene. The next morning she had found the baby-sitter still there, hunched over on the sofa, her face red and splotchy. Mrs. Stevens had embraced her, almost burying Emma in her soft bosom. She hadn't minded the hug so much, but a little voice inside whispered that something was wrong—dreadfully wrong. And when Grandma came with a suitcase—which was odd, since Grandma never stayed overnight—she eavesdropped on their whispered conversation behind the kitchen door.

"It was just awful," Emma had heard her say. "I didn't phone the house until three A.M.—and then only because the

Davises had promised to be home by one. Well, when the boss's wife said the party had been over for two hours I didn't know what to think because, well, the Davises do have their little spats, you know, and, of course, there's Mr. Davis's drinking. Now that I think of it, he must have been intoxicated when they left, because she said Mrs. Davis was doing the driving. Yet the police say there were no skid marks where their car left the road and went over the cliff, and no other vehicles were involved. It's all very mysterious . . . so sad for the poor little girls!" she had wailed.

All these years, Emma had hidden that conversation away in her heart, unable or unwilling to dredge it up and examine it. Tears streamed down her cheeks as she numbly acknowledged the truth.

She stepped out on deck. Outside, the sky was serene and cloudless, and a fresh breeze whisked through her hair and cooled her face. She stared out on the eastern horizon—where the blue of the sky met the blue of the sea. She felt as drained and empty as that vast space.

Then quietly, without warning, a surge of hope tingled through her. For the briefest moment, she felt herself cradled in the hand of God. These memories, this trip, even her painful encounter with Aaron—had a purpose. God's hand was on her life, and somehow He would see her through.

Fourteen

Northern Highlands, Papua New Guinea

"Thanks, Ian," said Josh as he loaded several odd-shaped bags and boxes into the back of Ian's rig. "I really appreciate your taking Miss Grouse back down to Lae. I wasn't planning a trip for at least another fortnight."

"Not a problem, mon," said Ian in his thick Scottish brogue. "That's what neighbors are for." He led Miss Grouse to the passenger side and helped her in. "I was heading down anyway. It'll be good to have some company."

Josh smiled slightly. Ian would be singing another tune if Miss Grouse launched into one of her nonstop monologues during the long descent down the mountain. On the other hand, even if she did, Ian McDowell was too polite to bring it up.

"Too bad about this," said Ian. "Must be hard on you and the children having to find another governess. Mary says you've been through several in the past few years."

"Six, to be exact." He gazed out over the coffee grove, squinting against the sun. "Guess this spread isn't very congenial to women."

"Except for Mary," said Ian with a twinkle in his eye.

"Right. *There's* one very rare exception."

"Speaking of Mary, she says to bring the children over anytime. She loves their company, and she could help with their studies. If only wee Holly were a bit older, they could all trek over the mountain on their own."

Josh frowned, bracing his hands on his hips. "Too dangerous these days—without an adult along, and I'm much too
busy—" Seeing the impatient look on Miss Grouse's face, he
clapped Ian on the shoulder and stepped back.

She rolled down the window and stuck out her head. "Say,
Ian," she called in a shrill voice, "are we leavin' or not? It's get-
tin' hot in here."

Josh walked over and forced a smile. "Well, hope you find
what you're looking for in the lowlands, Miss Grouse. Too bad
it didn't work out here."

She began to sniff, pulling a handkerchief from her purse.
"I'm sorry, Mr. Daniels, really I am. I'm going to be prayin' you
find a governess for those children—one that'll stay as long as
you need. Better still, I'll even ask the good Lord to send you a
wife!"

Josh blinked in surprise. Miss Grouse liked to bet on the
horses, and more than once, he'd caught her out on the back
porch, stubbing out a cigarette. But praying? The idea of Miss
Grouse on her knees before the Almighty was a bit of a stretch.
"I guess I never took you for a very religious woman, Miss
Grouse."

She gave him a withering look. "And I'm not, to be sure,
Mr. Daniels. But I've been known to pray every once in a while.
Especially when it seems there's a desperate need—like yours."

Ian winked at Josh. "That's a pretty tough order. Looks like
God's got His work cut out for Him."

"You two had better be on your way if you plan to make Lae
before sundown. Now, have a good trip. Thanks again, Ian. I
owe you one." He watched as his friend drove out of sight. Well,
who knew, maybe Miss Grouse's prayers would help. He certainly needed all the help he could get right now.

On his way back to the house, Josh did some mental cal-
culating. He'd used his shortwave radio to place classified ads
for a governess in newspapers, both in New Guinea and Australia, but it was probably too soon to hear anything. And by the
time he received resumés by mail, it would take at least another
month before he could count on anyone getting up here. Miss
Grouse might be right. Maybe he should send the children to

boarding school. Or maybe he should even consider selling—

Nope! That was really going too far. This plantation was his life. Lila couldn't take that from him, too. He'd fight to stay here. It was only a matter of time before his children grew up and moved on anyway. But the land was his. Solid and dependable, a constant. He had lived his entire life on this soil. Even if everything else in the world changed, the land would never let him down.

Right now, though, he was interested in seeing how Mina was faring with the children. This wasn't the first time she'd been left in charge. In many ways, he trusted Mina even more than Miss Grouse. At least, she seemed to love the children. But she was so young—only seventeen or so—and only a simple village girl at that. Bright enough, but one just couldn't expect too much from these people. That's what his father had always told him, and what Josh himself now believed, though some white people thought differently. Like Mary and Ian—what with their mission school. But then Mary and Ian were a bit too idealistic in Josh's view. Nice enough, to be sure, but to think that indigenous people could ever rise to the same level as Europeans was absurd.

Still, sometimes Josh wondered. In fact, one of his best workers seemed to be quite intelligent, although he had never finished his schooling. It had occurred to Josh that the native man might even be smarter than he. On the other hand, if Makiba was really so smart, why was he still working for Josh?

He walked around to the open window where he could hear voices coming from the little schoolroom on the end of the house. He had asked Mina to occupy the three children for the morning, having no idea what she'd do with them. She'd only said, "No worries, Mr. Daniel." Now he positioned himself so he could listen without being seen.

"Miss Sara," the girl began in a voice reflecting her new authority, "you must write a story about you garden. And you can draw picture of plants."

"All right," said Sara.

Sara seemed willing. *So far, so good*, Josh thought, grinning to himself.

"Now, Mr. Matthew," began Mina, and Matt groaned loudly, "Miss Grouse say you must work on you maths."

"You're not a real teacher, Mina. You can't make me!"

Josh was about to speak up when he realized that he'd only give away the fact that he'd been eavesdropping right outside their window. Besides, he didn't want to undermine Mina's efforts. She was doing the best she could, under the circumstances. He would speak to Matt later.

"Now, Mr. Matthew, you must not draw in you book. Books are like friend—"

"They're not *my* friends!" This, followed by what sounded like a book falling to the floor. "And you are not *my* teacher!"

At that moment Josh saw Makiba waving to him from the shop. Not wanting to be caught spying, Josh pretended to be examining a gutter, then strolled toward the shop.

This thing with Mina helping in the classroom wasn't going to last for long—at least not with Matt mouthing off like that. Well, Matt was getting to be a big boy, and maybe it was time he started to work in a man's world. After all, the local villagers initiated their sons into manhood at about this age. It was either that or boarding school. Josh flexed his jaw. He'd not ship his son off to school—not if there was any way in the world around it.

Fifteen

Lae, Papua New Guinea

This time Emma sat by the window and watched the treetops looming larger until at last the plane swept over them and landed on the airstrip directly below. She could feel the bumps in the tarmac, more noticeable since she was flying in a small, twin-engine Piper rather than a commercial Jet Liner.

"Welcome to Lae," announced the Australian pilot, extending a hand as she climbed down from the plane. The way he pronounced the name of the town sounded like *lye*. She had such difficulty understanding these Australians with their thick accents, almost as if they spoke another language.

She was thanking him for the informative flight when a small, barefooted black man hurried over and scooped up her bags, adeptly loading them onto a rickety metal cart.

"Thanks, Tamu." The pilot spoke first in English, then in some language that had a familiar ring, though she couldn't make out a single word. "I told him to call a cab for you," he translated as the little man scurried off. "Go along, and Tamu will set you up. Good day."

Feeling that the pilot was her last link to civilization, Emma was reluctant to leave. Shaking off her apprehension, she followed Tamu to a building roofed in corrugated tin and waited inside. Slow-moving ceiling fans, their rotating blades almost hypnotizing her with their steady rhythm, stirred the warm, moist air. A few idle workers stared openly, chatting and laughing among themselves.

"Meesus, you seet down here," directed Tamu. "I ring cab man now." He smiled, revealing wide gaps between teeth stained with tobacco, she decided.

She sat down next to her bags, rummaged in her purse, and retrieved the paper Charlene had given her. She'd told the Millers good-bye on board ship last week, promising to drop them a note when she was settled. Then she'd spent three marvelous days with Angeline in Sydney, staying with the wealthy uncle and seeing the local sights. She'd flown out early this morning. Between layovers and flight delays, it had taken all day to reach her destination.

Emma wasn't used to how early it got dark in the tropics. The warm weather made her think it should stay light longer.

"He here now, Meesus. You come." Tamu waved at her, indicating the waiting cab, then rushed to collect her bags and load them in the beat-up old car, which didn't resemble a taxi in the least. The dark man in front turned and smiled toothlessly. Trusting that he could read, she handed him the name and address of the guesthouse.

"Yesa, yesa," he said. "Me know dispela place."

She smiled and nodded, hoping that meant he could get her there.

After a short drive, he pulled up to a two-story complex and let her out. Her Australian currency satisfied him, and he drove off, rattling down the rutted dirt road. It was dark now, but the guesthouse was well-lit, giving it a welcoming appearance. Still, the heavyset woman who answered her knock seemed less than friendly.

"Yes? What do you need?"

"I was given the name of this guesthouse, by a friend."

"Well, we're full up right now. Did you ring for a reservation?" The woman stared at Emma as if she were some kind of vagabond.

"Well, no, I didn't. I wasn't aware I needed reservations. Maybe you could suggest another place to stay." Emma turned and eyed her bags piled out on the footpath, then glanced hopefully at the woman, who was already closing the door in her face.

"Norma, what is it?" A tall, skinny man walked up behind the woman. His lanky frame reminded Emma of Ichabod Crane, but he pushed the door open and smiled warmly.

"This lady wants a room, but I keep telling her we're full up." The woman threw up her hands and stormed off. "Why don't you take care of it, Ed?"

"Won't you come in?" he offered kindly. "I'm Ed Grimes, and that's my wife, Norma. She gets cranky this time o' day. We run this guesthouse—been doing it for over twenty years now. Norma's telling the truth, though—don't have a single vacancy. But there's a good hotel in town. I can ring them up for you, if you like. Would you be stayin' for tea?"

Emma didn't want to impose. "Tea sounds lovely, if it's no trouble. I'm Emma Davis, a friend of Fred and Charlene Miller. They recommended this guesthouse to me."

"Yep. The Millers are good folks, and tea's no trouble. You just sit down, little lady, and I'll tell Norma."

Emma took a seat in a stiff plastic chair in the tiny office and waited for what seemed much too long to make a simple phone call and fetch a cup of tea. She glanced at her watch uncomfortably. Had he forgotten her? Her stomach growled, and she remembered that she hadn't eaten since her morning flight from Sydney to Brisbane.

"Tea's ready," announced Ed, pointing to the door behind him.

Emma hadn't intended to intrude. "Oh, I can drink it here."

He squinted. "I can tell you're a Yankee, but you must be new to these parts." At her nod, he went on, "Yep, I can always spot 'em. But come right along. Tea's awaitin'."

He led her to a large dining room where others were just sitting down, a family and several adults. He pulled out a chair for her and grinned. "You see, Emma, what you Yanks call dinner, we Aussies call tea."

Her cheeks reddened as she slid into the chair and unfolded the napkin. She hadn't meant to invite herself to supper!

Across the table from her sat a man whose ruddy complexion

told her he was an outdoorsman. The deep creases at the corners of his eyes told her he smiled a lot. It was his name—Ian—that stuck after all the others were introduced.

After tea, she noticed Ed and Ian glancing her way.

"Ed here says you need a ride into town, miss. I happen to be heading that way. I could give you a lift, if you say the word." Ian spoke with a Scottish accent. The "r" rolled musically off his tongue.

"I wouldn't want to impose. . . ."

He looked back up with aquamarine eyes and said, "Not a problem at all." He loaded her things into the back of a dust-coated Land Rover, then extended a strong, tanned hand to help her into the seat. "Sorry 'bout the dust. I just came down from the highlands to deliver someone into town and pick up some supplies. It's amazing how much dust you can accumulate on some of these roads. Oh, let me move that box so you can sit down."

He chuckled. "That's a case of fancy orange marmalade from France—a surprise for my Mary. It has to be handled with care, so I buckled it into the seat belt," he added sheepishly. "I'll put it in back now."

"It's kind of you to give me a ride like this." Emma glanced over at the big, shy man as he jumped behind the wheel, and wondered if Mary was his wife.

Ian didn't seem very talkative, so Emma kept the conversation going. It was still new to her—this more assertive role. But she'd observed Angeline speaking effortlessly, and now was the time to practice the tips she'd picked up. She rambled on about the stops she'd made on her recent cruise and her short stay in Sydney with her friend and her friend's uncle. In no time, it seemed, they had pulled up in front of the hotel.

"It was nice to meet you, Ian. Thanks again for the ride."

He carefully placed her luggage by the hotel door and tipped his broad-brimmed hat. "I wish you a pleasant visit in Lae." With a smile glinting in his aquamarine eyes, he was gone.

Ed, as promised, had called ahead to secure her room, so they were expecting her. She was shown to the third floor by a boy who didn't look older than ten or eleven. Together they trudged up the stairs, lugging her heavy suitcases, the boy handling the bulkiest.

"What is your name?" she asked, enunciating each word slowly and plainly.

"Jonathan," he replied in flawless English. "My papa manages this hotel, and Mama is the head cook for the restaurant on the first floor. We have our own room behind the kitchen." He beamed with pride as he dragged her suitcase to the door of room number 31 and inserted the key.

"How old are you?" she asked, as he opened the door to a small, neat room.

"Thirteen, ma'am." He pulled her suitcases in, then quoted, "There's a lavatory in your room, and the bathroom is at the end of the hall. Can I get you anything else?"

Emma glanced around. "Everything looks fine. But maybe you could locate me a map of the town." She handed him a generous tip, and his dark brown eyes widened. But he didn't refuse.

She stayed up late, unpacking her bags and arranging her room. Most of her clothing needed laundering, but she could see about that tomorrow. She'd have to ask Jonathan.

Too excited for sleep, Emma turned off the bedside lamp and lay in bed. It was too hot, even for the lightweight sheets. But she'd have to get used to it. She would be living in the tropics now—at least for the foreseeable future. As for what she'd be doing here, she still hadn't a clue. But at least she was here—really here. Far from home.

Home. The thought crept in, but there was no longing or regret. She'd called Fran when the ship had docked in Australia, learning with relief that everyone there was well. Grandma had resigned herself to cooperating with Bernice, and according to Fran, the two old women watched TV or played double solitaire by the hour.

Though Emma had been relieved to hear it, strangely enough she was also a little uneasy. She'd always been needed at home. But now, it appeared, they were getting along just fine without her. She should be celebrating her newfound freedom! Instead, she was feeling sorry for herself.

ॐ   ॐ   ॐ   ॐ

She awoke late, started up in dismay, then relaxed against the pillows. What time she chose to start her day made absolutely no difference. Her time was now completely her own. No schedules. No routine. No one to please but herself.

Outside, the tropical sun shone brightly. Emma leaned onto the windowsill and looked out on the busy street below. What appeared to be an open market was situated across the street, but the people seemed to be packing up their wares and produce already, loading baskets and large string bags and moving on. She'd have to get up earlier if she wanted to do any shopping.

Turning to dress, she glanced down and noticed a shiny pamphlet. She picked it up to discover a map of the city, along with a handwritten note from Jonathan, listing the local highlights.

She dressed hurriedly, eager to find a cooler spot. Although it was only a little after nine, her room was already uncomfortably warm. With no air conditioning in sight, she closed the louvered windows and pulled the shades to block the light—then spotted the ceiling fan! It would come in handy.

The little dining room downstairs was empty when she arrived. Just as Emma was wondering if they were still serving breakfast, a plump, dark-haired woman waved from behind the counter.

"Eets all right, Meesus," she said. "You come. You eat now." She showed Emma to a table and handed her a menu listing three breakfast entrées. She selected the second one, and the woman bustled off.

Emma studied the map Jonathan had marked for her. It reminded her of the way Angeline had always been their tour guide. She missed Angeline. Missed her sharp mind and her warm, caring nature. Missed having a friend to pal around with.

The woman was back with a platter of bacon and eggs, served with scones and garnished with a grilled tomato. "Eets all right, Meesus? I cook for you." The woman seemed overly anxious.

"It looks delicious. You must be Jonathan's mother."

She grinned, exposing a missing front tooth. "Yesa, Jonathan my son. He's good boy, work hard."

"Yes, he's a fine boy. I'm Emma Davis, and I'll be staying with you for a while. Do you know where I can get my laundry done?"

"Yesa. We have laundry here. I send Jonathan to get it after school. You put in bag by door."

Emma smiled and thanked her, but something about the way the workers treated her gave her an uncomfortable feeling. They were so solicitous, tried so hard to please. *Too* hard. She didn't like it. But for now, she'd put it down to one of the many things she'd have to become accustomed to.

※　※　※　※

She spent the day touring the small coastal town, taking in the local sights. The War Memorial. The botanical gardens. And, finally, the seashore. To her disappointment, the sand was a dingy gray—nothing like the clean white sand on the beaches of Hawaii, or even Sydney. In this heat and humidity, she'd hoped for a swim, but she wasn't tempted. Instead, she sank down onto a bench and gazed out across the steely water. Suddenly she was seized with a loneliness as stifling as the thick, moist air.

The clouds continued to press in over the horizon, low and heavy, until it started to rain. The large droplets were not cold, as one might normally expect of a "spring" shower, but rather body temperature. In fact, she almost couldn't feel them at all. But the moisture was refreshing. With no one around to see, she didn't even mind that her thin blouse clung to her like cellophane. It was almost as if she were invisible. Or, maybe, the only person on earth. . . .

Suddenly, she stood and stretched her arms high, as if reaching for the heavens. Looking up to the leaden sky, she allowed the tepid rain to bathe her, trickling down her neck. Had God sent this rain just for her? As a sort of baptism? Or maybe a promise of something to come.

Then, almost as quickly as it had begun, the shower ended and the clouds passed. The sun's sharp rays quickly dried her blouse and erased all traces of the rain—at least on the outside.

Sixteen

*E*ach day, Emma had high tea at the Bird of Paradise Tea Room. High tea, she'd quickly learned, not to be confused with dinner "tea," was actual tea with cookies, or biscuits as they called them, and pastries and such. This daily event brought her a small sense of connection to the human world, because so far most of her time had been spent in solitude. And solitude, while an interesting way to get in touch with herself, could only be tolerated so long.

After two weeks in Lae, she knew the town inside and out. Some of the local people were beginning to recognize her, though no true friendships had been established. The closest thing to a friend was Louise Thompson, owner and proprietor of the Bird of Paradise. Louise always chatted with Emma in an open and personable manner, and Emma always looked forward to seeing this no-nonsense Australian businesswoman. She reminded her of Marie back at the coffee shop in Des Moines and made her think maybe it really was a "small world."

"Good-day, Emma," Louise hailed her, using the typical Aussie greeting that sounded exactly like "good-eye." "What's up with our local Yank?" she asked as she showed Emma to her regular table by the front window.

Louise pulled up a chair and, without waiting for Emma's reply, launched into an update of the local gossip. Slowly names had become familiar, and though Louise's colorful descriptions were undoubtedly embroidered by her own imagination, Emma enjoyed it.

"You know, Louise, you really should write books," said Emma when Louise paused for a breath.

"Oh, on with you now, Emma Davis!" Louise shoved a strand of gray hair off her damp forehead.

"No, really. You're such a good storyteller."

Louise stood and waved her hand in dismissal, but returned with a fuller-than-usual biscuit tray and a generous dollop of her prized raspberry preserves on the side.

"Had any luck finding yourself a job yet, Emma?" asked Louise, pouring fresh tea. "How 'bout the one with the shipping company?"

"Well, they offered me the job, but I'm not interested in another clerical position. I promised myself I'd find something different here." Emma stared down into the copper-colored tea, swirling it around in the dainty china cup. Her finances were rapidly dwindling and, if she didn't find work soon, she'd have to go home. The very idea sent a wave of dread through her.

"Well, Josh Daniels is here in town. Don't reckon I ever told you about him, did I? Hear he's looking for a governess. Seems the last one just up and left with hardly any notice."

Emma felt a prickle of curiosity. Being a governess could be interesting. Not that she was really qualified, unless babysitting her sister's kids would count.

"Tell me about it, Louise."

"Well, Josh owns a coffee plantation east of here, in the highlands. Beautiful country that—not so hot as down here." She fanned her warm face with a menu. "Seems his wife mysteriously disappeared a few years back. Most folks think she ran off with Josh's best friend who'd come to help out on the plantation. In a way, you can't blame a woman for running off—it's so isolated up there." Louise poured herself some more tea, then swatted at a mosquito that had landed on her plump forearm.

"The gist of it is, Josh was left with these kids to bring up, and he thinks he needs a white woman to keep them civilized. Can't say's I blame him. I knew of a missionary family who left the raising of their kids to the indigenous. The children turned out wilder than all get-out—regular little animals."

"Meesus Thompson," called one of her helpers. "Samino need you in kitchen now!"

Louise didn't seem to be in any hurry, but eyed Emma expectantly. "So shall I tell him you're interested?"

"Yes, I suppose I could—"

"Meesus Thompson!"

Before Emma could finish, Louise had rushed back to the kitchen where general pandemonium had broken out. Emma didn't wait for Louise to return, but laid down her money with the bill and left.

She took her time getting back to the hotel, feeling like every step was in slow motion. Everything about this town was so familiar to her now, yet she didn't fit in. She had no purpose here. She was like a visitor who had worn out her welcome. Of course, the local proprietors liked her money. She'd purchased and sent home plenty of souvenirs.

She mused over the possibility of becoming a governess. The timing of the opportunity seemed more than coincidental, and jobs in Lae weren't exactly plentiful.

Jonathan met her in the hotel lobby with a parcel of clean laundry and walked with her up the stairs, carrying the bundle. At the door, she thanked him and gave him a tip.

"How is it you are so rich, Miss Davis?" he asked with wide brown eyes. Jonathan always came straight to the point, a trait she admired, though his question left her groping for an answer. She knew she must appear wealthy, having money without apparently working for it. But she didn't want to mislead him.

"In my country, I went to school just as you're doing. I worked hard to put myself through college. Then I got a good job and saved my money for a long time—just so I could come here."

"And why did you come?"

She laughed nervously. "Jonathan, you ask too many hard questions." She opened her door and reached in to flick on the ceiling fan, then turned to face the boy. "I'm not sure why I'm here. But when I find out, you'll be the first to know."

※ ※ ※ ※

"Miss Davis, Miss Davis! Are you awake?"

She pulled on her robe and cracked the door. "What is it, Jonathan?"

"A letter for you. The man say I must give it to you immediately!" He handed her a folded paper, then disappeared down the hallway.

Dear Miss Davis,

Louise Thompson has informed me of your interest in the governess position I'm offering and has recommended you highly. Therefore, I am willing to try you out. I must leave town at 10 A.M. Please be ready.

Sincerely,
Josh Daniels

"Ten A.M.!" exclaimed Emma. "That's less than three hours from now! Try me out? What does he think I am? A piece of athletic equipment?" Just the same, she jerked her bags down from the top of the closet and started to pack, grumbling with every breath. Yet beneath the complaints fluttered the anticipation of a new adventure about to unfold. She was ready for a change!

Somehow she managed to pack, settle her bill, and have breakfast—all before Mr. Daniels arrived. Jonathan carried her bags down to the lobby while she made certain she hadn't overlooked anything in her room. She checked herself one last time in the mirror. Did she look like a governess? Maybe she'd look more authoritative with her hair up.

But before she could locate hairpins in her purse, a sharp knock on the door startled her, and she opened it to find a tall, dark-haired, and extremely handsome man standing before her.

"Miss Davis?" he asked solemnly, as if disappointed.

"Yes, I'm Emma Davis."

"I've already loaded your things." The frown lingered. "Are you sure you're interested in this job?"

She nodded, feeling foolish. But he only looked at her skeptically, then turned sharply on his heel and started off down the hall.

"Excuse me, Mr. Daniels," she called out firmly, halting him in his tracks.

"Yes?" He studied her in the semidarkness. "What is it?"

Now what did she say? "It occurs to me that I know very little about this position. I don't even know how many children I'll be responsible for."

"Three. Two girls and a boy."

"Very well." She could handle three. And if he'd said, "Eleven," would that have stopped her?

Seventeen

The Highlands

*F*or a change, Josh appreciated his Land Rover's loud rattle as the ancient vehicle climbed the winding road. It made conversation nearly impossible, and he had no desire to chat. What had Louise been thinking to recommend this fragile-looking Yankee? Why, this woman didn't look like she'd last a week on the plantation.

He gripped the steering wheel tightly, but kept his gaze straight ahead. He should've known better by now. The highlands were no place for any self-respecting woman—how many times had Lila told him that? But then she'd always hated being away from the big towns and the action.

He studied the landscape unfolding before them. He still couldn't understand how anyone could prefer a noisy, stinking town to all this. Lush, green trees and thick vegetation covered the rolling hillsides, which slowly transformed themselves into the rougher, more mountainous terrain. This region was so different from the steamy lowlands. He rolled down the window and took in a deep breath, enjoying the freshness of the clean mountain air. For the first time since he'd met her, he felt his frown diminishing slightly. He glanced over at her from the corner of his eye. She, too, seemed to be enjoying the scenery. Maybe he had misjudged her. But then again, most people could appreciate the beauty—at least at first.

"Nice country, eh?" He forced himself to speak. This silence couldn't go on forever. Even if she only lasted a week or two, he could be civilized.

"Yes, it's absolutely beautiful. And the fresh air is invigorating," she spoke loudly over the din of the truck.

But her pasted-on smile reminded him of a tooth-polish ad, and it was all he could do not to chuckle out loud. Poor, unsuspecting woman. She had no idea what she was getting into. He drove on in silence, but at least now it was a somewhat comfortable silence. He glanced over once and caught her staring at him, but she quickly looked away.

He stopped for lunch in Morokai. Being a rough mining town, it wasn't the best place for a woman, but she was safe enough with him. And it would be a good eye-opener for her.

The only place open was a tiny kiosk right next to the police station, and they sat outside in folding metal chairs pulled up to a rickety card table. He hadn't noticed how grimy the table was until her eyebrows went up, and she gingerly folded her hands into her lap. But at least she didn't complain. He wondered how old she was. At first, he'd thought she was much too young, but now he wasn't so sure. Mid-twenties or maybe even older, he guessed. And she was pretty. Not beautiful, perhaps, and certainly no eye-popping, gorgeous sheila. But still too pretty to be cooped up on some coffee plantation taking care of someone else's kids. And that's what bothered him most. That—and the fact that she was a Yankee.

He ordered for her, and she didn't complain. Fortunately, the pastries weren't too bad, and the tea was hot and strong. He watched as she ate. At least she had good manners. He couldn't say that for the last governess, but at least Agnes had lasted for nearly six months. He was certain Miss Davis wouldn't make it a fortnight. A heated outburst interrupted the otherwise silence of their meal. He wondered if she could understand the words. It wasn't anything a lady should hear.

"Do you speak Pidgen?" he asked, jerking his head toward the noise.

"Not more than a word or two, but I'd like to learn. Is there a problem over there?" Her eyes were wide, but they didn't seem fearful, perhaps only curious.

"It's just the men in the calaboose," he said, without going into detail.

"What's a calaboose?"

"You know, a jail—prison." He looked at her curiously.

She nodded dumbly, then took another bite. She seemed embarrassed, as if searching for something else to say. He knew he wasn't making it easy for her. Well, life wasn't easy up here.

He followed her gaze to two indigenous policemen as they swaggered importantly up to the kiosk and ordered tea.

"I still find it so strange that men wear shorts and knee socks here," she said as she studied their uniforms. "Where I come from, that's how a young schoolboy might—" She stopped herself short, staring down at Josh's bare knees. He was wearing his usual—shorts, high socks, and hiking boots. He resisted a smile as he saw the truth register, watched her face redden with embarrassment again. He knew the kind thing would be to make some light comment and let her off the hook. But he wasn't ready to be kind. He was still irked that he would probably be hauling her back down to the lowlands in a few days. This might be a good time to make her agree to giving a fortnight's notice or forfeiting her pay. Well, they could discuss that later.

The second half of the trip continued as quietly as the first, but at least the scenery was improving. He wondered if she'd noticed. Glancing at her profile, he figured she had, but he could also see a little shadow of apprehension in her eyes. The price for their panoramic view was paid in steeper, narrower roads, complete with hairpin curves and drop-offs down precipitous cliffs. Most folks got a little uptight when traveling this road for the first time. He regarded her for a quick moment, hoping to reassure her that he'd traveled this road more than a few times. Then he devoted his entire concentration to the steeply twisting road, securely gripping the wheel. At one point he glanced over to see that she had simply shut her eyes and was clinging to the edge of her seat with white knuckles. Well, she wasn't complaining. At least not yet.

Feeling a bit sorry for her, Josh pulled over on a high lookout point and turned off the motor. He could feel her relax a bit next to him as he scanned the countryside. Strands of misty clouds settled between the gaps of the familiar mountain peaks. It was always reassuring after a trip to the lowland towns to see this mountain range still stretched out before him. His dad had always stopped here on the way up. Dad had often compared it to an ocean with multicolored waves. And today that's just how it looked—a green wave that blended to blue and then faded to a hazy shade of violet.

"It's spectacular."

Her voice caught him by surprise. He'd almost forgotten she was there. Josh stared at her for a moment, then abruptly turned on the ignition and jerked the jalopy back onto the road. He wanted to make it home before dark.

The sun was just setting when he turned off onto the single-lane drive. Like old friends waiting to greet him, the groves of short, rounded trees lined both sides of the driveway. They grew in neat little rows, faithfully growing and blossoming and bearing nice red beans in season. The trees, unlike people, were dependable. He could always count on them. No surprises. No disappointments.

He took a deep breath of the air. Clean, pure, and lightly laced with the sweet musky smell of soil and vegetation. Oh, how good it was to be home again! There was no place on earth like this. No place he would rather be. He could easily imagine growing old here. He knew his children would probably leave. No one ever seemed to stay. No one but him. But he was content to grow old here all alone. He was used to loneliness. It suited him.

⁂ ⁂ ⁂ ⁂

Even in the dusky light, she noticed his dark eyes spark ever so slightly, and the corners of his mouth lifted in the semblance of a smile. She experienced a faint flicker of hope. Maybe some warm blood flowed in those veins, after all.

His continued silence was unsettling. It seemed as if he resented her. But why? He didn't even know her. She almost expected him to dump her next to the road before they ever reached the plantation. If Louise hadn't been such a good friend to help her find this job, and spoken so highly of this strange man, Emma might have taken the initiative and actually jumped out.

They passed several outbuildings and finally pulled up in front of a large house with lots of windows that was wrapped in a sprawling, screened porch. Emma's heart twisted slightly at the sight. It could have been her dream house! In a flash, the front door burst open, and three children spilled out. Seeing her, they hesitated on the porch—a cluster of shadows silhouetted in the brightly lit doorway.

"Give me a hand, Matt," called Josh as he unloaded her bags. "Take Miss Davis's things to her room, then meet me in back to unload the rest of this stuff."

Matt obeyed without question, and Emma picked up the remaining suitcase and followed the boy up the steps. It appeared Josh wasn't much for introductions. The two girls stood together, the smaller one nearly hidden behind her sister, only the pink hem of her nightie showing. The older girl wore long dark braids and glasses that looked too large for her serious face. Emma detected blond curls on the small one's head as she pressed her face into her sister's back.

Emma put down her bag and sat on the top step. She searched desperately for something clever to say, but her mind was as blank as the darkening sky. The children, like their father, were obviously not given to idle prattle and didn't appear the least inclined to make this any easier for her. Instead, they stood staring as if she were from another planet.

"Hello," she said finally. "I'm Emma Davis, and your father has brought me up here to be your new governess." Still they said nothing. Matt stepped up to the porch and set down her bags. He looked at her and frowned, and Emma realized how much he resembled his father.

"You mean you're a Yankee?" he demanded with clear disdain in his voice.

Emma laughed nervously. It was a phrase she'd heard a lot and wasn't particularly fond of. "I guess you could say that. I am from the United States. Anyway, I've told you my name, but you haven't told me yours. Of course, I know you are Matt." She looked to the girls.

"I'm Sara," said the older girl in a voice that seemed too low and sober for a child her age. "And this is Holly."

Emma smiled. "How old are you, Sara?"

"I'm nine and Holly is four. Matthew is ten."

"Nearly eleven," he stated proudly. "I'll be eleven in a month." With this vital information dispensed, Matt scooped up her bags and disappeared into the house.

Emma stayed on the step, breathing in the cool night air. "It's certainly beautiful up here," she spoke to no one in particular. "I've been in the lowlands and it's always so muggy and hot down there. This place feels almost like heaven." Sara stepped closer, leaning against the banister. "And look," said Emma, trying to keep Sara's attention. "There's the moon coming up over the mountain there. What a fantastic view you have. I can hardly wait to see it by daylight."

"Would you like me to show you your room?" offered Sara without looking directly at Emma. Then Sara took Holly's hand and opened the screen door for Emma, and they entered a spacious front room. Contrary to the rustic ranch-style look of the exterior, this room had an unexpected air of elegance. Emma admired the shining dark wood floors and vaulted ceilings. The walls were whitewashed and adorned with a couple of carefully placed and well-chosen paintings. Some large, leafy plants flourished in the corners, swaying slightly in the breeze of an overhead fan. The oversized furniture was wood-framed with large tapestry-covered cushions, and on the floor lay a splendid oriental carpet in rich jewel tones. The girls led her down a hallway that passed by the kitchen and turned right. It must've been an addition, because the ceilings were lower here. At the end of the hall, Sara opened the door to a roomy suite complete with a private bath. Her other bags were already there, situated next to a large pine armoire.

"This is a lovely room," she exclaimed honestly. A wicker chair and table were situated in a corner that was encased by a wide band of windows, and several fluffy white sheepskins were scattered about the floor.

"I'll tell Mina, our house-girl, to fetch you some linens," said Sara, sounding more and more like the lady of the house. Holly by now had poked her head out from behind her sister to sneak a peek at this new governess. Emma was careful not to look her way, not wishing to frighten the young child.

"Thank you, Sara."

"We've already had our tea, but I'm sure Tabo will fix you and Father something. Tabo is our cook, and, well, she kind of runs things around the house." The way Sara's voice trailed down sounded like she didn't care much for Tabo. But nothing more was said and she took Holly's hand and silently left.

Emma unpacked her bags. Suddenly she wondered what in the world she was doing here and would she really stay? It almost seemed as if Josh really didn't want her, although it made no sense since he obviously needed someone to look after the children. The idea of making that winding trip back down to Lae filled her with dread, and she hoped to at least stay a few days.

She ate dinner alone in her room. Tabo, a large woman with a deep scowl-line carved into the center of her forehead, brought a tray. But she shared no greeting, no welcome, and no explanation about anything. Emma didn't mind, though. The mere thought of sitting alone with Josh at his table and silently eating his food made her stomach knot. Oh, why had she come?

Mina came, just as Sara had mentioned, bringing fresh sheets and towels. The girl quickly stripped and remade the bed, but unlike Tabo, Mina seemed cheerful as she bustled about the room, glancing bashfully at Emma from the corner of her eye. Emma inquired whether Mina spoke English.

"Yes, I do! I learn at the mission. Mrs. McDowell, she teach me good." Mina held her chin down and smiled shyly with sparkling black eyes.

"Have you worked for the Daniels long?"

"Yes, I work here long time. I think—" she scratched her short-cropped hair and looked towards the ceiling. "I think about five years. Yes, I come here before Miss Holly is born. Yes, that's right, five years." Emma observed how pretty Mina was with her smooth bronze skin and high cheekbones.

"Yes, I come here when I am twelve years old. Mrs. Daniels,

she teach me how to be good house-girl. And she say, I smart—
I learn fast." Mina face saddened, as if recalling something unhappy. Emma wondered if Mina missed Josh's wife. "Before
that I stay with Mrs. McDowell at Pomotia—over the hill."
Mina pointed to her right as if that explained it, then tied the
used linens into a neat bundle.

"The big generator—it shut down at nine o'clock. Then you
must use this lamp." Mina pointed out the large kerosene glass
lamp on the dresser, then smiled and left.

Emma liked Mina. So far, she was the only one who seemed
happy to have Emma come. Maybe she could get better acquainted with Mina tomorrow. And maybe Mina could explain
some things. It seemed she might even know something about
the story behind Josh's missing wife. Perhaps that could help
shed some light on the subject. Because whatever the cause,
there seemed to be some dark spirit of sadness locked into this
family. And already, although she had only known Josh for a
matter of hours, and the children much less than that, Emma
had begun to care.

Eighteen

The sun poured through the thin glass louvers and cast bright stripes of light onto the ceiling above Emma's head. It was still early, yet she was ready to get up after a surprisingly good night's sleep. Compared to the lowlands, the room felt chilly, but she had purposely left the windows open, savoring the welcome change. She dressed quickly and, for the first time in weeks, put on a cotton sweater, enjoying the feel of the soft nubby knit against her bare arms.

She slipped past the kitchen, but not in time to avoid Tabo's observant eye. She knew it was Tabo, because she'd been told that the woman ruled the kitchen. And one glance told Emma that here was a force to be reckoned with.

She was immense, solid as a brick and taller than average. Beady, black eyes were set deeply in ebony skin, and her strong features seemed carved in granite. Here was a face that had forgotten how to smile, Emma thought—if it had ever known how. At the moment, the woman was boring a hole right through Emma.

"Good morning. I'm Emma, the new governess." She smiled, attempting to sound friendly. The woman said nothing and scowled darkly. Suddenly Emma felt like she was on foreign turf and clearly not welcome. She quickly exited out the back door. In the future she would have to remember to avoid Tabo's kitchen.

From the back porch, she could see an open area with various sheds and buildings carefully laid out. Everything on the plantation had a well-planned and deliberate look to it, bearing the no-nonsense stamp of Josh Daniels. Even the thick poinsettia hedge along the driveway appeared purposeful in its rigid uniformity, like a regiment of soldiers in red, guarding the house. Emma still couldn't get used to the idea of a Christmas flower blooming so profusely and with no apparent regard to the time of year.

She wandered back behind the house to find a well-tended garden with even rows of pineapple plants and assorted vegetables. Opposite the garden grew a small grove of banana trees. Walking nearer for a better look, she caught a glimpse of something on the other side of the glossy green foliage. Parting the wide green leaves, she found a lovely circular flower garden, blooming in a riot of extravagant color. In the center, on a pedestal, stood a large mirrored-glass sphere, reflecting the beauty surrounding it. A little rock path bordered the entire garden, with a worn wooden bench situated in a secluded corner. A secret garden!

Suddenly she felt like a trespasser—an intruder. She turned and left reluctantly, wondering who the gardener might be.

When she neared the house, she spotted Josh and Matt working side by side, loading crates onto a truck. Matt struggled to hoist the crates, while Josh stacked them in the flat bed. It seemed hard work for a young boy, but Matt stuck to it.

As Emma looked on, a bell rang, probably signaling breakfast time, and Josh pulled a handkerchief from his pocket and wiped his brow. The two left their work and headed for the house. Not wishing to be observed, and still feeling like a spy in the land, Emma followed from a distance.

They ate quietly at the scrubbed-pine table, and Emma wondered if every meal was eaten without conversation. Only Mina's wide smiles brightened the mood as she brought platters of hotcakes and sunny-yellow scrambled eggs and bacon. Whatever else might be said of her, Tabo was a fine cook.

After breakfast, Josh scooted his chair back and spoke to the children. "Miss Davis will oversee your lessons today." Matt groaned, and Josh shot him a withering look. "See to it that you mind her. Matthew, you may join me in the north field after you finish your studies. Sara, show Miss Davis around."

He stood and left without a good-bye. Was that the only job description she could expect? And why hadn't he addressed her directly?

Sara showed Emma to the narrow room at the other end of the house—obviously a makeshift classroom—with one wall accommodating a sparsely filled bookcase, and a world map and chalkboard occupying another. Sara took a seat at one of the two library tables, while Holly went to the bookcase and removed a shabby box of crayons and a well-used tablet from one of the open shelves.

In a corner of the room, where a shortwave radio was sitting on a low table, Matt was already fiddling with the dials, adjusting the volume through crackling static until an Australian accent could be heard, twanging into the otherwise silent room.

"Good day, pupils," came a female announcer's voice. "This is Sally Cyphert from Port Moresby. In our lesson today, we will continue with Australian history. Yesterday we learned about Arthur Phillip who commanded the expedition to Port Jackson in 1787—"

The metallic tone droned on and on until Emma wondered how the children could stand listening to another word. On the other hand, there was no television here, so maybe their attention span was longer. She noticed Sara's gaze focused intently on her lap, and peeked over the young girl's shoulder to see a Nancy Drew book, concealed by the table's ledge. Feeling Emma's eyes on her, Sara snapped the book shut, but Emma didn't scold her. Holly watched it all with wide, blue eyes and a sober expression. When the child smiled—if she ever smiled—Emma suspected it would be like sunshine coming out after a cloudy day. She tried her own best smile on the little girl, but Holly bent over her tablet and resumed her coloring with bold, dark strokes.

When Sally Cyphert signed off, the two older children pulled out workbooks and started in. Emma eventually located the teacher's manuals high on the bookshelf and began to skim the pages. She couldn't fathom what drove these children. They didn't really seem to need a governess. Just the same, she strolled the room, observing their work.

So far, this job was a breeze, and she enjoyed the notion of being a teacher, imparting helpful information to young minds. After a while she noticed Holly whispering something to Sara—the first time Emma had seen the little girl speak.

"She needs to go to the loo," explained Sara apologetically.

"Well, of course she's excused." How strange—that these children had to ask to use the bathroom in their own home.

"You see," began Sara, "the rule is: you can only use the loo before class and at break."

"And who made this rule?" Emma frowned, disturbed by this revelation. "Is there a list somewhere?"

"Miss Grouse had scads of rules," complained Matt. "But I don't think they're written down. She invented new ones every day."

"Well," said Emma, treading new territory, "we'll have a new set of rules, but we'll work on them together." The two older children stared, open-mouthed, and Emma thought she spotted a sinister gleam in Matt's eye. She'd have to be careful just how much slack she cut that young man.

"Who's helped you with your studies recently? . . . I mean, since Miss Grouse left?"

"Father does lessons after tea sometimes, but not every night," Matt spoke up. "And I like that better." He looked her straight in the eye as if tossing down the gauntlet.

"Miss Grouse has only been gone a fortnight, and Father really doesn't have time to teach us," explained the ever-practical Sara. "We used to go to school down in Koroke—it's about fifteen kilometers from here. But that school shut down last year—there weren't enough kids—so many have moved away, you see . . ." Her voice trailed off, and it was evident what a lonely existence this must be for the children, isolated up in the highlands like this.

"Father's been talking about sending me down to some stupid old boarding school in Lae, but I'm not going!" Matt stuck out his chin, thudding his fist on the desk for added emphasis.

Before things got completely out of hand, they'd better get on with their lessons. Although getting acquainted was important, Emma wasn't willing to face Josh if they didn't finish, especially on her first day.

She slid into a chair beside Matt and examined his open arithmetic book. "Now, this looks like a tough one." She pointed to a large decimal multiplication problem.

Matt frowned and bit into the end of his tooth-marked pencil. "Nah, I can do it." He went to work, and she watched him calculate, following along mentally. His answer was correct, except for the decimal point.

When she tried to explain his error, he slammed the book shut and shoved it away. "I hate decimals!" he growled.

Emma glanced at Sara, but Sara quickly returned to her own work. "Why do you hate decimals?"

Matt only scowled, his lips pressed tightly together.

"The thing is," continued Emma slowly, groping for a way to reach him, "you worked the problem perfectly. It was only the decimal point that was in the wrong place. You see, Matt, those silly little dots are awfully important." He rolled his eyes. "Take your father, for instance—" Matt looked up, his expression still sour. "Suppose he was selling a truckload of coffee beans for fifteen hundred dollars, and the buyer switched the decimal by two points—like this." She scratched the figures onto the paper.

Matt leaned over and took a look. "Why, that'd only be fifteen dollars! That would be stealing!" Impressed, in spite of his attempt to cover it, he tossed her a sidelong glance and reopened his book.

Bingo! Emma smiled inwardly, then checked Sara's work, which was correct and meticulously done, just as she knew it would be. Holly had returned and now sat silently on a large chair, bare legs dangling. Emma longed to scoop up the silent child, who seemed scarcely more than a baby, but resisted the urge. Her instincts warned her she must first win this small one's trust.

The lunch bell rang, and the children closed their books and went to wash up. Emma wasn't surprised when Josh didn't join them for lunch, but instead had his meal delivered to the fields. The man was a complete enigma. He seemed to want to cover all his bases as a father—all, except giving his children his own time and attention.

Emma and the children worked for another hour after lunch until their lessons were complete. Then Matt promptly disappeared, while Sara lingered, Holly on her heels.

"My little sister usually takes her rest now," informed Sara.

Emma studied Holly's face, wondering if a nap was really necessary. "Would you like for me to read you a story first?" she offered. The little girl's eyes lit up, and though she clung to Sara's hand on the way to her room, she went willingly.

The girls' quarters were not quite as spacious as Emma's, but the whitewashed walls and large windows gave the same airy feel. None of the rooms were overly decorated or cluttered, and every piece of furniture was sturdy and functional. The only adornment on the walls was a shepherd girl print and a cross-stitch sampler of the Twenty-third Psalm.

The twin beds were covered with matching comforters in a yellow floral print, with three porcelain dolls arranged on one bed, a well-worn bear and a Raggedy Ann on the other. The tall bookcase between the beds housed a large assortment of children's books and a collection of model horses. Holly went straight to the shelf and removed a book, holding it close to her chest, head down.

"May I sit on your bed, Holly?" asked Emma, picking up the bear and noting he had only one eye. "Oh my, he certainly looks loved." When Holly snatched the bear away, Emma realized her mistake. "Oh, I'm sorry, Holly. I should have asked first—it's just that he reminds me of a stuffed animal I used to have. My bear's name was Bluff, and he had a missing eye, too. What's your bear's name?"

Holly muttered something inaudible, and Sara translated, "Cocoa."

"Perfect, since his coat is just the color of cocoa." Emma sat down and reached for the book, careful not to make any sudden moves. Holly handed it to her, but didn't sit until Sara did, and then kept her distance.

The book was a Winnie the Pooh story and Emma read slowly, with expression. She knew Holly was having a difficult time seeing the pictures, and edged nearer, seemingly unaware of what she was doing. Before the story was half over, she'd snuggled up beside Emma, pulled a tattered blanket from under her pillow, and popped her thumb in her mouth. And by the time the story ended, the little girl was fast asleep.

Sara and Emma slipped quietly from the room, Sara looking uncertain. "Miss Grouse always took a nap this time of day, too—" The sentence was left dangling, and Emma wondered if it was a statement or question.

"And what do you usually do?"

"Oh, not much. Usually just poke around or read or something. I'm supposed to stay inside—"

"Would you mind if I poked around with you?" Emma was a little hesitant, not wanting to force her companionship on this quiet girl.

But Sara broke into a wide grin. "I'd like that, Miss Davis." Emma noticed how pretty Sara's eyes were behind her glasses, fringed with long, dark lashes.

Obviously feeling important, Sara took Emma on a complete tour of the grounds, pointing out the coffee trees and other interesting areas as thoroughly as a trained guide. Finally, they circled around back, winding up in the vegetable garden.

"Would you like to see my special place?" asked Sara shyly, and Emma nodded, following her through the hedge of banana trees and into the secret garden.

"This is exquisite!" Emma exclaimed when they entered the garden, not revealing she'd already seen it. They walked slowly around the path, and Sara told her the names of the flowers.

"My nana in Melbourne sends me packets of seeds and starts and things. But lots of them don't grow good, and I have to keep trying. I like to read about gardens, too."

"So you did this all by yourself?" asked Emma in amazement.

"Not exactly. Tomari, our garden boy, helped me get it started, but then I took over. Nana sent me the garden globe last Christmas," she said, standing to walk to the center of the garden where the large sphere rested on its pedestal. "I can't believe it made it here without breaking, but she shipped it in an enormous box full of cotton wool."

"I don't believe I've ever seen anything like this, Sara. It reminds me of an English garden you might read about in an old-fashioned book."

Sara beamed. "It's a constant battle to keep the bugs out, but Father sprays sometimes." She stooped to pull a tiny weed. "You're welcome to come here anytime you like, Miss Davis. It's a good place to read or just sit—" Her eyes brightened. "Or better still, we could take afternoon tea out here. I could get Holly after her nap and we could have a real tea party!"

Emma smiled at the rare display of enthusiasm. "What a great idea!"

"Good. Now you must go to your room, Miss Davis, while I get everything ready. Then we'll meet back here—all right?" Sara asked, looking more like a mischievous child than a miniature adult. "At exactly four o'clock."

At "exactly four o'clock," Emma, wearing a flowered sundress she'd bought in Lae, joined the little girls in the garden. A small table, covered with a pink linen cloth, was set with delicate china dishes. Holly and Sara were already seated, both wearing wide smiles and flowers in their hair.

Holly's face, as Emma had imagined, now shone like sunlight. Emma wished she'd brought her camera with her, but didn't want to spoil the moment by going back to fetch it.

"Please sit down, Miss Davis," said Sara, pulling out a chair. Emma sat at the little table and admired the pretty dishes. They looked a bit fragile for outdoor use, but she didn't mention this.

Sara carefully poured tea from the dainty pot. "Do you have white in your tea, or lemon?"

Emma, now familiar with this terminology, shook her head. "No, I'll have it black, thank you." The girls had theirs white and with sugar, then Sara put the cozy back on the pot and passed a plateful of store-bought shortbread and cookies, or rather, *bickies*, as they called them. They munched companionably while the cicadas buzzed loudly in the trees, and Emma knew it was one of those moments she would cherish for a long time.

After tea, the girls strolled around the garden gathering flowers, then Sara stood behind Emma's chair and carefully arranged them in Emma's hair. Emma sat peacefully with Holly's eyes upon her as Sara gently poked little flower stems into her hair. Emma sighed and thought she could live like this forever. She'd never had times like these as a child, at least not after the accident, and anything before that was still foggy in her mind and perhaps it was best to remain so. Holly was standing very close to her now, and finally rested a tiny pink hand on Emma's knee. Emma didn't move and hardly dared breathe, for this was a momentous occasion. She studied the delicate fingers with their tiny, creamy nails. The hand was warm and as light as a rose petal, and Emma's heart reached out for this motherless child, but her arms remained at her side.

Nineteen

*J*ow was school today?" asked Josh when Matt came outside to help.

"All right, I reckon," said Matt as he set a short stack of pallets by the back wall.

"Learn anything?" This time Matt stopped and stared up at him with a curious expression, and Josh felt a small stab of guilt. It wasn't often he carried on a conversation with his son, especially when they were working. It was a habit that was deeply ingrained—a habit Josh wasn't sure how to break. Wasn't sure he wanted to break. It was the way the Daniels men had always done things. His dad—and his dad's dad before that.

"Yeah, I reckon I learnt something. Miss Davis is all right—for a Yank that is."

Josh nodded. "Go ahead and move the rest of these pallets. Then I want you to go check the irrigation ditch on the west side. Niko was complaining about it this morning."

"Sure, Dad." There was a plaintive tone in Matt's voice today, as if he were pleading for something. Something Josh didn't know how to give.

"Thanks, Matt. You're a good bloke."

Josh headed back toward the house. He didn't want to appear to be checking up on the new governess, but as a parent, he did feel responsible for his children. It hadn't been *his* choice to parent these three alone. Sure, he had always wanted children, but he'd expected them to have a mother, too. Life had dealt him a poor hand. But then, maybe that was his fault. He had married Lila against his parents' wishes. And look where it had gotten him.

Just before he stepped onto the back porch, he heard the sound of soft, feminine voices coming from the direction of Sara's garden. He peeked through the foliage of banana trees without rustling a leaf. As a child, he had learned to sneak about the bush without making a sound. It could mean survival for a villager, and he had been taught by the best.

He had to admit they made a pretty picture sitting there together. A regular garden party. And for a change, the two girls looked almost happy. Or at least pleasant and serene. And that was something. It was so seldom that Sara actually smiled. And Holly—well, that was more than he cared to think about right now.

Emma looked right at home with them—like three little girls playing together. He wondered again how old she was. Although Josh wasn't even that close to forty, he'd begun to think of himself as middle-aged a couple years back. And for some reason, this Yankee woman seemed a lot younger than that. He just hadn't expected it, and he was not a man who appreciated surprises.

So far, every governess he'd brought up here had been much more grandmother-like, at least in appearance. Unfortunately for the children, none of them had half the heart of their own grandmother, his mother. How many times had she offered to come back up here and help with the girls? And each time he'd flatly refused. She had her own life down under now, and he had no right to ask her to leave it. No, his mother had done her time up here. And as Lila had always said, this was no place for a civilized woman.

He studied Emma as she held a china teacup high and crooked her little finger. And to his surprise, Sara and Holly both giggled. He swallowed and turned away. It just wasn't fair! She'd stay around only long enough to break their hearts. And then what would he do? Perhaps he should take her back down the mountain tomorrow. That Louise! And he'd thought she was his friend.

He slipped away as silently as he'd come and went into the

house for a flask of fresh tea. Tabo was busily scrubbing vegetables in the sink. She turned and regarded him darkly, and he
didn't bother to greet her. It made little difference with her.

Everyone wondered why he put up with her. Fact was, she
was one of the best indigenous cooks around, trained by his own
mother while he was away at university. And despite Tabo's sour
disposition, she was worth her considerable weight in gold.

He'd never really taken to her, nor she to him. But she
cooked and he paid. And after Lila ran off, he had come to depend on Tabo to help run the household. She did so with more
authority than efficiency, but he knew better than to complain.
Tabo was a woman who knew how to get even. And he had no
desire to be on her bad list. He'd even heard rumors that she
had some kind of strange power, but he'd heard many strange
things over the years. Probably somebody's overactive imagination.

Still, while not necessarily afraid of her, Josh did allow her a
fair measure of respect. Mostly he tried to stay out of her way,
and now he realized by her stony, dark stare that it was time to
get out of her kitchen.

Twenty

*T*he next few days fell into a tranquil pattern, and Emma wondered if she'd landed in paradise. Other than a few power struggles with Matt, the children were a breeze, and Holly warmed up to her more each day. Josh remained aloof and absent, rarely speaking to her personally and usually addressing her through the children's instructions. It seemed to Emma he purposely avoided her and this filled her with irritation. How could he expect her to care for his children without his input or cooperation? She couldn't understand his relationship with them, either. Although he and Matt spent much time together, Sara received little attention, and Josh seemed to totally ignore Holly. This last thing made Emma indignant, for Holly's withdrawn reserve seemed to her a pitiful plea for parental love.

One evening, Emma and the girls gathered in the living room to read. Sara put some classical music on the cassette player, and Emma settled back into the sofa to catch up with her correspondence. Although her sister had only written once and then briefly, Melinda had sent a nice letter, and Angeline, true to her word, had faithfully written several times. And it was Angeline she now wrote to, explaining the uncertainty of her situation and how Josh's attitude disturbed her. It was a relief to have someone to confide in and she felt comforted when she finally sealed the envelope. As soon as Emma laid her stationary box aside, Holly approached her with a small stack of picture books and, for the first time, climbed right into Emma's lap. Emma acted as if this were completely normal and opened the top book, but inside her heart sang. Sara sat on the other side with a book of her own. As usual, the men were gone. Emma had no idea what they did in the evenings, but she came to accept and even appreciate their absence. She knew how much it meant to Matt. Besides, it made things more relaxed before bedtime and allowed her these quiet moments with the girls. Mina brought in a tea tray and situated it in front of the three.

"Thank you, Mina," said Emma. "It looks very nice." Mina grinned and left.

"How come you always tell the servants 'thank you'?" asked Sara, glancing up from her mystery book. The question didn't surprise Emma. In fact, she was glad Sara asked. Already Emma had noticed no one ever seemed to thank the domestic help, and it bothered her that everyone else seemed to take them so much for granted, almost as if they were slaves. Now was her chance to make a point.

"I thank them because I appreciate their work. This place wouldn't run half as nicely without them. And you know, Mina is a person with feelings and she likes to be appreciated, just like you." Sara's eyes fell and Emma realized she may have hurt the sensitive girl's feelings.

"You see, Sara, I used to work someplace where I was taken for granted—no one ever said thank you or anything—and sometimes it made me feel bad, like I wasn't even a person. You know what I mean?"

Sara looked up and nodded. "I guess I haven't thought of it quite like that. I'll start telling them thank you, too. Maybe it will help Tabo not to be so cranky."

Emma grinned. "Maybe, but don't count on it." They giggled and Holly pushed another book into Emma's hands.

"Please, Miss Davis, can you read one more?"

Emma read five books to Holly before she declared bedtime. Emma tucked Holly into bed and sat next to her, reaching out and moving a wayward curl from the small girl's face. Holly no longer backed away from Emma's touch. Instead, she smiled.

"Miss Davis," she asked softly. "Why do you never pray?" Emma looked at Sara for an explanation as Sara pulled her long flannel nightie over her head.

"She probably means like Miss Grouse. She always made us do our prayers before bedtime. You know, 'Now I lay me down to sleep' . . ."

Emma could tell Sara hadn't enjoyed bedtime prayers, and Emma had never liked recited prayers, either. Yet she still wasn't comfortable with any type of spontaneous prayer. In fact, she'd never actually prayed out loud before. She wasn't even sure she could.

"Did you want me to pray?" she asked Holly with uncertainty, hoping Holly would decline. But the blond head nodded eagerly. "All right, I'll try." Emma paused and took a deep breath. "Dear God, please watch over this family as they sleep, and please hold them in your hands—and thank you for letting me come to stay with them. Amen."

"That was nice, Miss Davis," said Holly.

"Yes," agreed Sara. "That was a real prayer." Emma tucked in Sara, then lingered a moment.

"Would you like me to kiss you good-night?" The words, as if self-willed, came out before Emma had a chance to even stop them. But Sara nodded and Emma bent over and kissed the girl on the forehead.

"Me too," came a little voice from the other bed. Emma smiled and happily kissed Holly, too.

"Good night, girls," she called happily as she switched off the light. "Sleep well." She slipped out to the front porch with a feeling of achievement. She liked being a governess. She liked the two girls.

Soon her eyes adjusted to the darkness and a million stars shone above. She sat down in the wicker rocker and listened to the night. These sounds were becoming more familiar each night. She felt almost perfectly content.

Usually Josh came in the house through the back door because it was close to his room, but tonight she saw him strolling up the path toward her. She knew Matt had already headed for bed, and Josh was alone. He might not see her sitting in the darkness if she didn't move. And so she sat there silently, hoping he'd walk right past without observing her presence. And yet another part of her wished he'd pause to speak.

He started slightly and she knew his keen eyes spotted her. "Oh, I didn't know anyone was out here," he said quietly.

"Sorry to take you by surprise. I was just enjoying your sky."

"*My* sky?"

"Well, I guess it isn't really *your* sky."

He shifted his weight as if deciding whether to continue this conversation or just leave. "You seem to be getting along all right around here, Miss Davis."

When he said "Miss Davis," it reminded her of something she'd wanted to ask. "Mr. Daniels, I really wish the children could call me Emma. *Miss Davis* sounds so formal and not a bit friendly." She felt foolish, wondering if he thought she obsessed over these trifle things on a regular basis. And he surely had more important matters to think about.

"Hmm? I was raised to believe that polite children always addressed elders with a proper title. Is this some new American way?" His voice took on a belligerent tone now, almost as if he was challenging her national allegiance. It reminded her of when Matt hadn't wanted to finish a section of his literature this morning.

"Well, I do agree children need to respect grown-ups, but I would really prefer for the children to call me Emma, if you don't mind." She said it so forcefully she surprised herself.

"And what shall I call you?"

"You may call me Miss Davis if you like; it makes no difference to me." That was a lie, but she didn't care right now. She'd decided to maintain her guard as far as Josh was concerned. She had already begun to categorize him with men like Aaron Fitzpatrick. Too handsome, too controlling and authoritative. The kind best kept at a distance.

"And so, Miss Davis . . ." He paused, it seemed, for dramatic interest. "When do you plan on leaving us?"

Now this caught her completely off guard. What did he mean by that? Did he want her to leave already? Had she done something wrong?

"I, uh, I don't understand—" She searched his face, half hidden in darkness, as if to find a clue.

"You don't need to play games with me, Miss Davis. I knew

the moment I laid eyes on you—you wouldn't stay." His voice was ice-cold now, and his words as sharp as a knife.

"What do you mean?"

"I'd just like to know how long you intend to stay, in order to line up another governess. Or maybe I should start straight away?"

"Why? Do you think I'm not doing the job well enough?" She heard a catch in her voice and was thankful for the darkness. It seemed her pleasant little world was rapidly coming unraveled.

He laughed, low and cynical. "Look. Don't you understand what I'm saying? I know you won't stay—not for more than a fortnight, anyway."

"And just how do you know that?" she demanded.

"Well, you're just not right for the job. Louise was way off on this one. Like I said, I knew from the bloody moment I saw you. What I can't understand is why you bothered to come up here with me in the first place."

"Well, why did you bother to bring me?"

"Because I was desperate."

"Thanks a lot! That's pretty flattering. Maybe I should include it in my next resumé!" She stood and faced him with clenched fists. "So just what exactly were you looking for in a governess? You knew I didn't have experience. What did you expect from me?" Her voice was growing louder.

"Someone more mature for starters, more experienced and—older—and certainly *not* a Yank." His voice rose to match hers.

"Oh, I see, you wanted an Australian granny."

"Yeah, that's right. And I guess it's my business if I did, so like I asked earlier—when are you leaving, Miss Davis?"

The front door burst open and Sara came out and threw her arms around Emma. "No, Father, please don't make Miss Davis leave," she sobbed. "Please, Father, let her stay. She's the best governess we've ever had!"

Emma stroked Sara's smooth dark hair and felt her heart twist oddly. Suddenly she felt protective of Sara in a way she'd never experienced before.

"Sara, get inside—right this minute! This has nothing to do with you!" His voice sliced the night air and, Emma felt sure, Sara as well. And for that Emma hated him. She gently nudged Sara toward the door, whispering it would be okay.

After Sara went in the house, Emma began again, this time in a low voice full of suppressed emotion. "Fine, I can leave tomorrow if you like. But before I go, I *will* give you a piece of my mind. First of all, I *am* doing a good job. I adore your children and they like me, and I could've stayed here for a long, long time. But you wouldn't know that, Mr. Daniels, because *you* never speak to me. Secondly, and more importantly, Mr. Daniels, you are a neglectful father! Sure, you spend time with Matt—working, that is. But as far as the girls go, well, you don't treat Sara much better than a house girl, which is another subject. And you totally ignore poor Holly—it's almost as if you don't even like her—"

"That's quite enough! You know nothing—"

"No, it's not. Not quite enough," she cut him off. "Because if you don't change the way you're treating them, they'll soon grow up and leave you altogether! And then you can live here all by your lonely old self!"

"Ha! And you don't think they will anyway? You don't know anything about this, Miss Davis. And that's furthermore reason why you should leave!"

"Perhaps you're right. I only wish I could take your daughters with me." Her words astounded her, but in her heart she knew it was true. If she could, she wouldn't hesitate to take Sara and Holly for her own children. An uncomfortable silence fell over the two of them, like a thick, heavy tarp. Emma could think of nothing more to say. She heard her pulse throbbing in her ears, and her fists remained tightly clenched with her nails digging into her palms, but that meager pain was almost soothing compared to what she felt inside. She knew she'd stepped way over the line on this, but she no longer cared.

Josh sank down onto the porch steps, his elbows on his knees and head hanging between his hands. Emma stared at him for some time. What had she said? What had she done? And then, quite unexpectedly, a trickle of compassion began to course through her. Suddenly he no longer seemed the authoritative plantation owner, but rather a confused and overgrown boy. She guessed his life must've been difficult, and she assumed he had good reason to be the way he was. Yet somewhere along the line, he had become the enemy in her mind. And in all fairness, he hadn't made it easy for her. Now she felt a pang of guilt for all her stinging accusations. After all, she was the newcomer, and there was much she didn't know.

"I'm sorry," she stammered. "I shouldn't have said—"

"No, what you said was mostly true." His voice was low, almost inaudible. She leaned forward, straining to hear. "I know I'm not a good father to the girls. I don't know how. Most recently, I left it to Miss Grouse, and she was actually better than the governess before her. But even so, she didn't ever really seem to—didn't really . . ." He paused and looked at the sky as if searching for words.

"Love them?"

He sighed and nodded. "Sure, she took care of them. She made them sit straight, mind their manners. I just don't think she knew how to . . . Maybe I don't even know how to . . ." She waited for him to finish the sentence, but the silence grew thick around them. She sat down on the steps next to him, searching for the right words.

"So now that you have someone who might actually 'know how,' as you say, or at least be willing to try—why do you want to get rid of her?"

"No, Emma, it's not that. I wasn't trying to give you the sack. I just wanted you to leave before the girls get too attached to you. Don't you think I can see it happening already? They follow you around like baby chicks. I mean, Emma, you don't belong here—you're young, you've got your whole life ahead of you. Why would you want to get bogged down with a lot like us—out here in the middle of nowhere?" Emma was smiling to herself. Not only had he called her "young," but he'd actually called her Emma instead of Miss Davis.

"Well, for starters, Mr. Daniels, I'm thirty-one, that's not exactly young, and so far my life hasn't been all that exciting, at least until recently. Besides that, I like it here. So if it's okay with you, I'd be happy to stay."

He sat silently, his face still cloudy, as though he was still going to turn her down and send her packing. "It's just that I can't bear to see them get hurt—anymore than they've already been."

"Were they hurt when Miss Grouse left?"

"No . . . not really."

"So what are you saying? Do you want someone to come work for you who doesn't love the children, so just in case they leave—the children won't be hurt?"

He moaned and ran his fingers through his dark hair. "No, of course not. I don't even know what I want."

Suddenly she understood. He was thinking about how his wife, their mother, had left. She had tried to blank out the missing mother, almost as if she weren't real or had never really been here, but now she felt consumed with curiosity about this woman. She longed to ask him, and yet all instincts warned her not to.

"You do what you think best, Miss Davis." His words carried a tone of finality in them, and she knew this conversation, at least for now, was over. And she knew that, at least for now, she would stay. For how long? She would think about that later.

Twenty-one

No, no, Miss Davis. I do that." Mina gently pulled the sheet from Emma's hand. "Making bed my job."

Emma could see the hurt look on the girl's face. "I'm sorry, Mina. I just wanted to help. It seems you have so much to do." She had been hoping for an opportunity to bring it up, and now here it was. "Have you always done all the chores yourself? Or did Mrs. Daniels help . . . before—before she left?"

"Mrs. Daniels show me plenty things." Mina beamed and smoothed the sheet. "But soon I learn and do myself."

"So when Mrs. Daniels left, you just kept things running?"

Mina nodded, head down, as she bundled the laundry into a neat ball.

"How long has she been away?"

"Almost three year now," Mina answered softly, and Emma sensed she didn't like to talk about it.

"Do you think she'll ever come back?" When the girl did not reply, Emma touched her arm. "I'm only asking because it may help me understand the children better. I just can't see why Mrs. Daniels left her family and her home. It doesn't make sense."

Mina nodded sadly. "It so sad—" She broke off abruptly, looking wild-eyed past Emma's shoulder toward the doorway.

Turning in the direction of Mina's gaze, Emma saw Tabo disappearing down the hallway, the quiet thuds of her bare feet following her.

"I get to work," said Mina, hastening from the room.

Emma sighed and walked over to her window. It was so beautiful out today, and yet she stared blankly, forgetting to appreciate the view. Who could answer her questions? She hated to bring up the subject with Sara or Matt. The memory must be excruciating for them. And as for Josh—she was aleady treading on thin ice with him. Maybe later . . .

༺ ༺ ༺ ༺

That afternoon they finished their lessons early. Matt, as usual, took off to join his dad. Emma still wasn't sure if it was because Matt enjoyed working with Josh, or because it was expected of him. But Matt never complained about helping on the plantation.

Yesterday, though, Emma had observed the boy chastising a worker about dropping a couple of seedling coffee trees along the drive. She couldn't understand what he was saying, but she was shocked to hear him use such an arrogant tone of voice with an adult. The worker said nothing in return, although Emma was sure she'd detected resentment in the smoldering glance he'd sent Matt's way.

"Miss Davis, would you like to go for a walkabout today?" asked Sara as she straightened the table and put her books away. Sara had been carefully observing Emma all morning, as if searching for some sign that all was well after last night's little spat.

"Let's see. A walkabout—that's a hike, isn't it? Sounds great, Sara. But shall we wait for Holly to have her nap first?"

Holly groaned. "I'm not sleepy, Miss Davis. Truly, I'm not."

Emma grinned and tussled the blond curls. "Okay, how about only a short rest—after your favorite story?"

Both girls followed her to the bedroom and willingly sat down on the bed beside her, one on either side. Even Sara seemed eager for the now familiar story hour.

After the story, Emma laid the book aside. "I've been thinking. Now that we're friends, hadn't you rather call me 'Emma'?"

Sara nodded. "Emma is a beautiful name. But is it really all right with Father?"

Emma turned a meaningful look on the girl. "Yes, Sara, it is. Your father agreed last night."

At this secret signal that the argument had been resolved—at least for now—Sara beamed. "Thanks . . . Emma."

While the girls rested, Emma stopped by the kitchen to collect provisions for their walkabout, only to receive another hard glare from Tabo. Trying to ignore the unsettling look, Emma perused the open shelves until she spotted several thermoses and a small basket.

"Tabo, your sugar biscuits are so delicious." Maybe the gloomy woman would respond to praise, as Mina did. Emma placed several on a napkin in the basket. "It's unusual to find such fine cooking up here in the highlands. Mr. Daniels must be very proud." Still no response. "Sara is taking us on a walkabout this afternoon. I'm not sure how long we'll be gone, but we'll be sure to get home in time for tea."

Tabo only grunted and returned to her cutting board, chopping the vegetables with a vengeance. Maybe it was useless to try to make friends with this woman.

Emma enjoyed watching Sara confidently lead the way. They first cut through the west grove of coffee trees, and then around a newly planted section of seedlings. The earth around the seedlings was rich and brown, and it reminded Emma of fresh-ground coffee. It was the first time she'd ever lived near any form of agriculture, and the sight of green growing things still filled her with a sense of wonder.

When they came to a wooden rail fence, they climbed over and found a well-worn trail on the other side. The trail sliced through a grassy meadow that gradually ascended. Emma was panting as the trail grew steeper. She couldn't see the top of the hill, but she trusted Sara's judgment and, after twenty minutes of steady walking, they reached the summit and paused under a lone, scraggly tree.

"This is One Tree Hill," announced Sara proudly. Holly

danced around the tree and then proclaimed that she was starved.

Emma opened up the basket, poured milk from the thermos, and they sat and snacked while Sara pointed out the landmarks. "That village over there belongs to the Osabe tribe." She gestured toward the large group of huts clustered in a corner of the valley below. Emma would never have noticed them. They blended like camouflage into their surroundings.

"They're kind of mean," Sara went on. "That's Tabo's tribe." Somehow this didn't surprise Emma. "The Osabes think Grandpa Daniels stole land from them, but Father says that's not true—that the land was purchased. Anyway, the Osabes don't understand it, so they're always sort of mad at us. Like an old feud."

Emma was puzzled. "I'm surprised Tabo would work for your father, under the circumstances."

"It's because she got thrown out of her village a long, long time ago. I heard it had to do with her making poison," Sara whispered while Holly gathered sticks for a large "nest" she was building. "But I'm not supposed to know that."

Emma gasped. "You mean Tabo poisoned someone?"

Sara giggled. "No, no, poison is—let's see, how do you say it—like a magic spell or something. See, the story is, Tabo's father sold her to a Sikani man, on the other side of the mountain, but her Sikani husband didn't like her. When he got very sick, the Sikanis said Tabo worked poison on him. They say she put poisoned bamboo slivers into the bottoms of his feet, and later he died. So Tabo had to leave the Sikani village, but then her own village wouldn't take her back."

Emma's head was reeling from the bizarre story, but Sara wasn't through.

"My Nana Daniels took her in. They say Nana was the only person Tabo has ever cared for. And last year when Nana came to visit, Tabo was almost nice for a change."

"Interesting," said Emma, trying to put the pieces together. "What's that village over there?" She pointed to a smaller grouping of rounded huts nestled against the opposite hill. The tiny houses reminded her of mushrooms that sprout up during the night.

"That's Kubari. They're friendly. See that row of trees right next to it? That's where the McDowells live—the ones who run the mission school." Sara helped herself to another biscuit. "Mina's from Kubari. The Osabes don't like the Kubari, either. Father says to stay away from the Osabes."

Emma shuddered. "Wise man." She glanced around nervously. "Are you allowed to come here?"

"Oh yes. As long as a grown-up is with us." Sara brushed the crumbs off her lap and stood. "Do you want to meet the McDowells, Emma? It only takes another twenty minutes to get down there."

Emma looked at her watch. Still plenty of time before dinner—tea, that is. And the idea of adult conversation was appealing. "How about you, Holly? Can you make it?"

"Let's go! Let's go!" Holly tugged on Emma's hand as they headed down the hill.

When they reached the edge of the Kubari village, a handful of women and children approached them, staring openly at Emma. A few naked toddlers darted about, shrieking wildly. And from somewhere nearby, a rooster crowed.

This was Emma's first experience in a native village, and the appearance of the stark poverty surpised her. Outside one of the huts, a woman sat cross-legged on the hard-packed dirt, nursing a newborn baby at her sagging breast. Next to this mother lay a rough wooden garden implement and a string bag filled with sweet potatoes, or *kaukau*. To Emma's surprise, none of the people appeared malnourished and, in fact, they seemed healthy, their faces reflecting contentment.

An old woman emerged from a hut and spoke to Sara. Emma thought she picked up the word *Mina* and looked to Sara for verification.

"Yawasai is Mina's mother," she explained.

Happy to meet the woman, Emma bowed slightly, out of deference, something the girls could not understand. But they clung to her hands as they walked on toward the row of tall trees bordering the village.

Holly pranced along at Emma's side like a spirited pony. "We're almost there, Emma!"

Ahead, a group of indigenous men gathered around what appeared to be a woodworking class being conducted by a white man.

"Mr. McDowell!" squealed Holly, breaking free of Emma's grip and racing toward him.

"Holly just loves Mr. McDowell," explained Sara in a mature tone. "He always gives her horsy rides and lollies and such." Sara spoke as if such childish amusements were beneath her. Poor little thing. The girl had had precious little childhood.

The man set his hammer down and swooped Holly up, standing her up on the very table he'd just been making. "Aye, and 'tis been a long time since we've laid eyes on you, lassie."

The Scottish accent sounded vaguely familiar, and as they got closer, Emma recognized the ruddy face. "Ian?"

He looked up in surprise. "Aye. And you must be the new governess. If I recall, I gave you a ride to the hotel in Lae. Emma, isn't it?"

"That's right. But I didn't realize we'd be neighbors."

He shrugged his broad shoulders. "'Tis a small world, as they say. I'm just about to finish up here. Won't you go on in and meet my Mary and have yourself a cup of tea?" His blue eyes twinkled—like the ocean in sunlight—and he turned back to his class.

The girls led Emma to the house, where a little woman was waving off a group of village girls with what appeared to be sewing baskets on their arms. Emma thought it looked a little incongruous to see these barefoot villagers carrying proper English sewing baskets.

"Hello there, Sara and Holly, have you brought your new nanny to meet me? Come in, come in. I'm about to make tea."

Emma liked this friendly woman on sight. Ian had good taste in women. "I'm Emma Davis, I hope you don't mind our dropping in like this."

"Not a'tall. It's not like you could ring first. Sometimes I long for a telephone, but then I remember the interruptions, and I bite my tongue and thank the good Lord for my peace and quiet." She chuckled and led them into a dainty little parlor that could've been transported, intact, directly from Edinburgh.

"I'm Mary McDowell, as the girls may have told you. We've just finished our sewing class. You see, we don't have school on Fridays. Instead, the girls come here, and I read from the Gospels while they sew—it's rather like a captive audience." She laughed again, her voice reminding Emma of a songbird. Somehow Emma wouldn't have imagined Ian McDowell's wife being anything like this refined little lady, living out here in the bush. It was strange to stand here in this well-furnished room—such an absolute contrast to Yawasai's hut only just yards away. And yet both women were kind and hospitable by their own customs.

"Come into the kitchen, Emma," called Mary. "The girls know their way around the house." Already, Sara was examining a jigsaw puzzle spread across a library table, and Holly had made herself at home with an old-fashioned dollhouse.

"The girls seem right at home here," commented Emma as Mary filled the kettle and threw some kindling into the big woodstove.

"Aye, we try to be like family to them. But I've been missin' the dear girls since they got their new nanny. I was about to get a wee bit jealous." The twinkle in Mary's eyes gave her away. "So, Emma Davis, how did you manage to link up with the likes of Josh Daniels?"

Emma could tell by the woman's tone that she didn't really disapprove of Josh. It was more like friendly banter. Emma tried to keep her story brief, and Mary nodded, seeming to understand even beyond the sketchy explanation.

"Aye, Josh needs a good nanny, no doubt about that. I hope you can stay long enough to make it worth his while."

"I have no reason not to."

Mary seemed slightly skeptical, her skepticism softened by a smile. "Good then. You must know by now that it's not an easy life up here. But it has its own rewards."

"I think it's beautiful up here," said Emma quietly. "I've never seen anything quite like it."

"And I suppose you'll be wanting to hear what became of Lila Daniels." Mary looked at Emma from the corner of her eye.

"That is, unless you already know." Mary glanced in the other room as if to see if the girls were fully occupied.

"Lila . . . Daniels?" whispered Emma. "Josh's wife?" Emma sat down on the kitchen stool, eager to hear.

"Is—or was—depending upon how you look at it. Lila disappeared a few years back. Rumor has it, she ran off with Skip Banliff, but I never quite believed it myself. I'll grant you that Lila may not have been the best wife in the world, but I'll never believe she'd willingly abandon those children. It's a pure mystery, Emma."

Mary climbed on a well-worn stepstool to reach a tray and a teapot. "Josh tried to hunt them down. I think he would've killed Skip at one time. Maybe Lila, too. You see, Skip was his best friend, went to university in Melbourne with Josh. Skip came out regularly to visit and help Josh with the plantation. Everyone knew Skip and Lila got along real well, but still it's hard to believe Skip would have done such a thing."

She shook her head sadly, filling the pot with water from the faucet. "The fact is, no one's seen hide nor hair of them since they left. Josh figures they're hiding out somewhere down under, too ashamed to return. He won't even speak of it anymore. Can't really blame him. It was odd—truly odd. I've tried to believe the best of Lila, but to be honest, there have been times when even I've had my doubts about her."

"Hello," called Ian from the back porch. "Am I too late for a cup of tea?"

Just then the kettle whistled, and Mary poured the water into the pot, right over the loose black leaves. Emma watched curiously, eager to learn the proper way to make tea. As Mary looked up and smiled at Ian, the steam curled around her head like a halo.

"No, Ian, you're not too late. You're just in the nick of time. But wipe your feet first." It was such a wifely remark, and Emma smiled to herself.

Ian came in and sat at the table to have his tea, and Mary called for the girls. The couple chatted companionably, being careful to include the girls, while Emma sorted through the bits of information she'd just gleaned about Lila Daniels, unwilling to lose a single thread. But when she looked across the table, she found Ian's steady gaze on her. She glanced nervously at Mary, who seemed not to notice, or to mind.

"Have you ever gone spelunking?" asked Mary, pulling Emma back into the flow of conversation.

"What?"

"Spelunking. Ian is an avid spelunker." Mary grinned.

"Caving," interpreted Ian. "I like to explore caves."

"Oh, I see. No, I've never even been in a cave."

"Really?" Mary poured Emma another cup of tea. "Ian is planning a little trip for tomorrow. Maybe you'd like to go along."

Emma didn't know what to say. "But—the children. I'm not sure—"

"I happen to know that Matt's been wishing to go, and Sara might even enjoy it as well," continued Mary. Sara nodded in eager confirmation. "And I could keep Holly for you. Ian's been trying to get in as much spelunking as possible before he returns to Scotland."

"Oh, I didn't realize you were going back—"

"Yes," said Ian. "I take about a month or two off every year to visit Mary, but then I must get back to make sure the farm is still running."

Emma was thoroughly confused, and looked from one to the other. "But what about you, Mary—I mean, do you stay here all alone the rest of the year? Isn't that awfully hard on your marriage?"

Ian laughed—a throaty, hearty laugh. "Now, that's a rich one, Emma. You don't understand. You see, Mary's my big sister." He caught Mary's eye and winked. "I just come over to check on her and to lend a hand with some classes—woodworking, agriculture, that kind of thing. And when I can work it in, I do some spelunking."

Mary and Ian McDowell were sister and brother, not husband and wife? "But—but aren't you afraid to stay here alone?"

"Oh, I'm never alone, dear." Mary hastened to cover Emma's confusion. "I've all kinds of friends in the village and, of course, my Lord is always with me. I'm never afraid." Emma shook her head in wonder at this small woman's large faith.

"My Mary's quite a lass," observed Ian with open admiration. "She's been here nearly twenty-five years now. She's put up with tribal wars, independence, untimely deaths, and all manner of other exciting adventures. But she's also made a difference, she has. Has seen a lot of kids through school. Some who've gone on to take up trades and find employment in the local towns. Many who have even attended university and entered various professions. One young man is about to become a doctor—"Ian turned to address his sister—"and how many pastors have you sent out, Mary?"

"At latest count, eleven, I believe."

"Oh, Mary, that's wonderful!" Suddenly realizing that dusk was coming on, Emma rose. "I didn't realize we'd been here so long. I'm afraid we'll barely make it home before dark."

"Don't worry, Emma. I'm sure Ian would be happy to escort three lovely ladies back home."

"That I would!" Ian shot to his feet. " 'Twould be my pleasure."

His grin spoke volumes, and Emma found herself blushing. "Thank you for everything, Mary. It's nice to know I've got good neighbors not too far away."

Ian picked up the empty picnic basket left over from lunch, took her elbow, and steered her outside. "Not far a'tall."

Twenty-two

I was about to send out a search party, Miss Davis," Josh said with obvious irritation. "I had no idea where you three had disappeared to."

"I'm sorry, Mr. Daniels. We went visiting and completely lost track of the time. Surely Tabo told you of our walkabout."

"She did not." He turned to Ian and shook his hand. "Evening, Ian. Care to join us for tea?"

"No thanks. Mary is expecting me back. Say, Emma, how about tomorrow? We've planned a spelunking expedition," he explained to Josh. "Sara and Matt are welcome, and Mary will keep Holly. Maybe you'd like to come, too."

Josh seemed more snappish than usual. "No, I've got work to do. But the kids can go if they want."

"You know what they say, Josh—all work and no play makes for a dull boy—"

"Well, this plantation won't run itself."

Ian laughed and clapped Josh on the back. "Believe me, mon, I do know what farm work is all about. But I've also learned there's more to life than growing things. My father worked himself to death on the farm, and I canna remember him smiling much."

"You don't depend on your farm for your living. You're a 'gentleman' farmer."

Ian hooted. "Well, now, just don't tell my cows, Josh. They might lose their respect for me." Ian turned to Emma, who was fascinated by Ian's way with words. Maybe some of his good cheer would rub off on Josh. "I'll be by at seven to pick you up then, Emma."

"We'll be ready, Ian."

"Then, I'll be sayin' a good evening to you." He tipped his hat and left.

As soon as Ian was out of sight, Josh spoke quietly but with a trace of anger in his voice. "I would appreciate it, Miss Davis, if next time you would let me know your whereabouts. I don't believe you fully comprehend the dangers of this country."

"Really? Then maybe you should explain them to me." She hadn't intended to toss off such a flippant retort.

"Aren't some things obvious? We're the minority here, living in a country with a history of headhunting and cannibalism. Do I have to explain everything?"

With a sinking heart, Emma recalled Tim Miller's comments about that very thing, but she wasn't about to give Josh Daniels the satisfaction of knowing he was right. "Well, Mr. Daniels, you must realize that so far you've told me precious little. I'm simply playing this out by ear. I still don't know what you expect or want from me. Couldn't we sit down and discuss it like civilized people?"

Just then the dinner bell rang, cutting through the silence. "Perhaps you're right, Miss Davis. But tonight is obviously not the time since it appears you have an early engagement tomorrow."

Dinner, as usual, was a quiet affair. Matt, though clearly excited about the spelunking trip, contained himself until they were finally excused from the dining room.

Then he stopped Emma in the hallway. "Did Mr. McDowell say what we should bring?"

"Not really, but I assume you'll need some heavy shoes and maybe some protective clothing. Why don't you lay out everything tonight, Matt? Then you'll be ready in the morning."

"All right, Miss Davis." Matt grinned, and Emma was pleased to see this new enthusiasm in the boy.

"You know, Matt, I told the girls to call me Emma. It sounds a little friendlier, I think."

"Truly? Father doesn't mind? All right then, Emma." Matt walked off with a spring in his step. "Good night."

"Good night, Matt. Happy dreams!"

Emma, too, was beginning to anticipate tomorrow's adventure with eagerness. She helped the girls prepare for bed, suggesting that Sara gather what she'd need for the next day.

"I wish I could go with you and Mr. McDowell," Holly complained as Emma tucked her in. "I'm not too little to go spunking."

"It's spelunking," corrected Sara from the other bed.

"Oh, I think it's very special to be staying with Mary," Emma reassured. "I'm sure she has lots of plans for the two of you."

"Truly?" Holly's blue eyes widened. Of the three children, only this one had fair complexion. She must resemble her mother, Emma thought as she turned off the lamp, because she looked nothing like Josh. Lila was probably a blond beauty with translucent skin. No doubt she and Josh had made a striking pair.

Although Emma put the children to bed early, she felt restless and not the least bit sleepy. She had discovered a letter from Angeline on her dresser after dinner, but had only taken time to scan it before getting the girls off to bed. Now she re-read it, feeling more and more concerned for her friend. Poor Angeline. Her hopes and expectations for Australia seemed dashed. Her uncle's movies were, as Angeline put it, "nothing but trash," and she and her aunt didn't get along at all. Now Angeline was struggling with serious doubts about her decision.

Emma ached for her friend. But it was almost more disturbing to discover that her idol—the woman Emma still tried to emulate—had feet of clay.

She wrote Angeline a long letter of encouragement, telling her all about the children and their plans for tomorrow's expedition. She mentioned Ian McDowell, too—an eligible bachelor. But she decided not to say anything about Josh. She wasn't sure how to put her feelings about Josh into words.

Finally, she invited Angeline to consider coming for a visit, hoping Josh wouldn't have a fit if she did come. Or, if there were some objection, hoping Mary would put her friend up. Oh well, she'd cross that bridge later. She sealed and addressed the letter and prepared for bed.

Emma hadn't meant to, but her glowing comments about Ian had set her mind racing. His gentleness put her at ease, and she had to admit he was attractive in a Spencer Tracy sort of way. She wondered why he wasn't married and what his place in Scotland might be like. Suddenly he was all she could think of, and she fell asleep with Ian on her mind.

❧   ❧   ❧   ❧

"Emma." She was awakened by a trembling voice penetrating the murkiness of sleep. When she opened her eyes, Sara's pale face was peering down at her.

"What's wrong?" Emma sat up. "Is it Holly?"

"No, no. She's still asleep. I'm sorry to wake you, Emma." Sara's voice choked into sobs, and Emma pulled the girl toward her, holding her close.

"It's okay, darling," she whispered, stroking the dark head, waiting for Sara to open up. And after a while the sobbing ceased.

"I had—a bad dream, Emma. About Mummy. It was horrible." Sara shivered.

"Would you like to sleep with me tonight, Sara?"

"May I?"

"Of course." Emma opened the covers, and Sara crawled in beside her. Emma turned to study the girl's profile, silhouetted in the colorless moonlight. She looked so much like Josh. "I used to have nightmares as a child, Sara—in fact, sometimes I still do."

"Truly, Emma?

"Yes, truly." Emma paused, wondering how much to tell this child, who was already wise beyond her years. "You see,

Sara, my parents both died when I was six. After that, I often dreamed . . . the dreams were so very real—"

"Yes, Emma, that's just how it is. I see Mummy. She's hurt and bleeding and yelling my name—it's so awful, Emma. Father doesn't want us talk about Mummy—he says she doesn't care about us anymore—that that's why she went away. Do you think it's true, Emma?"

"Oh, darling, I don't think so. I can't imagine a mother not caring—"

"Then why did she leave, Emma?"

Although Sara's voice was almost a whisper, the anguish in her question screamed for an answer.

Emma had always thought that if she had ever had children of her own, she would never be anything but honest with them. No half-truths. No evasion. Just the plain truth. But what was the truth?

"I know how you feel, Sara," she began haltingly. "You see, when my parents died, it felt as if my mom had left me, too. I know it's not exactly the same, but that's how it felt. At first, I felt guilty, like it was somehow my fault. And then after a while, I got angry because I thought my mom could have prevented the wreck. I thought she would have still been alive if she'd really loved me and my sister. But the simple fact is, Sara, I'll never really know what happened.

"What I'm trying to do now is to trust God and get on with my life. Maybe that's what you should do, too."

There was a gentle sigh. "Thanks, Emma. I've never had anyone to talk to before. Sometimes it feels like I might just explode." She turned to throw her arms around Emma's neck. "Oh, I'm so glad you came to be with us, Emma. I hope you never, never leave. . . ."

This last phrase was like a knife to Emma's heart, and suddenly she knew exactly what Josh had meant. But how could she have known that she'd be stepping into a situation where she had the power to bring even more suffering? The heavy responsibility was almost suffocating. How could she ever leave? How could she stay? Caring for Grandma had been a walk in the park compared with this emotional minefield.

Even after she could tell, by Sara's even breathing, that the child had finally fallen asleep, Emma lay awake, her thoughts in turmoil. This was far more than she'd bargained for that day in Lae when she'd agreed to come here.

She cried out to God in the deepest places of her heart. *Help me, Lord! Give me Your wisdom!* And she prayed for this fragile little family she had grown to love. For how long? Only God knew. All *she* knew was that she was walking a very precarious path. And more than ever, she needed Him to guide her—every step of the way.

Twenty-three

Six o'clock came early. Not wanting to awaken Sara after her disrupted night's sleep, Emma dressed quietly in the darkness. She nudged Sara just in time for her to dress and eat a hasty breakfast.

Matt was already up and raring to go. He'd set the picnic basket, prepared by Tabo last night, on the porch. Now he was perched on the rail, watching for Ian's truck. Mina would take Holly over to Mary's before lunchtime.

Emma noticed that Josh was hanging around the house, fiddling with insignificant little tasks, and Emma wondered if maybe he'd changed his mind about joining them. But just before Ian pulled up, Josh disappeared. Though somewhat disappointed, Emma was relieved. For some reason, when Josh was with them, the children seemed tense and anxious.

The drive in the dawn's fresh light was pleasant. The morning mist trailed over the valleys, rolling along like ocean-bound forks of an ethereal river. Matt was quiet in back, and Sara was soon sleeping again.

"What part of Scotland are you from, Ian?" asked Emma, hoping to stir up some conversation.

"Just north of Dundee. An agricultural community. Do you know Scotland?"

"No, not really."

"And where are you from, Emma?"

"Ever hear of Wilsonville, Iowa? Actually, it's close to Des Moines."

Ian nodded and inquired about the climate. Between them, they managed to occupy their time until Ian pulled down a narrow dirt road and parked.

"This is it," he announced, and the kids tumbled from the back of the Land Rover. No one was around, but Ian locked the rig just the same.

He opened a knapsack and handed each of them a flashlight. "Now, remember, we must stay together. We'll take it slow and easy. This cave is supposed to drop for quite a ways before it exits on the other side of the mountain. But it gets pretty tight in spots, and since we aren't wearing helmets, we won't go too deep."

Ian placed a notebook with their names, date, and cave plan outside the entrance, then led the way, followed by Sara and Matt, with Emma bringing up the rear. The entry tunnel was less than five feet tall, but once inside, the cavern opened up to a large chamber.

Ian pointed out some rock formations with his flashlight. "The way to remember the difference between stalagmites and stalactites is to think about a creepy, crawly bug—"

"Ugh!" groaned Sara, grabbing Emma's hand. "Why's that?"

"Because that will help you to remember that when the mites go up, the tights go down. You see, the stalag-*mites* grow up and the stalac-*tites* hang down."

"Who could forget!" Sara moaned.

As they ventured farther and farther from the opening, the cave was still surprisingly spacious, though much darker now. But at the idea of being underground, Emma had to take a few deep, calming breaths. Already, she was pretty certain spelunking wasn't her cup of tea, but she could be a good sport about it. The air smelled damp and moldy, and soon they turned a corner to enter a smaller area about eight feet square.

"Now, just for the fun of it, let's turn off our flashlights." This, from Ian.

They all did as he suggested, and were plunged into total darkness. Emma caught her breath, attempting to adjust to the smothering blackness, but she couldn't see her hand in front of her face.

Something clattered to the floor, and the rustling of hundreds of wings could be heard overhead. Sara screamed, and the flashlights flicked on in time to illuminate a colony of bats disturbed by the intruders. Most were still hanging upside down from the ceiling, some were fluttering their wings, but a few had swooped down dangerously near.

"Squat down and cover your heads," instructed Ian calmly. "Everyone remain quiet, and they'll settle back down pretty soon."

Sara held on to Emma, and she wrapped her arms around the trembling girl. Her light illuminated the thick layer of bat manure coating the rocks beneath their feet, and Emma closed her eyes in revulsion, longing for the sunlight. At last the bats quieted down.

"I—I'm sorry," whispered Sara, obviously trying to be brave. "I dropped my light and that must've set them off."

Ian's deep masculine voice at their elbow was reassuring. "It's all right, Sara. Are you too frightened to go on?"

Emma took note of the pale face, but the child nodded bravely. Leading the way, Ian and Matt moved forward, and Emma took Sara's hand and followed. The small hand was cold as stone.

At this point, they entered a narrow, tunnel-like hallway, and Ian instructed them to crouch low, but halfway through, Sara froze.

"What's wrong, Sara?" asked Emma gently, suspecting Sara had had enough of spelunking for one day.

"I'm scared, Emma," she gasped. "I can't breathe."

"Everything all right back there?" Ian swiveled in the cramped space to aim his light in their direction.

"Ian, I hate to break up the party, but I think Sara and I should turn back. We'll find our way out, and it's not far. You and Matt go on. We'll be fine."

"Not on your life, Emma," called Ian cheerfully. "Come on, Matt. We'll escort the ladies out, then we'll come back." Matt moaned, but went along.

"The first rule of spelunking," continued Ian, ignoring Matt's complaint, "is safety. You might think you know your way, but even an experienced spelunker can get lost in this underground maze. That's why I leave these markers—" he indicated a small yellow cone on a rock—"so in case anything happens, someone could track us."

When they reached the entrance. Emma squinted into the bright sunlight, gratefully gulping in the fresh air.

Ian handed her the keys to the Land Rover and tucked some food from the picnic basket into his pack. "Matt and I might decide to eat in the cave, if you don't mind. But there's a stream over there—" he gestured toward some brush—"and a nice picnic spot alongside."

"Oh, don't let us spoil your fun." She shooed them off. "You two stay as long as you like. Don't worry about us."

"It's almost noon," said Ian. "I think we could see quite a bit and still finish by around two-thirty. But don't be worried if we're not back. And don't call out the troops until at least four." He laughed his rumbling laugh again, and Emma was buoyed by his confidence. He had a way of making her feel so safe, so protected. . . .

She and Sara waded in the cool stream for a bit, then sat down and ate their lunch in the shade of a mangrove tree near the creek.

"Look, Emma." Sara pointed out a bird of paradise perched on a tree on the opposite bank, and Emma studied the colorful plumage, which appeared iridescent in the sunlight that filtered through the trees. This was just like the exotic bird she'd seen in the travel brochure at home. It seemed another lifetime ago. Again, she had to pinch herself. She was here in the wilds of New Guinea, seeing with her own eyes what others would only see in travel posters! She'd have to be sure to write Linda about—

With a swoosh, the regal bird plummeted from its perch and splashed into the water below. The body was instantly swept downstream in a spiraling trail of red, quickly erased by the bubbling current. Emma gasped and Sara clutched her arm tightly, placing a hand over her mouth in warning. Then Sara silently pulled Emma back into the screen of brush nearby, cautioning

Emma, with a gesture, to be perfectly still.

Emma's shock was replaced by outrage when she heard whoops of triumph and the splash of hunters retrieving their prey only twenty yards away. Peering through the underbrush, she spied several dark bodies, gleaming with sweat, trekking up the hill beyond the creek. Suspended between them was their trophy, still impaled by the lethal arrow and dripping with blood. The scene was nauseating. How dare they?

Sara waited until the hunting party was out of sight before she spoke in a whisper. "Killing the bird of paradise is illegal, Emma. If they'd known we were here, they might've—"

The reality of their dilemma struck Emma with a force that left her gasping. "Sara, I didn't know we were in real danger. If you hadn't stopped me, I would have yelled at them." She shuddered at the thought.

"Miss Grouse told us about this missionary who reported some illegal artifact smuggling, and he was later found murdered—with his eyes cut out."

Emma felt her knees weaken. "Oh, how horrible!"

"But Father says Miss Grouse sometimes exaggerated."

"Well, just the same, I think we should go wait in the Land Rover."

Sara didn't argue, and they locked themselves in the vehicle and began a game of Twenty Questions to pass the time. Before long, Sara's early-morning start caught up with her, the dark circles under her eyes magnified by her glasses.

"Why don't you lie down in the back and have a little nap, Sara. Here, use my sweater for a pillow."

Sara climbed into the backseat and was soon fast asleep. Glancing at her watch, Emma saw that it was not yet two-thirty, and there was no guarantee that Ian and Matt would return by that time anyway. She leaned back into the driver's seat and sighed, thinking to catch a nap herself.

But something caught her eye in the rearview mirror. It was the poaching party, still armed with bows and wicked-looking arrows, and heading straight for the Land Rover. From their kinky hair protruded colorful plumage, evidence of their earlier conquest. Her heart beat wildly as visions of blinded missionaries loomed in her imagination.

If she only knew how to drive! What a stupid fool she was. Any other half-witted adult could drive. Even Matt could handle the tractor. But not her! She glanced at Sara, sleeping sweetly in back, and felt completely helpless.

God, help us! she begged silently again and again as the men drew nearer. By the time they were within ten feet of the vehicle, she could clearly see their expressions, and they weren't happy. In desperation, she put her hand to the horn and let out a long, deafening blast. Startled, the men turned suddenly and disappeared into the brush. She blinked her eyes in astonishment, wondering if God had indeed sent angels or if it had been the horn that frightened them away.

While she was pondering, Ian and Matt appeared. "What are you two doing?" It was Matt, pounding on the window.

Tripping the latch, Emma opened the door, while Sara launched into a detailed account of the poaching incident, though still unaware of the final chapter. Emma decided not to tell Ian, at least not while the children were listening.

"Then it was probably wise to wait in here." Ian nodded approvingly. "Though I suspect you'd like to stretch your legs a bit before we go."

"I suppose so—" Emma glanced about uncertainly—"but let's stay together."

They found their spot by the stream, Sara replaying in vivid color the entire episode as she knew it. Then, while the children waded, Emma filled Ian in on the rest. "While Sara was asleep, those men came back. They walked right up to the Land Rover. That's why I honked the horn. But I really think what stopped them was you and Matt coming back when you did. What do you suppose they were up to?"

Hearing this version of the story, Ian stood abruptly and whistled for the kids. "I don't know, but I don't think we want to stay around to find out."

They piled into the Land Rover and, to distract the children, Emma asked them to teach her the song "Waltzing Matilda." Ian joined in, but hampered by his Scottish burr, he stumbled through the lyrics as clumsily as she. And though Sara and Matt teased them both unmercifully, clearly enjoying every minute of the ride back, there was an underlying current of tension. The poaching incident had left her with a feeling of vulnerability, just when she'd begun to feel at home in this strange and savage land.

Twenty-four

With the children all tucked in after bedtime prayers, Emma took her cup of tea out to the porch and settled into a rocker. She listened as its friendly, rhythmic squeak blended with the night sounds. She hadn't seen Josh since they'd come home, and she was eager to hear his thoughts about their eventful afternoon. But when he didn't appear, she took her empty cup and went back inside.

When she sank into her bed, she was bone-weary but her mind was racing. Then through the open window came a weird, whining noise, unlike anything she'd heard before. At one moment, it sounded wild and beastly; the next, almost melodic. She sat up, straining to hear, and decided it must be some kind of native musical instrument. But where was it coming from?

She pulled on her robe and slipped through the darkened house. Standing on the back porch, she strained her ears to hear better. The sounds—both mysterious and beautiful—seemed to be coming from the hills behind the house, as if floating on the air toward her. She froze, not wanting to miss a note.

"Nice, isn't it?" Josh's voice, soft and gentle for a change, startled her, coming unexpectedly out of the darkness.

"Yes," she said, recovering quickly. "What is that? I've never heard anything like it."

"It's Ian, playing his bagpipes. He plays every once in a while on a clear night. Says the highlands provide the perfect acoustics for the pipes." He paused. "Just listen. . . ."

There it was again—low, guttural tones supporting the high-pitched melody, rising and falling, reverberating across the mountains, the valleys giving back the sound.

"I had no idea Ian was a musician."

"Yep, Ian's quite a guy." Josh's voice fell suddenly flat, though he continued to praise his neighbor. "Yeah, Ian's got a huge spread in Scotland—thousands of acres where he raises sheep, cows, crops—a little of everything. He inherited a large estate and a bundle of money to keep it up, so he can come and go as he pleases. Yep, he's one lucky bloke."

There was a hint of jealousy in Josh's voice, but no malice. Emma sensed that Josh admired Ian, but maybe coveted the man's freedom. By comparison, Josh's life might even appear dismal. After all, he had been born and brought up right here on this plantation, never venturing far from home. In many ways, his life may have even been more sheltered than her own. That thought took her by surpise.

She asked, "Have you traveled much?"

"Hardly!" he said with a sarcastic laugh. "Just down under for university and then the occasional visit to Melbourne. Can't get away from the plantation. And, of course, there are the children—" He stopped abruptly, gripping the railing and staring out across the moon-washed grounds.

"But you love this plantation, don't you, Josh?" She hoped he wouldn't notice her slip of the tongue.

He stood in silence as the sounds of the pipes drifted over the valley. "I suppose it's a bit of a love-hate thing. . . ." He eyed her as if only now realizing she was there.

It dawned on her that she was in nightclothes, and she tightened her sash, stepping back into the shadows.

"Yeah," he continued without taking his eyes off her, "Ian's one lucky bloke. Did you know he's never been married? Reckon that would make him quite a catch." Josh gave a low whistle, as if making an important discovery, then turned on his heel without another word and left the porch, heading for one of the out-buildings.

Emma stormed back to her room, uncertain as to why Josh's words had upset her so. She paced angrily in her bare feet until she decided to put her energy to better use. She'd spill it all to Angeline in a letter.

Scribbling furiously, she told her friend about the spelunking trip, rhapsodizing over Ian's incredible musical talent as if he were the man of her dreams.

Josh's final words tumbled through her head: *"Quite a catch . . . quite a catch. . . ."*

❧ ❧ ❧ ❧

The next morning, Josh and Matt were missing from the breakfast table.

"They went to pick up a part for the truck," Sara explained.

"Can we go to the McDowells' for church?" Holly was unusually insistent. "Today is Palm Sunday. Mary told me all about it. Please, Emma, please."

Emma glanced at Sara. This was the first she'd heard of church.

"Miss Grouse used to take us sometimes—like at Christmas and such. Father even went a couple of times. It's all right, if you want to go, Emma."

Emma frowned. "I'm not sure about the weather—" She really shouldn't neglect the children's spiritual training. "But why not? What time does church start?"

"Usually not until noon. But we should leave early, just in case."

On the way to the McDowells', the sky darkened ominously, and Emma wondered if they'd make it before the clouds burst. She prodded the girls to walk faster, but by the time they reached One Tree Hill, drops were falling in heavy splats. This rain, unlike the lowland rain, was cold, and with a chill breeze blowing up, they were soaked to the skin in minutes.

While Emma could have kicked herself for bringing the girls out on such a wet and stormy day, they didn't seem to mind in the least. They laughed as they slipped and slid through the mud on the way down the hill.

Still, Emma was relieved to see the lights burning in Mary's house. Mary herself ran out to greet them. "Oh, you wet darlings! Kick off your shoes and come inside before you catch your death!"

"We came for Palm Sunday," said Holly, her hair curling in tight ringlets around her cherubic face.

"Oh, you did, did you, lassie?" Mary laughed as she toweled Holly's dripping hair. "Well, I fear the weather may have put a damper on our service today. But we can have church in here by the fire."

Ian stomped up the front steps at that moment, tossing his wet mackintosh on the porch. When he opened the door, the wind blew in with him. "It's really coming down out there. But looks like the weather washed us in some company." He tweaked Sara's wet braid and winked at Holly.

"We came for the Palm Sunday service," said Sara seriously.

"Sorry, kids, but the church is just a roof with no sides, you know. And right now, it's more like a giant swimmin' pool, with the storm whipping through like a monsoon. Unless it clears up, I doubt that anyone will be comin' . . . although I did see a couple of frogs who showed up."

Holly, her eyes shining, giggled with delight, and even sober Sara grinned at his foolishness.

"Now, then, let's get you three into some dry things," said Mary briskly, leading them into a tiny bedroom. She pulled out a dress of her own for Sara. " 'Twill be a bit big for you, I know, but at least it's dry." A knit tunic served as a dress for Holly.

"You're certainly not going to find anything in there to fit me." Emma laughed, thinking that next to Mary's tiny frame, she must look like an Amazon.

"You never know what I might find." Mary pulled out a garment bag, unzipped it, and removed a pale-yellow linen dress trimmed in crocheted lace. It was obviously old, but quite pretty. Emma fingered the soft fabric, admiring the satin-covered buttons and careful handwork. "It was my mother's," Mary explained. "I'd love to see it on you."

"Yes, Emma, please try it on," begged Sara. "It's beautiful."

Emma gave in to their pleas, and Mary shepherded the girls from the room. "We'll give you some privacy, dear, while I put on some tea."

As soon as they left, Emma peeled off her soggy clothes and dried herself, rubbing some warmth back into her limbs. She slipped the dress over her head and buttoned it. It was just a little too big, but not so one would notice.

She stood before Mary's maple vanity and studied her reflection in the mirror. The dress appeared to be a style from the late forties—long, flowing skirt, sweetheart neckline, snug waistline. She tried to imagine the woman who'd worn it as she toweled her hair into a mass of curls. Her cheeks were flushed from the walk, and she noticed that her skin had a healthy glow. No longer the pale, sallow complexion of her Des Moines days. Probably due to all the fresh air and sunshine.

Mary and the girls were in the kitchen making tea and decorating some yeasty hot-cross buns when Emma entered. She did a dramatic turn, modeling the dress with a theatrical flair and pointing a bare foot.

"Oh, Emma, you look beautiful!" gushed Holly, wrapping her arms around Emma's waist. Emma patted the still-damp curls and smiled down at the child.

"That was my mother's engagement party dress," Mary explained. "Her first long skirt after the War. She and Father married a year later. The dress looks well on you, Emma. My mother was a beautiful woman, too."

Never having thought of herself as beautiful, Emma blushed at the veiled compliment.

"Is this a private party—females only?" asked Ian as he brought in a small armload of firewood and shook off the rain. "It looks like we should start building an ark. Holly, do you think you could round up the animals like Noah did? Two by—" Spotting Emma, he paused in mid-sentence.

"That's Mother's old dress, Ian," said Mary without missing a beat. "It was all I had to fit Emma. But isn't it lovely?"

Ian nodded as he laid the wood in the box by the kitchen stove, his eyes still fixed on Emma. Avoiding his open gaze, she turned to watch Sara ice the currant buns, marking them with crosses. Mary continued to chatter, but Emma barely registered a word. She was too busy replaying the look on Ian's face. And Josh's words from last night. *"Quite a catch,"* he'd said.

They sat down to tea, and Emma did her best to act natural—a difficult feat with Ian's eyes still burning into hers. She was relieved when he stepped out onto the porch for more wood to stoke the fire.

While Mary got out some cross-stitch samplers for the girls, Emma escaped to the kitchen to wash up the tea things. But she wasn't prepared for Ian to join her there.

"Here," he said kindly. "We can't have you burning yourself, now can we?" He showed her how to get the hot water out of the wood stove, then reached for a towel to dry the dishes as she washed. Their conversation took on a comfortable cadence, and she began to relax. Even his admiring glances didn't disturb her anymore. In fact, she decided she rather liked them.

She was beginning to enjoy his attention when Mary came into the kitchen, carrying a cardboard box. "Look, Ian, I found a picture of Mother wearing that very dress."

Mary set the box on the table and lifted out a framed photograph. Emma removed her apron and went to take a closer look. The black-and-white photo showed an attractive woman wearing the linen dress and holding a basket of flowers. A tall, handsome man, the image of Ian, stood proudly by her side. Dazed, Emma stared, for a split second feeling she was the woman in the picture. Not that she resembled her that much, she decided. It was the dress. But it gave her an eerie sensation just the same.

Absently, she thumbed through the other photos in the box. "Are these all family photographs?"

"Oh, a little of this and a little of that," said Mary as she picked up a handful. "One of these days, I'm going to get them organized and properly mounted in an album."

Just then a color photo caught Emma's eye, and she reached for it. The man in the picture was definitely Josh, though it was a little hard to tell, since this man was actually smiling. He looked much younger as he leaned casually against the rail of

Mary's front porch. But who was the dark-eyed brunette with him?

Emma had to know. "Who's this with Josh? She almost looks like she could be his sister."

"Oh, that's Lila," said Mary. "That picture was taken a couple of years before Holly was born."

"Lila?" All this time Emma had believed Holly must be the image of her mother—blond and fair. This dark-haired woman couldn't be Lila. Puzzled, she stared at the picture.

While the girls played, the three of them sat at the table and rummaged through the box, finding a few more snapshots of Josh and Lila—several with Matt and Sara at various ages. In one picture, Josh and Lila were joined by a blue-eyed man with pale blond curls.

"Skip?" she whispered to Mary, who nodded, giving a slight frown of warning.

Emma held the picture closer and studied the man's features. Could it be possible? Then she examined Josh's eyes, not smiling here. Instead, there was a haunted look, as if tortured by some dark knowledge. It was the way he always looked.

In a blinding flash of insight, Emma felt his pain. She swallowed the lump in her throat.

Ian was looking over her shoulder at the photo still in her hand. "It's a shame," he muttered. "A dirty, rotten shame."

"Oh, Ian, now we don't know anything for sure," Mary cautioned him, jerking her head toward the two.

Ian just shook his head sadly.

Twenty-five

Josh and Matt didn't make it back to the plantation until mid-afternoon. The unexpected deluge had turned the roads into a bog, doubling their one-hour return trip. He was always glad to get home on a gray day like this. Loved the warm, welcoming glow of lights in the windows. The spiral of smoke from the chimney, signaling a cozy fire in the fireplace.

But when he pulled up in front of the house, there was no evidence of life. The place looked dark and abandoned.

"What's wrong, Dad?" called Matt as Josh leaped out and ran up onto the porch.

"Wait there, son. I'm just going to check the house. It appears that no one's home." It was a sorry explanation, but it would have to do. It would only worry the boy if he told Matt that some of the local tribes had been behaving unpredictably lately, some of them resorting to random acts of violence. It hadn't been like this when he was Matthew's age.

Fortunately, his son wasn't one to press, and Josh unlocked the door and entered the house, calling out for Emma and the girls. Since it was the hired help's day off, there was no use calling for Tabo or Mina. There was no answer, but everything seemed normal, nothing out of place. Still, where could they have gone on such a stormy day?

He walked around the house, searching for clues and finding none. Then he checked the kitchen, suddenly recalling his foolish words to Emma the previous night. What an imbecile he had been—going on and on about Ian being such a great catch.

What in the world had gotten into him?

Josh retraced his steps, making a more thorough inspection of every room. This time he noticed a sheet of unfamiliar stationery on his desk. He picked up the paper, embossed with violets, and examined the signature. It was from Emma, and his heart thudded. Her resignation? A notice that she'd taken the girls and run off with Ian McDowell after his foolish baiting last night?

He had to laugh when he saw that she had only walked the girls over to the mission for the Palm Sunday church service. Vastly relieved, he took a minute to study the handwriting. Small, controlled, feminine. It figured. He refolded the note and stuffed it into his pocket, catching a whiff of some delicate perfume.

"Well, Matt," Josh said, climbing back under the wheel. "Looks like we'd better go pick up the girls. They've gone over to Kubari. Must have started out before the storm hit."

Although it was a forty-minute hike to Kubari—thirty minutes by vehicle on a dry day—in weather like this, it could take an hour. That is, if there were no mud slides to stop them altogether. On the way, Matt kept quiet. He wasn't much for talking, Josh had observed. At least, he hadn't opened up much to *him*. But right now Josh welcomed the silence. This kind of driving required one's full attention, and he needed to watch for potential trouble spots along the mountain road. At least there were no landslides brewing, he noted, glancing at the steep incline for the telltale signs of loose rocks or a stream of water flowing down the mountainside.

He didn't really want to replay last night's scene with Emma—that foolish comment he'd tossed at her, but he couldn't seem to let it go. He could still see her staring back at him in the moonlight. She'd looked so vulnerable, so young . . . and pretty. And then he'd gone and stuck his foot in his mouth with all that Ian nonsense. She'd looked completely crushed. And he'd regretted it instantly. But all the same, he'd taken off without so much as a "Good night."

"What's wrong, Dad?" asked Matt.

"Oh, nothing, son. Just this lousy weather is all." Josh

shook his head. Yeah, it would serve him right if Emma did run off with Ian. But if she was going to do it, he wished she'd hurry up and get it over with before the children got too attached to her.

"What do you think of Miss Davis, Matt?"

Matt shrugged. "She's all right, I reckon."

Josh had never heard Matt say this about any of the other governesses. "She a good teacher?"

"Reckon so. Doesn't make me feel stupid like Miss Grouse used to do. And she makes stuff like history and geography seem more interesting because she says she's learning, too. Since she's a Yankee, she never learnt much about Australian history and geography. Sometimes, *I* even know more than *she* does." Matt chuckled.

It had been a long time since Josh had heard Matt laugh. In fact, this was one of the longest conversations he could remember having with his son. "Sounds like you had a fine time yesterday."

"Yeah, Dad. Spelunking's great. You'll have to come sometime." Matt rambled on for quite a while, Josh catching phrases now and then. Maybe this was a reminder that he ought to start planning outings with his children, instead of sending them off with someone else. Still, there was always so much to be done on the plantation. So many things that just wouldn't wait. He glanced over at Matt, who had finished his soliloquy and was sitting quietly, gazing out the window now. He probably wouldn't wait, either.

Life seemed so complicated right now. Josh had always considered himself a self-sufficient man—able to handle almost anything that came along. Anything but Lila, that is. To be honest, his confidence had been shaken long before she left. But somehow during those hard years, he'd managed to create a facade, a thick, protective shell that kept others from knowing how he felt. Lately, though, he was beginning to believe his shell was seriously flawed, ready to crack—like the eroding of the mountain just before a major landslide.

Oh, God, he prayed in silent desperation. *Help me before everything falls completely apart.* It was a pretty poor excuse for a prayer, but maybe it wouldn't hurt to ask.

Twenty-six

The photo box was put away, and Mary brought out a well-used Scrabble game. Ian let Holly help set up his tiles on the board, and Mary consistently made long words no one had ever heard of. Emma entered in half-heartedly, unable to get the photo of Josh, Lila, and Skip out of her head.

Outside, the rain fell in heavy sheets, and she realized that they should be heading back. But Mary's house was warm and cozy, and the girls were having such a good time that she hadn't the heart to end the party. Finally, when all the tiles were used, the victory was conceded to Mary.

"We really should be going now," Emma said, picking up the empty cocoa cups.

"Oh, not just yet. Since the lassies came over for a Palm Sunday service," Mary hurried on, " 'tis only fitting that we have one. Ian, perhaps you'd read of Jesus' triumphal entry into Jerusalem, and then we'll sing some hymns."

Emma glanced at Ian, curious as to how he'd react to this request. But he merely reached for the Bible on the coffee table, quickly located the passage, and began to read in a clear voice. His Scottish enunciation added distinction to the words. Never having heard the Bible read in this way, Emma listened intently. Yet it wasn't Ian's voice alone that made it so special.

The story was simple enough—Jesus, astride a colt, people praising Him, waving palm branches along the route. Suddenly she wished she had been there. . . .

Emma had been aware of some subtle changes taking place

in the past two months in the deepest part of her. She couldn't describe this wonderful thing that was happening. But she knew it was real—she felt it now more than ever.

Now Ian was telling the story in his own words—words so basic and elementary that even Holly could understand. Emma's eyes filled with tears. It was like she was hearing Jesus with her own ears. She felt Mary press a handkerchief into her hand, then move to the little Wurlitzer to accompany some Easter hymns.

Finally Mary ended with a short prayer—not too wordy or flowery but succinct and to the point. When Mary finished, Emma looked up in time to see Josh's flatbed truck pull into the driveway.

"Come on in, Josh!" Mary swung the door wide. "Bring Matthew in, too."

"No thanks, Mary. We can't stay. We just came to give the girls a ride home." He glanced across the room at Emma, frowning in impatience—or was it bewilderment?

Suddenly she remembered her unusual apparel—and her bare feet. "Oh, we'd appreciate a ride," Emma rushed to cover the awkward silence. "Do you think our clothes are dry yet, Mary?"

"I doubt it. That drying rack by the stove takes forever and a day—it's times like these I wish for an electric clothes dryer. But you go right ahead and wear those things—"

"Oh no, Mary, I couldn't—not out in that rain!"

"Here now, use my mackintosh," Ian offered.

Josh scooped up both girls, and Emma ran through the rain to the passenger door. Matt leaped out of the truck, motioning Emma in while Josh stuffed the girls in behind her. Emma wanted to sit by the door, but Josh slid into the driver's seat. They were packed like sardines, and she was wedged up against him.

She held her breath as he carefully backed the truck. The driveway resembled a lake, and the windows were fogging up with every breath. These highland roads were bad enough on a clear day, but a day like today could spell disaster. She'd heard of giant mud slides that had buried cars and taken days to unearth. The girls sat without speaking, and Matt swiped the window clear with his palm.

Emma felt Josh's muscles tense as he navigated the steep and winding road. In some places they forded what appeared to be small brown rivers coursing over the road, now nothing more than slick clay. Against her will, visions of her parents' car careening over the cliff flashed through her mind in realistic detail—as in her dreams. But this time she shut her eyes and sent up a silent plea, asking God to help. When she opened her eyes, Josh was slowly taking a hairpin curve, and she felt the rear of the truck veer to the outside edge, but to her amazement she was no longer terrified.

She exhaled and leaned back in the seat, studying Josh's profile out of the corner of her eye. His forehead was creased in concentration, and his jaw tensed.

When the worst of the road was behind them, Emma felt Josh relax beside her, and instantly she became conscious of their closeness. His muscular arm gave her a sense of warmth and security, but she was thankful he couldn't discern her fickle thoughts.

All too soon they were home. Normally the driveway was about twenty feet from the front porch, but today the house resembled a small castle surrounded by a muddy moat. Matt carried Holly, and Josh shuttled Sara to the covered porch. Emma lingered in the cab for a moment, trying to adjust the skirt of the heirloom dress in order to protect the hemline.

She'd just stepped out into the ankle-deep puddle when Josh splashed over to her. He swooped her up without a word and transported her effortlessly to the porch. She stared at him, completely dumbfounded, as he set her on her feet. Then he tipped his soggy, broad-brimmed hat, and almost smiled, a hint of warmth in those dark brown eyes. It was enough to drive away the damp chill of the rainy day.

※ ※ ※ ※

After a late supper, Emma herded the children to bed. Holly was so exhausted from the day's activities that she didn't even request a story, only a prayer and a kiss. Emma tiptoed from their room and cracked the door. Lingering for a moment, she observed Sara slipping a Nancy Drew from under the covers and flicking on her reading lamp. Emma smiled to herself, remembering how she'd done the very same thing at Grandma's house.

She jumped at the light tap on her shoulder and turned to see Josh right behind her. He held a finger to his lips, then motioned her to the living room.

A fire crackled in the fireplace, warming the room. The rain was still falling steadily, clattering on the corrugated roof—a sound Emma loved. She settled onto the couch, wondering what this was all about.

"You said you wanted to know what I expect from you as a governess," said Josh in a let's-get-down-to-business tone. "And so I've written some things out. Not very official, but I think it'll do." He handed her a few sheets of notebook paper, carefully drawn up in his crisp businessman's hand. He went over everything, point by point, in meticulous detail.

"Any questions?" He leaned back in his chair and steepled his fingers, gazing at her curiously.

"Everything seems pretty clear," she answered, looking over the papers once more.

"I considered having you sign a contract, but I'll settle for a list of references instead. I know you've had no experience as a governess, but I'd like something just the same—for the files."

"That's understandable," said Emma, trying not to be offended by his impersonal tone.

"I usually check all the references before I hire a governess, but since Louise recommended you—"

She stopped him with an uplifted hand. "No need to explain. If they were my children, I'd do exactly the same."

Josh's face brightened a little, and Emma went on, hoping to build a small bridge of trust. "And even though I've never been a governess before, I want you to know I'm trying to care for Matt and Sara and Holly as if they were my own. That is—" she flushed under his scrutiny—"I—I really do care about them, and you can trust me to do whatever is best for them."

"I know. . . ."

"You take tea in here, Mr. Daniel?" asked Mina quietly from the hall by the kitchen.

"Uh . . . fine," Josh agreed briskly, watching as the dark-skinned girl carried in the tray and set it before them on the rosewood tea table.

Emma made it a point to thank Mina, commenting on her clever arrangement of scones and biscuits. Josh said nothing, and Emma sensed his disapproval. In fact, he seemed irritated.

"I'm trying to teach your children that employees deserve respect and appreciation, too," said Emma in what she was afraid came across as a defensive tone. She poured the tea, while Josh stared at the floor in stony silence. Maybe this was the time to change the subject before she killed the conversation completely.

He made it so difficult. It was as if he'd buried himself in the heart of a mountain, with layers of rock all around him. Why couldn't he be more like Ian—easygoing and relaxed? The memory of her times with Ian were somehow unsettling, and she glanced uneasily about the room, searching for something to spark the conversation again.

"This is such a pleasant room," she said, feeling defeated before she began. "So tastefully decorated . . . yet cozy."

Josh only scowled, and Emma realized that she'd probably picked the wrong subject. Sometimes trying to communicate with Josh Daniels was like walking through a minefield.

"The decorating was Lila's doing." His eyes traveled the room absently, and she knew he wasn't seeing his surroundings. But at least he had finally spoken his wife's name aloud. Although the way he pronounced it—as if it were poison—made her feel that the name itself left a bitter taste in his mouth.

"Well, Lila has very good taste."

Josh grunted, then took a gulp of tea. "Yeah, I suppose she's got good taste—unfortunately, it's insatiable."

"Really?" Emma hardly expected a response. She was fully aware that their conversation was balancing in a very precarious position. She watched him closely as he studied the oil painting hanging above the fireplace. A melancholy, earth-toned rendering of peasants loading hay onto a two-wheeled cart, and mounted in an ornate gold frame. Somehow Emma didn't think the frame quite suited the picture.

Josh answered in a monotone. "Lila always wanted more— much more . . ."

"How did you meet?"

"At university. She was one of the only women enrolled in the school of business, and we studied together. Funny, we looked so much alike, some people actually thought she was my sister." He leaned back and Emma nodded, remembering the photo. "We didn't exactly date at first, but we did things to- gether—the three of us—"

"The three of you?"

"Yes, Skip and Lila and me." He laughed, an ugly, cynical laugh. "Yeah, good ol' Skip, my best friend." Josh was staring at the ceiling now, and Emma was afraid she'd heard the last for a while.

She'd give it one more try. "So if you weren't really dating, when did it get serious?"

He didn't respond—just sat staring into space. Emma won- dered if he had heard the question.

"Well," he began with a sigh, "when Lila heard I was the son of a prosperous plantation owner, she perked up." Another snort. "Yeah, Skip was jealous at first—I was fairly certain he'd had his eye on her. But he denied it and stepped out of the pic- ture. Before I knew what had happened, it seemed we were en- gaged."

He continued without intonation or any sign of emotion, rising to pace in front of the fireplace. "We got married in Jan- uary, right after graduation, and she came back here with me. For a while, I actually thought we were happy. My father added the north suite for us—the room you're in now. My mum had been so happy to add a daughter to the family. But Lila and Mum didn't get along at all. Lila wanted to be in charge of everything—" Josh stopped unexpectedly and peered at Emma as if checking to see if she were still listening. "I don't know why I'm telling you all this."

She felt his gaze boring into her, as if trying to read her mind. She paused. How far should she push? "I'd hoped we could become friends, too. Don't you think it's better for *them*—the children—if we trust each other—just a little?"

"I reckon you're right. But trust doesn't come natural for me." He sat back down and placed his booted feet on the coffee table. "If I tell you my story, I'll expect you to tell me yours in return. You know, I don't know very much about you, either, Emma."

She liked the sound of her name, drawn out in his Australian accent, almost like a caress.

He continued more easily now, letting his guard down a bit more. "About a year after Lila and I got married and came back here to live, my father had a stroke." Emma could detect pain in his eyes. "He never recovered. Lila was expecting Matt at the time, but Dad didn't live to see his only grandson. Not too long after Dad passed away, Mum returned to Melbourne to live with a spinster aunt. About a year after that, Sara was born. Life was pretty good for us in those days, but my hands were full. What with taking over the management of the plantation, keeping the accounts straight, I suppose I didn't give Lila enough attention. Still, I tried to make her happy. And money made her happy. So I was even busier, expanding the plantation, trying to secure bigger contracts. . . ." His lips thinned.

"She spent it faster than it came in. She wanted to travel, wanted to entertain. She told me life on a coffee plantation wasn't the life she expected." He raked his fingers through his hair. "And then Skip came back into the picture. He'd come up every few months on holiday, telling his big-city stories about Sydney, parties, the celebrity circle. And Lila ate it up. She'd sit up with him for hours, talking way into the night. Then—when she became pregnant with Holly—Well, you see, Lila and I hadn't been getting along. And when our little fair-haired, blue-eyed girl was born the week before Christmas—it all added up. She didn't deny it, and it was then I knew I didn't love her anymore."

She listened in growing horror as Josh paced again, his words flowing like mud down the mountainside. "I couldn't believe it when Skip showed up back here the next spring. But, of course, he didn't know about Holly. I couldn't bear to look at him—was actually afraid I might kill him." Josh turned to Emma, his eyes tortured. "But you know something—I almost felt worse over Skip's betrayal than my own wife's." He shook his head as if trying to figure it out. "I told Lila to get Skip out of here—he was no longer welcome in my house. I threw his bags in the Jeep and told Lila to take him to Kainanti. And . . . they never came back."

Emma let out the breath she was holding. "And you never heard from her again? She never tried to claim the children? Not even Holly?"

Josh's eyes flashed at the mention of the name, and he put out a hand. "I know what you're thinking . . . but it's not true. It's not Holly's fault. It's just that sometimes I see Skip in her, and it's like a boot in the gut. Poor little tyke. And don't think I don't see what's happening with Sara and Matt . . . but how do you tell kids that their mother doesn't want them anymore?"

She waited for what seemed an eternity, the fire still burning brightly as if in defiance of the darkness in this room. "I can't answer that," she said in a hushed voice. "All I know is they have you—and as long as you'll have me, they have *me* . . . to help them through it. There's a purpose in all this somewhere, Josh. We just can't see it right now, but God won't let us down."

For the next few minutes, she shared her story, confiding in this man what she had never shared with another human being: her deepest suspicions about her parents' accident. Her fragile new faith. Her hopes for the future. When she was done, she was surprised at how easily the words had flowed, how orderly—like reading a bedtime story to Holly. When she finished, the fire was only smoldering embers, darkening to smoking coals.

"Well, I guess you'll never know for sure, Emma," he said quietly, pinching the bridge of his nose. "Maybe we just take some things to our graves unresolved. Life's full of mysteries, and I've almost given up on finding a lot of the answers."

Not wanting the conversation to end on such a note of futility, Emma added, "I'm not really looking for answers anymore, but somehow just telling you about my suspicion makes it easier to bear. Now I almost think I can set it aside, trust God, and move on—instead of letting it haunt me the rest of my life."

Even as she spoke, it seemed some load had been lifted. "Thanks for listening, Josh."

Josh rose and faced the lifeless fire, jamming his hands deep into his pockets. "Yeah, I thank you, too, Emma," he said over his shoulder.

There was no logical reason to feel happy, but she did. Holding herself in check, she told him good night and went to her room.

There, she asked God to nurture their friendship, to heal the hurt in Josh's heart. She knew she cared deeply for the man. And something else begged acknowledgment, but she wasn't ready to face it. A riot of emotions, like lightning bolts, charged through her, reminding her of the electrical energy that had leaped to life in the cramped truck. Like a hot coal, that moment burned in her memory.

But she'd been burned before. By a careless passion for a man on a ship. It hadn't been a serious burn, but it had taught her not to play with fire. Not only for her sake, but for the sake of the children, she would guard her heart, not giving it away to the wrong person.

Josh was still a legally married man. Emma wondered if he might even forgive Lila if she were to show up here one day. He might do it . . . for the children. Josh knew better than anyone how badly they needed a mother. And surely, someday, Lila would want to see her children again. In fact, she could return at any time to claim what was hers.

These thoughts were sobering, and Emma's final prayer was for God to do whatever was best for the children. In the meantime, she would do the same. As for Josh—she would simply be his friend.

Twenty-seven

*T*he next week went smoothly, and Emma sensed that she and Josh were developing a bond of trust between them. At the same time, she maintained a safe emotional distance. They had never discussed her salary, but on Monday morning, she'd found an envelope under her door, with a generous check inside. It was more than she'd expected to be paid for only two weeks, but it was reassuring just the same. It had told her he was pleased with her, that he valued her work. Still, caring for the children she was growing to love did not feel like work anymore. In fact, she felt almost guilty for taking the money. Then again, she reminded herself that she was not truly a part of this family. She was expendable, a mere employee. Remembering this helped her to maintain her objectivity.

Mealtimes had become much more pleasant affairs as the five of them began to act more like a family—or at least how Emma imagined a real family might act. The children seemed more relaxed, with friendly exchanges occurring between father and children. A bit louder than before, but it was a pleasant sort of noise, and Emma didn't think Josh minded.

One evening Josh and Matt joined them in the living room before bedtime. Matt was patiently trying to mend the wires in his remote control car, and Josh was browsing through an agricultural journal. After a while, Holly picked up a storybook and walked over to Josh's chair. Silently she held out the book. Emma observed discreetly, holding her breath as she watched Holly before him, looking up with wide, hopeful eyes. Emma ached for the little girl and prayed that Josh would not turn her away. Then slowly, haltingly, he laid his journal aside and reached out for Holly. Pulling her onto his lap, he opened the book and began to read.

Emma heard his voice reading the story as she tried to finish her letter to Linda, but her vision was foggy, and her pen refused to move.

❧ ❧ ❧ ❧

On Friday afternoon Ian dropped by the house with a basket of freshly laid eggs from Mary's hens and a couple of paperback books for Emma.

"Mary thought the children might like to dye eggs for Easter," he explained to Emma. "And here are a couple of simple yet profound books I've enjoyed over the years. They were written by an amazing Chinese Christian named Watchman Nee— ever heard of him?"

"No, but I'm always looking for something to read. Thanks, Ian. Let me run get the clothes Mary loaned us last Sunday." She'd spot-cleaned and pressed the old dress until it looked as good as new, then wrapped it in tissue paper. When she brought out Mary's things, she found Josh and Ian visiting on the porch.

"I was just telling Josh that Mary would like for you all to come over for Easter—if you've not made other plans, that is. We'll be having dinner after the service." This, to Emma, who looked to Josh, not wanting to speak for him.

"Sounds fine, and I know the children would enjoy it," Josh said with a smile. How different his face looked when he smiled. Only a few years her senior, he usually seemed so much older. Sometimes she almost felt like she was one of the kids, and Josh the dad.

"Hopefully, the service won't be rained out this week," continued Ian, glancing up at the clear blue sky, "though you can never tell. I'm heading over to Obanti right now to pick up a roast. Anything I can bring you, Emma? Or maybe you'd like to come along, if you haven't made the trip before."

Emma eyed Josh uncomfortably. "No, I haven't—but I uh, well the children, you know—"

"No problem, Emma," Josh answered lightly, though his smile had lost some of its sparkle. "You go on ahead with Ian. Mina will watch the girls. You're not expected to work seven days a week. Go have some fun." He slapped Ian on the back and strolled away.

Emma felt trapped. She hadn't really wanted to go. Somehow, she suspected Josh didn't want her to go, either. But now she had no excuse. And Ian was standing there, waiting expectantly.

"Sure, Ian. Just let me tell the girls."

Holly was waking up from a long nap when Emma reached their room, and Sara had arranged her horses around a home-made stable, with tiny fence posts forming a corral. "I'm going to Obanti with Ian," she told them lightly. "I'll see you later."

"All right, Emma." Sara peered up at her curiously, a slightly troubled look across her brow. "When will you be back?"

"Oh, later tonight, I suppose, I don't really know—"

"No!" screamed Holly. "Don't go, Emma! Don't go!" Holly leaped from her bed and entwined herself around Emma's legs.

Emma knelt and looked into the stricken face. "I'll only be gone a few hours. Mina will be here—and Sara and your dad and Matt. You'll be fine, honey."

Holly pouted, her lower lip protruding, and she took a jagged breath. "I don't want you to go, Emma."

Emma hugged the little girl close. "I'll be back before you even know it. I promise." She peeled the little hands off her legs. When she looked around, she noticed Josh lingering in the hallway and knew he had been watching this little scene. Why hadn't he stepped in? But already he was gone.

"I'll bring you both back a surprise from Obanti," she promised, "and tomorrow we'll make colored eggs for Easter."

"Colored eggs?" Holly was intrigued. "What's that?"

"You'll see." Emma winked at them, then left to join Ian.

Outside, from the corner of her eye, she could see Josh leaning against the storage shed. He was still watching as the Land

Rover rolled down the drive. Even from a distance, his face looked dark and angry. Well, it was his own fault she was going off with Ian. Was this more of his "good-catch" thinking? Or maybe she was just imagining things.

Yet even so, leaving the children made her a little sick inside. Almost as if she were abandoning them. Maybe it was silly, but she wished she'd turned Ian down.

He, on the other hand, appeared oblivious to her worries. "Obanti is an interesting place, but it has its rough element. That's why I didn't invite the children to come along. It's what you Americans might call a 'boom town'. There's a gold mine close by that employs a lot of indigenous fellows who think they've struck it rich. Unfortunately, with abundance comes trouble." He looked over at her with a reassuring smile. "But it has some fine r-r-restaurants." The Scottish burr, purposely emphasized, she decided, made her chuckle.

She sighed and leaned back, determined to make the best of this trip. Her worries about Josh and the kids were ridiculous— a good sign she really needed to get away. "It sounds interesting, Ian. I guess I just feel a little guilty for leaving the girls like this. I know it's silly. . . ."

"Not a'tall, Emma. After all they've been through, those children have latched on to you. But you must take time for yourself, too."

"I know you're right, but it's still a little overwhelming sometimes. I want to do a good job, but being a governess is not a normal, everyday job. It's really rather frightening at times."

Ian nodded. "A big responsibility, to be sure. Know what I do when I feel overwhelmed?"

She was ready for some sound advice, and she could trust this man. "No, what?"

"I remind myself that Jesus said to take one day at a time."

"Jesus said that?"

"Yes, He did. 'Tis my favorite Scripture. Matthew 6:33 and 34. My version says: 'But seek first his kingdom and his righteousness, and all these things will be given to you as well. Therefore do not worry about tomorrow, for tomorrow will worry about itself. Each day has enough trouble of its own.' One day at a time, doing the best you can, and trusting God for the rest. It doesn't do any good to worry anyway. Worrying is a lot like rocking in a chair. It may keep you moving, but you'll never get anyplace."

"Exactly!" She pulled a pen and notepad from her purse. "I want to remember that passage. You know, Ian, I feel like I'm just beginning to wake up to so many things. I didn't even bring a Bible to New Guinea, but suddenly I'm ready to read one. Do you think I might find one in Obanti?"

He laughed. "Wouldn't be surprised. With God, all things are possible, you know."

They stopped at a hydroelectric plant straddling a fast-flowing mountain river and got out to examine it more closely. Ian explained its construction and the power it could produce. "Electricity's a relatively new phenomenon in this part of the world. This plant provides energy for Obanti and several other towns nearby."

A group of women, the long handles of heavily loaded *bilums*, or string bags, slung over their heads, walked by, eyeing the two of them and giggling. "High fashion for New Guineans," Ian explained. "Handy for transporting garden produce or firewood—" A baby cried as the women passed. "Infants too."

"I can't get over it," she whispered to Ian. "These women work so hard and have so little. Yet they seem happy. Maybe they've mastered the art of living a day at a time."

"Perhaps, but their lives are also shortened by the mere strain of survival. It's not easy for men in the highlands, but women have it doubly hard. That's why I respect Mary's outreach. In fact, I've considered moving here permanently—to help out. It's just that I promised my father, before he died, that I'd keep up the estate."

"Well, Ian, I'm not one to preach, but don't you think God might have a reason for all this?"

Ian laughed again, a hearty laugh that echoed off the hills

beside the river. "Well, now, I believe you're right, Emma. He may, indeed. For one thing, the estate supports Mary's mission school. Not only that, but I'd miss my bonny Scotland if I never returned to her."

Obanti appeared to be a rugged town, and Emma was thankful to have Ian at her side. Tough-looking characters loitered about the streets, and every business seemed to be a bar, a tavern, or a gambling room. At the marketplace, they shopped for the children, then stopped at a steakhouse run by a little Asian man named Sammy Lee.

Sammy wore cowboy boots and spoke with an Australian accent. They selected choice cuts of beef and watched as their steaks were grilled over an open charcoal pit. The aroma was tantalizing. While they waited, Emma admired the colorful paper lanterns suspended on strings above the covered patio. Asian-style music played over a tinny sound system.

When they were served, they ate with relish, finding unexplored topics of conversation. "Tell me how Mary came to be in New Guinea, Ian," Emma asked as she poured him a cup of jasmine tea.

He sobered. "It's a rather interesting story, that. Mary is ten years older than I, and I've always looked up to the girl. In fact, I've rather thought of her as a saint. And I wasn't the only one. Seems a certain young man, studying to be a missionary to New Guinea, felt the same and asked her to be his bride." Emma leaned forward, forgetting to eat.

"She lost him, a week before the wedding, in a rock climbing accident. He died a hero, though, saving the life of another chap."

He sketched in the details, and Emma realized why she'd been so drawn to the delicate woman, not to mention her younger brother. She cast Ian a speculative glance over the table, hearing him tell of the life work he and his sister had chosen. Any woman would be proud—

Realizing the direction of her thoughts, she looked down just as Ian was concluding his tale. "Poor Mary," she said. "I had no idea she'd had such a tragic life. She's such a happy person."

"Aye, that she is. But she'd be the first to tell you that 'twas not always so. It took time to get over losing Conrad. And even so, she made a vow not to marry. But Mary, God bless her, looks at life differently from most. She's truly secure, rarely frets. God has used her to help so many."

She leaned back against the padded seat and wiped her mouth. "Thank you, Ian. It seems I'm in your debt again. I've learned so much today. I know now how much I needed to get away. I only wish I'd been able to find a Bible."

Ian smiled and reached inside his jacket. He pulled out a small flat box and handed it to her. "While you were getting Matt's model at that curio shop, I ran across this." She opened it to find a smooth, black leather-bound book. "It's only a New Testament," he apologized. "But it has Psalms and Proverbs. It's a start."

"I'm touched, Ian. How thoughtful." She was thinking what a good friend he was when she opened the cover and noticed an inscription on the flyleaf: *To Emma, Remember Matthew 6:33–34. Love, Ian McDowell.* Reading those words reminded her of the tender moments she'd spent with this man. Josh was right. This was a very special guy.

☙ ☙ ☙ ☙

When they reached the house, Ian carried her packages to the porch. The house was dark now, and everyone must have been sleeping. Emma felt something like a renegade teen, sneaking in late. She whispered a thank you to Ian and watched as his taillights disappeared down the road. Then she opened the screen door, being careful to avoid the squeak.

"Why are you tiptoeing around?" Josh's voice came unexpectedly from inside, and she dropped a parcel. He picked it up and handed it back to her, his fingers grazing her hand.

"It was late and I—uh—didn't want to disturb anyone. It's so dark—"

"That's because the main generator is off, and I haven't lit a lamp yet. Did you have a good day with Ian?"

He sounded a little perturbed. Then she remembered, with

mild irritation, that he'd pushed her into going in the first place. "Yes, in fact, I had a wonderful time. Thank you very much." Her answer was determinedly cheerful. "Good night," she said as she groped her way down the hallway, too proud to ask for a lamp.

When she finally found the door to her room, her eyes had adjusted to the darkness. Instead of lighting the kerosene lamp, she prepared for bed by the light of the moon. She was still fuming, feeling frustrated.

She lay in her bed, wide awake. What was the matter with her? She'd had such a pleasant evening with Ian, a perfectly wonderful man. Ian had a way of making her feel safe and protected, totally at ease. Yet running into Josh was like a head-on encounter with a prickly porcupine. But why should she let him spoil her whole day? Why couldn't she just shake it off?

These thoughts tumbled in her head until she recalled the verses Ian had shared earlier. She decided to put them to good use. Maybe God would quiet her heart if she asked Him to.

Just as she was beginning to unwind, she heard the sweet strains of some haunting melody floating through her open window. Ian again—out on the hills with his bagpipes. She imagined him in a Scottish kilt, strolling the highlands with his pipes. Smiling, she drifted off to sleep.

Twenty-eight

Josh was off before dawn the next day, but Emma kept her promise to dye eggs. The children, especially the girls, were intrigued by the idea, probably never having experienced such frivolity. Emma was determined that they wouldn't miss anything more—not while she was still around.

Tabo was another matter. Obviously disgruntled at having her kitchen invaded by little people engaged in such a useless project as tinting chicken eggs, the perpetual scowl on her face darkened. But when they finished, Emma sent the children to clean themselves up while she and Mina returned the kitchen to its former spotless condition.

"Nice," murmured Mina as she gently placed the last pastel egg in a wicker basket. "What we do now?"

"Have you ever heard of an Easter egg hunt?" Mina looked puzzled, and Emma explained. "Well," she began mysteriously, "first we hide the eggs, then the children try to find them. It's an Easter tradition in the States."

Mina's eyes twinkled. "Yes, we must do that."

Together the two women hid the eggs all about the yard and in Sara's garden. Mina giggled as the children searched, pointing out the easy ones for Holly. With squeals of delight, the two girls discovered the hidden treasure, while Matt clowned around, cracking one of the eggs on his head and howling with pretended pain. While they were still chattering away, Mina served tea in the garden.

Emma noticed Josh approaching them. She waved, but then

he turned abruptly. Mina sprang up quickly, silently gathered the tea things, and hurried back to the kitchen with them.

Emma waited for Josh, but when he didn't put in an appearance, she instructed the children to clean up the eggshells from the lawn before she, too, went back inside.

As she stepped onto the back porch, she heard Tabo's voice raised in anger. The target of the scolding was Mina, who cowered in a corner of the kitchen. Emma had begun to learn the sing-song trade language and could now recognize a few words. But this wasn't Pidgen.

Tabo ceased her tirade the moment Emma entered the kitchen. Still her dark face smoldered with ill-concealed rage.

Even with Mina's head lowered, Emma could see the tear-streak glistening on the smooth, bronze cheek. Somehow Emma suspected that the scolding had something to do with *her*.

A movement caught her eye, and she noticed Josh in the shadows, propped against the door that led to the dining room. He motioned for her.

"See what comes of fraternizing with the hired help?" He spoke quietly, but his tone was clearly accusatory. And she knew he had overseen their little tea party. "Maybe you'll understand from now on."

She glared at him. "You seem to forget, Mr. Daniels—I, too, am 'hired help'!"

He frowned and turned away, and she instantly regretted her impulsive words. She'd tried so hard to win his friendship, earn his trust. "I'm—sorry," she stammered. "But I don't really understand. Mina had helped all morning, and it only seemed right to include her in the festivities."

Josh peered at her curiously for a long moment. At last, he sighed, unfolded his arms, and stuffed his hands into his pockets. "Let's just forget about it, Emma."

The glimmer of a smile brightened her whole day. But she waited until Josh returned to his chores before slipping Mina a pretty pink scarf she'd purchased back in Iowa.

Mina backed away.

"Oh, come on, Mina. It's only a small gift, and the color is so good on you."

The dark-skinned girl took a reluctant step forward, eyes alight, and touched the silky fabric with one tentative finger. And when Emma looped the scarf around her neck, she held it to her cheek, the earlier conflict with Tabo apparently forgotten.

ॐ   ॐ   ॐ   ॐ

Easter morning dawned bright and clear, and Josh decided to capitalize on the fair weather by trekking over to the McDowells' place. Emma loved the clean feel of the sun's warm rays on her bare head. She really should start using a hat and sunscreen, but for the moment, she wanted nothing between her skin and the warm rays.

Josh and Matt led the way, their long strides easily outdistancing the others. Holly bounced back and forth between the two pairs of walkers, and Emma and Sara more leisurely brought up the rear. Both girls had on their best dresses today—new frocks from their Nana in Melbourne. Sara's was pale blue eyelet; Holly's, fluffy and yellow. She resembled a baby chick, Emma thought, as the child skipped back and forth along the trail.

Upon arriving, they found that the casual Easter service was to be held in the "church house"—an open-sided building covered by a thatched roof, with rough-hewn log benches situated in neat rows on the packed dirt floor. The space was filled to capacity, and the mostly barefooted congregation sang with unbridled enthusiasm, more than compensating for their inability to carry a traditional western tune. It was oddly heartwarming to hear the familiar hymns chanted rather than sung. Mary plucked away at the portable organ in the back, but the instrument's melody was overpowered by the nasal tones of the "singers." Still, Emma felt it was the most sincere worship she'd ever experienced.

Midway through the service, a group of schoolchildren performed a short play, with lots of prompting from Mary and stifled giggles from the audience. Emma could make out only a few words, but their sincere and happy faces transcended the language barrier, and she had to fight back tears.

Following the play, Ian stepped up to the bamboo podium and read a Scripture passage in Pidgen, the story of Jesus' death and resurrection, she figured. The listeners seemed deeply moved and listened with rapt attention. She read in English, using her New Testament, amazed at Ian's ability to preach with such ease in a second language.

Dinner afterward—baked ham with fresh pineapple, along with some traditional Scottish dishes—was served buffet-style. Emma had heard that Mary regularly entertained each villager in her home once a year, an impressive accomplishment considering the fact that the population numbered around three hundred! Emma wondered what Josh thought of that. She couldn't see how it was any different from sharing tea with Mina. In fact, Mina was a guest here today.

"Good sermon, Ian," said Josh after the service. "Didn't know you were a preacher man, too."

Ian chuckled good-naturedly. "Actually, I'm not. But the local pastor was detained over in Lae, and they called on me in desperation."

"Desperation or not, it looked like everyone appreciated it," Emma put in. "Of course, I still have trouble with my Pidgen, although Mina has been helping me." She tried to avoid Josh's quick frown. "I'm pretty dense when it comes to foreign languages."

"Don't worry, dear," said Mary. "Once you catch on, you'll be amazed at how simple Pidgen is."

By late afternoon, dark clouds had rolled in again, and Josh suggested they head home to beat the rain. This time Josh and the two older children led the way, and Emma walked with Holly, the little girl's cheeks still flushed from a game of tag with some of the village children.

It wasn't long before Holly's steps slowed. Soon the two were lagging far behind the others. Emma glanced toward the leaden sky and urged her to hurry, but Holly only whined, "My legs hurt, Emma."

One look at the forlorn, dirt-steaked little face told Emma that the child couldn't take another step. The fluffy yellow chick looked as if she'd been mauled by a wild dog. Emma suppressed her laughter, then looked up just in time to observe the others clearing the crest of One Tree Hill, out of shouting distance. She picked Holly up and hurried along the trail in hopes of catching up with them.

Holly wasn't very heavy, but soon Emma tired and slowed to a plodding walk. The heavy sky seemed ready to burst above her head, and now that they were in unfriendly territory, she couldn't resist a furtive look about them.

"I'm sorry, Emma," muttered Holly in a weary little voice.

Emma only hugged the child closer and picked up her pace. The trail would turn to mud once the clouds let loose, and the top of the hill was still a fair distance away.

Just as she considered turning back, Emma noticed Josh bounding over the crest of the hill, running toward them like a madman. What could have gone wrong? One of the children?

"Emma," he said, panting for breath as he reached them, "you shouldn't be carrying Holly. She's much too heavy for you." He easily removed her small burden, swinging Holly onto his shoulders, much to the child's obvious delight.

Josh adjusted his pace to match Emma's and they continued up the hill. "We didn't realize you weren't with us until we were halfway down the other side. I sent Sara and Matt on ahead."

"Holly's legs got tired," explained Emma, "and now I know how she feels."

"Well, let's slow down, then. We're in no hurry."

This Josh was so much more approachable than the man who had seemed so distant last night. They walked in companionable silence for a while.

Overhead, the sky grew darker, and soon giant raindrops splattered the ground in quiet thuds, leaving puffs of dust where they struck. Josh took no notice of the rain as he walked along, pointing out some of the nearby villages to Emma. Out there somewhere was the notorious Osabe village, the ones with a grudge against him. He didn't seem particularly worried, and Emma relaxed, allowing her gaze to stray to his wet, dark hair, curled in wet ringlets around his face. He looked quite content with Holly riding on his shoulders.

Just as the clouds dropped their burden, they were home. *Home!* The word flashed through Emma's mind, pulsing like a neon sign. Home wasn't a concept she'd ever had much use for. Even back in Iowa, she'd often referred to the place where she lived as "the apartment" or "Grandma's," rarely *home*. Still, it bothered her to think of Josh's place in this way. And so, like many other unreconciled thoughts regarding the enigmatic Josh Daniels, she tucked this one away in some dormant recess of her brain.

❧ ❧ ❧ ❧

The following week a letter from Angeline arrived, announcing that she was taking Emma up on her invitation to visit the plantation. She was thrilled, of course, but questioned what Josh would say to the idea of a houseguest who had given no idea of a departure date. Everything had gone so smoothly the last few days, and she hated to risk displeasing him again.

She shared her concern with Mary on Friday, when she and the girls walked over for their weekly visit.

"Why, your friend is welcome to stay here," she offered. "Ian can sleep in the back room of the schoolhouse, and she can have his room."

"You're so generous, Mary. But I'm hoping Josh won't mind. Besides, I'm willing to pay room and board, or she could sleep in my room—it's nice and large. It's just that I hate asking."

"You make Josh sound like a mean old ogre, Emma. I'm sure he'd enjoy having a houseguest. And if not, she can always stay here."

Ian walked in with a basket of fresh produce, the girls on his heels. "Who can stay here?" he asked as he unloaded the basket onto the kitchen table.

"Emma's friend is coming for a visit." Mary thumped an

enormous papaya. "I don't think this is ripe yet."

"Who's coming?" Sara's eyes were huge behind her thick glasses.

"Who, Emma, who?" Holly chimed in, sounding like an owl.

"A good friend of mine. Her name is Angeline."

"That's a pretty name," said Holly, her blond curls bobbing.

"Yes, and she's a very pretty lady. She has pretty blond hair just like yours. But even more than that, she's beautiful on the inside."

"That's quite a compliment," said Ian. "I can't wait to meet her."

Mary bustled about the kitchen, putting away the produce. "She sounds very nice. Do bring her over as soon as she arrives."

Emma was pensive as she considered Angeline's visit. "Now all I have to do is break the news to Josh."

Breaking the news to Josh was not the problem Emma had anticipated. Holly did it for her.

"Father! Emma's angel-friend is coming!" Holly burst out at tea before the first course had been served. "Emma says she's real pretty. Can she stay—"

"Excuse me, Holly," Emma interrupted, then turned to Josh with a conciliatory tone in her voice. "I had intended to ask you myself, but Mary says Angeline can stay with them if there's a problem."

He shrugged. "Of course she can stay here. Why not? Come to think of it—where would we put her?"

"I wouldn't mind sharing my room—that is, if you don't mind," Emma offered hopefully.

"Fine. Have Mina fetch a rollaway bed." He took a swig of tea. "When will your friend be arriving?"

"Next Thursday. But I'll need to make arrangements for her to get up here. I don't really know—"

He waved aside her concern. "I have a load of beans to deliver down in Wopak—that's not far from Lae. Maybe I could head down on Wednesday, drop off the load, spend the night, and bring your friend back here the next day."

Emma was overwhelmed. Why had she been so worried? It seemed she was always misjudging the man. "Well, if you're sure it's no trouble—spending the night away—"

"Oh, it's too long a trip for one day. Your friend's got good timing. Next weekend is the Obanti Sing-Sing."

"What's that?" Emma had never heard of the term.

"A sing-sing's like a big party," Matt said. "All these tribes get together and get dressed up—paint and feathers and leaves and beads and stuff—and then they dance all night long!" Turning to his father, he asked, "Can the girls and I go this year, Dad?"

Josh shook his head. "Sorry, Matt. Unfortunately, Obanti is no longer a very safe place for children. Too much drink and people out of control. Every year we hear some awful story. In fact, you and your friend may not want to go, Emma."

"I think it sounds exciting." Emma quirked her lip. "And Angeline is the adventurous type."

"Good. We'll plan on it then for next Saturday."

"Well, I don't see why I can't go at least," complained Matt.

"Maybe next year. But if you're all caught up with your lessons, maybe Emma would let you come with me on Wednesday."

Matt's eyes lit up. "No worries, Dad, I'll be all caught up."

ЖS   ЖS   ЖS   ЖS

Emma was helping Sara transplant some hyacinth bulbs when Josh approached carrying a parcel wrapped in brown paper.

"Mary's garden boy just ran this package over to you from her place. It's from Ian."

"Open it, Emma!" exclaimed Sara. "I wonder what it could be."

Emma studied Josh's eyes, unable to read his shuttered expression. She pulled off her garden gloves, slipped the paper off the box, and removed the lid. Inside was a mosaic-style picture of a beautiful bird of paradise, done in an intricate design of multicolored sand, tiny stones, and seeds.

She read the enclosed note aloud. " 'This picture reminded me of you and our spelunking trip. I hope it will help make up for the unhappy occurrence that day.' "

Omitting the "Love, Ian," Emma refolded the note, feeling her cheeks redden as she stared down at the colorful picture.

"Oh, Emma, it's so pretty!" breathed Sara. "Just like the one they killed that day!"

"What on earth are you talking about?" demanded Josh. "Who killed—what?"

"I've been meaning to tell you, Josh." Emma quickly recapped the poaching incident, playing down their terror as they'd watched the native hunters take their prize—or their frightening visit to the Land Rover.

"Every time I turn around, there are reports of lawlessness." Josh clenched his fists at his sides. "Ever since they got their independence!" There was a dramatic pause, and Emma knew Josh had more on his mind that an illegal hunting trip. "Go inside, Sara. I need to speak with Emma."

Sara scurried away, and Emma watched as Josh slammed his fist into his hand. "I sent Sara in so I could warn you—we're having trouble with the Osabes."

"I know, Josh, Sara told me about it."

He lifted his brow. "The old land dispute?" At her nod, he went on. "Well, there's more. Things are getting way out of hand—"

He stared off in the direction of the northern hills, then back, holding her gaze. "The children are never to be out alone—understood?" He waited for her breathless acknowledgment, then continued in a lethal tone. "A man was murdered last night, Emma—one of my own men!"

Twenty-nine

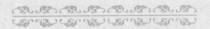

*R*ipples of shock ran through her. "A murder?" she gasped. "One of your men? Oh, Josh, what happened?"

"It was near the Osabe village. Some are saying it's because of this blasted land dispute. I know the Osabes are itching for a fight, but I've already shown the head man my legal papers. Still, you never know about these people. So for now, we must be very careful. I don't want the children outside unsupervised—ever!"

"Do—do you really think someone would harm them?"

He flexed his jaw, and she could see the fatigue shadowing his face. "The police will be around making sure everything settles down. But if I truly thought we were in danger, I'd send you and the children out of here. Just the same, we must play it safe." He paused, considering. "Do you think you should notify your friend?"

"Oh, Angeline's not afraid of anything."

"Well, then, will it bother you to be alone out here on Wednesday night while I'm gone?"

"Not a bit. We'll be fine." She hoped she sounded more confident than she felt. "Maybe Mina could spend the night."

Josh nodded distractedly, looking again at the picture in Emma's hand. "That was nice of Ian. He seems to think a lot of you." He narrowed his gaze in speculation, and Emma felt her cheeks grow hot.

"I think Ian realized how disturbing it was to see those poachers kill that beautiful bird," she murmured. Squaring her shoulders, she went on. "You say it was one of your men who was killed? Which one? Who was murdered?"

"Makiba." Emma heard the catch in Josh's voice and wondered if Makiba meant more to her employer than the other hired hands. "He was a good man—the best." Josh spread his legs and braced his hands on his hips. "And I think I know who did it. I made the mistake of hiring some Osabes a few years back, thinking it would help heal the rift—a sign of good will and all that." He snorted. "Well, it backfired. It's just a blasted shame it had to be Makiba!"

His gaze roamed the nearby grove of coffee trees, and she watched him inspecting the stubby, round shrubs and wondered if this land was worth the price of a life—any life.

"Just remember what I said about the children," he continued gruffly. "And watch out for yourself—don't go out alone!"

Back in the house, Emma told the children about their father's new rule—no unsupervised play outside—withholding the details. "I'll tell Tabo when she gets back from market, but Mina needs to know."

Emma sent the girls to search the house. Then, walking by the storage closet on her way into the kitchen, she heard a muffled sound. She paused and listened, putting her ear next to the closet door. Painfully aware of Josh's warning, Emma's heart thumped wildly.

The sound came again. A soft muffled sob. Holding her breath, she threw open the closet door. There, sitting on an inverted mop bucket, was Mina, tears streaming down her face.

Behind the locked door of Emma's room, Mina choked out her grief. "Ma—ki—ba!"

"Makiba? Was he a relative—your brother?"

"No," wailed Mina. "He working . . . to get bride price!"

Emma gasped. She had heard about the tribal custom of collecting livestock and other goods in exchange for a wife. "Mina . . . were you and Makiba planning to be married?"

The girl burst into fresh sobs.

"Was it arranged by your father?"

"No, my papa say Makiba too poor. He want another man—

old, rich man to have me, pay big price. But Makiba work hard, Makiba work hard—" she wailed, and Emma took Mina in her arms and held the girl until she stopped crying.

"Does your mama know about you and Makiba, Mina?"

"No, it our secret. Now . . . it always be our secret."

"There's Someone else who knows your secret."

Mina looked up with a troubled expression on her face. "Mr. Daniels? He know?"

"No. At least he didn't mention it to me if he does. I was thinking of God, who knows everything about us. Would it help if I prayed with you?"

Mina seemed more than willing, and they bowed their heads and lifted her heartache to the One who could help her most.

Then, taking Mina's hand, Emma briefed her on Josh's concern about a possible Osabi uprising and the new rule regarding the children's safety. "We must be very careful, Mina." She grimaced, feeling a stirring of the old anxiety.

This time it was Mina's turn to reach out, and when Emma looked up, the girl's gaze was steady. "You not alone, Emma. I help you."

&ear;&ear;&ear;&ear;

The next few days passed slowly. Word of Makiba's death seemed to affect everyone like a gloomy cloud hanging over the entire plantation. Josh attended the funeral but didn't speak of it afterward, and Mina became Emma's shadow, always helpful and close at hand. She reminded Emma of a frightened doe with her big, brown eyes still full of pain.

By now, Emma had heard the grim story of Makiba's death. Tabo had told Mina in graphic detail, seemingly gloating over the incident. Emma wanted to bring it up with Josh, but Wednesday came before she had an opportunity to see him alone, and he and Matt left early to deliver the beans and bring Angeline back.

Since her hasty invitation, Emma had had second thoughts about Angeline's visit. Especially now with the recent tragedy.

Contrary to Josh's earlier comment, the timing couldn't be worse.

But by the time she'd gotten out snapshots from the cruise to show the girls, Emma had changed her mind. Good old Angeline. The confident woman she remembered would consider this just another challenge. And maybe Angeline's arrival would give them all something more pleasant to think about.

Mina and the girls eagerly joined in the preparations for Angeline's arrival, waxing and shining and arranging flowers from Sara's garden. But when night fell, Emma found herself carefully checking all the locks on the doors and windows, and then checking them again.

Since Makiba's death, Mina had spent her nights on the plantation, sleeping on a rollaway on the enclosed laundry-room porch, rather than making the long walk back to her village. Tonight, Emma invited her to sleep in her room. And while Mina looked slightly surprised, she seemed happy to comply.

They talked for a while after the girls were settled, mostly about Makiba and the funeral. With the growing friendship between them, Mina opened up a little, sharing her dreams and now her fears. Her voice dropped and her dark eyes widened. "Makiba's uncle say he find killer and do payback."

Emma knew that a payback—much like the old "eye for an eye, and tooth for a tooth"—was serious business in this country. Although outlawed, it was still common practice in many tribes. Even in the case of accidental deaths, some tribes would attempt a retribution killing. And in the case of Makiba, a valued tribesman, it could easily escalate into something very ugly.

When Mina's soft, even breathing signaled that she was asleep, Emma lay awake in the darkness. To distract her thoughts, she found herself thinking of Josh and Matt. Without the two males of the family, she felt uneasy—alone and vulnerable. She reminded herself that God wasn't asleep, and she prayed for the safety of everyone on the plantation, and for traveler's mercies for the three returning from Lae tomorrow.

With all the windows closed, the air now felt stale and stuffy. Emma rose and tiptoed across the room to open the window. Outside, the sky was clear and a nearly full moon illuminated the sweeping view—a study in shades of black and slate and various hues of gray. Emma marveled at the beauty of the stark moonscape.

Carried along on the cool night air came the familiar sounds of Ian's bagpipes. She sighed. His music was a comfort, a reminder that her good neighbors were just over the mountain. She wondered if Ian might be playing especially for her tonight, knowing she was alone with the children. Whatever the reasons, his music soothed her, and she fell asleep.

❧ ❧ ❧ ❧

Emma rose early, anxious to finish last-minute preparations for Angeline's arrival. Mina had already informed Tabo that there would be another guest at the table. Emma hadn't known exactly how to interpret the rude response—an exasperated snort. She had decided that it wouldn't be the end of the world if Tabo decided to look for employment elsewhere. But by noon, it was clear that the tight-lipped woman had no intention of leaving her kitchen to be managed by novices and marauding children!

Late in the afternoon, the girls took turns watching for the truck from the front porch, though Emma cautioned them not to go into the yard alone. She also gave Tabo permission to go home as soon as she had completed the meal, since they would not be serving until Josh and the others had returned. Emma didn't really expect the woman to go, so she was a little surprised when Tabo left earlier than usual.

Sara and Holly had put on their nice dresses for the occasion, and now Sara was setting the table with the best china and crystal, while Holly drew a picture to give to "Angel," as she was already calling Angeline. Josh's elder daughter was amazingly resourceful for a nine-year-old. But maybe that's what came of living in a culture that was not glutted with such curses of civilization as movies and TV.

"Sara, since you seem to have everything under control, I think I'll go change, too," Emma told her.

Sara looked up with a heart-stopping smile. If only she'd do it more often. "We'll be just fine, Emma, really we will. I'll keep an eye on Holly."

With a quick hug, Emma left her and went to her quarters. In the shower, she turned the knob to tepid water. Conserving electricity was a way of life here. Funny how easily she had adjusted.

She towel-dried her hair, noting how her perm had loosened up in the last several weeks. Her hair seemed softer, more natural-looking, and it shone when she brushed it, with golden highlights from the sun. A towel still wrapped around her, she stared at her reflection in the mirror. She looked tanned and healthy. Even her eyes looked brighter. How much she had changed since last February. She blinked. Was this the same person—mouse-colored hair and personality to match—who had fled a small town in Iowa?

Turning to her closet, she thumbed through the garments. Not a lot to choose from, but she finally settled on a soft, gauzy cotton Angeline had talked her into buying in Sydney. The dress—both loose and clingy—had a romantic look to it, and she had never worn it, lest she send the wrong message to Josh. Not that the man could be swept off his feet—not with both of them planted firmly on the ground! With Angeline around, though, the dress was a safe bet. She slipped on some sandals and took another look at her reflection. Yes, it was a good thing Angeline would be here.

"Ooh, Emma," said Sara when Emma was back, "you look like a movie star."

Emma laughed. "Thanks, Sara. I'd almost forgotten this dress, but it seemed perfect for our special dinner tonight."

"I can't wait to meet Angeline," said Sara as she straightened the pillows on the couch. "This is such fun!"

Emma glanced around the room. "Sara, where's Holly?"

"I think she's in the kitchen with Mina."

"I'll check. Let me know if you see your dad's truck, okay?"

"No worries, Emma. I've been keeping watch."

"Need any help, Mina?" Sara glanced around, a little anxious now. "Where's Holly?"

"I think she with Sara."

With growing unease, Emma hurried back to the living area, checking every nook and cranny along the way. "Sara, Holly's not with Mina. I'm going to look in your room."

But the girls' bedroom was empty. Matt's too. And Josh's.

Alarmed, she raced around the house, calling for Holly. "Holly, are you hiding in the house somewhere? This is no time for games."

Mina met her in the hallway. "Holly lost?"

"Not exactly," Emma said, struggling not to panic. "We just can't find her at the moment. I'm going outside to look. You two wait here."

Mina gasped. "But Mr. Daniel—he say—"

"I know what he said, Mina. But we have to find her. I'll be right back."

Breathing a prayer for courage, Emma stepped outside the screen door. Maybe Holly was hiding in a corner of the big wraparound porch. But there was not a sign of her there.

Her heart in her throat, Emma left the porch and walked toward the driveway. Maybe the little girl, in her excitement to greet the travelers, had wandered out near the road. But after going around the curve, Emma could see no trace of her. Where was she?

She turned toward one of the outbuildings and caught a glimpse of a dark-skinned worker—one she didn't recognize. Feeling truly frightened now, she reversed her direction and headed for the other side of the house, praying in earnest, "Please, God, don't let anything happen to Holly!"

Maybe she should have Sara radio Ian. Or maybe she should round up the workers and organize a search party. But recalling the unfamiliar man, she realized she wouldn't know which ones to trust. Speaking of trust, what kind of governess left a four-year-old unsupervised while she dolled up for a fancy party?

Breathless with her rapid pace and near panic, Emma continued walking, taking the path to Sara's garden. Through the leafy hedge of banana trees, she could hear a little voice, sweetly singing.

She ran into the garden and threw her arms around the little girl, laughing hysterically. "Holly! I've been looking all over for you! Where were you?"

Holly held up the bouquet of flowers she was gathering, her smile breaking through like the sun. "I was right here."

It was all Emma could do not to smile back. "But you were not supposed to leave the house." She hoped she sounded stern enough to be convincing.

"I just wanted to get the Angel some more flowers."

Emma knelt, cupping the little face in her hands to look the child straight in the eye. "You must understand, Holly. No one goes outside alone. Not even Matt."

"Not even Matt?"

"That's right. Do you understand?"

Holly nodded soberly.

Emma sighed and rose, taking Holly's free hand in hers. "Let's go inside and put your flowers in some water."

Strange—in those few moments while Holly was missing, Emma had known sheer terror. A fear more profound than anything she'd ever experienced. She couldn't love this little one more . . . not even if she were her very own.

"You found her!" cried Sara when they reached the house.

And just in time. "Mr. Daniels—he coming now," called Mina from the living room. "I see he truck coming down the road."

Thirty

*J*osh had expected a quiet ride back to the plantation. He figured Matt would be tired enough to sleep, since they'd taken in a late movie in town last night. Then they'd gotten an early start this morning to pick up some tools before meeting Angeline Thomas at the hotel.

Josh glanced past Matt to the woman sitting in the passenger seat. She shot him a dazzling smile, revealing too-perfect teeth, and kept on with her nonstop chattering. For the moment, fortunately, her attention was focused on Matt as she recounted some kind of surfing story. The kid was hanging on every word, clearly mesmerized. Well, Matt probably wasn't too young for a crush, and the blond woman was pretty enough.

Josh glanced out the side window and smiled to himself. Funny to think of his son growing up so soon. Still, he supposed that Angeline was the sort of woman he might have been infatuated with, at one time—before Emma Davis had moved in to occupy his time and his thoughts.

It was disturbing how much she'd upset his well-regulated routine. But as hard as he tried, he couldn't get her out of his head. Not that he wanted to, exactly. But it had all come on so fast, and he wasn't used to fast. Everything about his life was rather plodding and slow. Predictable and planned. Seedtime and harvest. These feelings toward Emma had taken him by surprise, and Josh didn't like surprises.

"Dad?" Matt's tone suggested that this wasn't the first time he'd spoken.

"Sorry, son. I was . . . just thinking."

"Angeline was asking you a question."

Angeline laughed. It was a clear, tinkling sort of laugh, innocent enough, but slightly grating. "I was asking you about the Scotsman—the one Emma has been telling me about."

"You must mean Ian. Ian McDowell."

She brightened even more, if that were possible. "Tell me about this amazing man. Emma makes him sound like he's Superman or a candidate for sainthood."

Josh cleared his throat. "Ian's quite a guy, all right."

"Do you know him well?"

"As well as any. He's a good man. I have the utmost respect for him." Josh was aggravated now. Just what was she getting at? "What is it you'd like to know?"

"If he's good enough for our Emma, of course!"

"What do you mean?" Matt frowned. "Is Emma going to marry Ian?"

Angeline laughed again. "Well, you just never know. What do *you* think, Josh? Are they serious?"

Matt groaned and slapped his forehead with the heel of his hand. "And just when we finally get a good governess."

"That's enough, son." Josh was really ticked off. Who was this woman, and what was she talking about? "You don't know that Emma has made any such plans—"

"Any reason she shouldn't?" Angeline's big, blue eyes widened.

He returned his gaze to the road, which was growing steeper and would soon require all of his attention.

But Angeline wasn't ready to give up. "I mean, you said yourself that Ian was a good guy. . . ."

"No, I don't suppose there's any reason why Ian and Emma shouldn't—"

"Dad," complained Matt. "You just said—"

"I know," said Josh, cutting him off, yet still trying to conceal his irritation. This was a dumb conversation, but he had no intention of letting on how he felt. "I don't think Emma is making any big plans," he said in a controlled voice. "But she has every right to, if she wants. And Ian is a good bloke."

"What does he do for a living?" asked Angeline.

"He's rich," said Matt. Josh could tell by Matt's voice that he was getting into Angeline's little game. "He has some huge ranch or spread or something in Scotland, with all sorts of animals and stuff. He travels all over the world whenever he wants to. Right, Dad?"

Josh nodded. It felt like someone had transplanted a lead brick in the place where his heart had just been. "But for a rich guy, he's all right," Josh put in reluctantly.

"There must be a catch," said Angeline.

"Huh?" said Matt.

"He sounds too good to be true."

Josh shook his head, forcing himself to answer with carefully measured words. "No, I've known Ian McDowell for nearly twenty years. He's absolutely for real."

Who did this woman think she was anyway? Coming in here like this, as if she wanted to destroy Josh's entire world in one swift blow. But then, he reminded himself, he had no claim on Emma. She didn't belong to him. After all, he was still legally married to Lila. Lila. It was the first time he'd thought of her since that night he'd spilled his guts to Emma.

He glanced over at the blond woman, who was now looking placidly out the window, as if she had not a clue as to the hurricane she had just stirred up. Now he realized why he found her so aggravating. Something about her reminded him of Lila. Of course, they looked absolutely nothing alike, but there was something just the same. Maybe it was her attitude. He used to think that attitude was just a female thing—that all women were like that. Until Emma.

He drove along in silence. Only now he couldn't enjoy the breathtaking view as they climbed toward the coffee plantation. It was almost as if he could hear the wheels spinning in Angeline's head, and they were playing the "Wedding March"—for Ian and Emma. He gripped the wheel tighter. What was wrong with him? When had he suddenly become so possessive of his children's governess, and what possible good could come of it? He felt Matt begin to slump against his arm, the late night finally catching up with him. Well, maybe that would keep that confounded woman quiet for a while. He didn't want to hear another word from her about Ian McDowell.

❧   ❧   ❧   ❧

Dusk was coming on when Josh finally turned down the road to the plantation. Usually, he loved coming home. But now all he could think about was the possibility that Emma was going to leave him to marry Ian. Why had he trusted her? He'd known from the start she wouldn't stay. But she had led him to believe otherwise. Well, he could certainly live without her. After all, he'd gotten along without her this long, hadn't he?

The lights were glowing warmly in the house when he parked out front. He nudged Matt. "Hey, son, we're home," he said quietly, and Matt straightened, looking out the window with bleary eyes.

Josh climbed out, went around, and opened Angeline's door.

"I'll get her bags," offered Matt with a silly grin directed at the woman.

"Thank you, Matt," said Angeline sweetly. "Oh my, Josh, your place is lovely. And the air here is so clean and fresh. So much better than that muggy stuff in the lowlands."

"You're here!" Emma opened the front door, wearing something soft and white that seemed to hug her before falling into loose folds that almost reached her ankles. He stared at the picture before him. Backlighted by the golden glow from the house, Emma stood smiling, the girls at her side. She looked so right. So welcoming. And for one brief moment, it seemed the welcome was for *him*. Then her focus shifted quickly to Angeline, and soon the two women were hugging and laughing like a couple of schoolgirls.

When Josh stepped onto the porch, he was greeted by Sara and Holly. "Come see, Father," called Sara in a happy voice. "We've made everything all pretty for tea." She led him to the dining room. Flowers, china, candles—it had never looked finer. Not even when Lila was here. He swallowed hard and turned to

Sara. Her eyes were glowing even more brightly than the candles.

"It looks . . . loverly, Sara." It was a private little joke between them—back before things got bad—back when they'd been a family.

"Thanks, we all helped."

"Come see *my* flowers, Father," said Holly, pulling him back into the living room and pointing to a small, lopsided bouquet on an end table. "I made them for Angel."

"Beautiful, Holly," he said, tweaking a golden curl. "Now, if you ladies will excuse me for a bit, I'd like to freshen up for tea myself. It looks as if this is party night." The girls giggled as Josh bowed and walked out of the room. Well, at least everyone else was happy tonight.

He took a quick shower but dressed slowly. He wasn't eager to go back out there. The thought of Angeline spending time with Emma was disturbing. He wondered again what she could possibly see in someone like that. They were so entirely different.

Finally, he could put off the inevitable no longer. It was time to put on a party smile. He'd do it—for Sara and Holly. They were so excited about this evening, and for their sakes, he'd play Mr. Congeniality.

He found everyone seated comfortably in the living room, with a cheery fire going. He glanced down at the fireplace with a small wave of guilt. Fire-building was his job.

"I made the fire tonight, Dad," said Matt with a proud grin and—what? A slightly deeper voice? "Angeline thought it would be nice. She's been down where it's hot, and she thought it was a bit cool up here."

"Your home is gorgeous, Josh," gushed Angeline. "If you ever need a new nanny, let me know. I might be interested." She turned and winked at Emma.

But Emma only smiled. "I think I should go see how Mina is doing with tea."

"Is Mina helping Tabo tonight?" Josh arched a brow.

"Actually, Tabo left early. I was pretty surprised, knowing how she likes to run the kitchen."

"That seems odd," said Josh, frowning. "Anything wrong, Emma?"

She shook her head. "Not that I could see. If you'll excuse me."

He watched her leave the dining room and pass through the door into the kitchen. That was *some* dress. . . .

"I take it Tabo is your cook," Angeline said, not giving a man time to think.

"She's been with my family for ages. Couldn't get along without her."

Sara made a face, and Matt laughed. "She may be a good cook, but she's a real crank, Angeline."

"Tea's on." Emma was back, and the room lit up. Josh smiled a little as he stood, remembering how Emma had called it "dinner" for so long. She'd finally gotten it straight.

Angeline was taking his arm. He glanced at her in surprise, then remembered his resolution not ten minutes ago. All right. Mr. Congeniality it was. He escorted her into the dining room, pulling out the designated chair. Matt followed suit, helping Emma into hers. Holly had already scooted into her seat, but Josh noted with satisfaction that Sara had not.

"Allow me." Josh made a little bow, and Sara rewarded him with a rare smile. Funny. He'd never thought of her as a particularly pretty child before. He sat down and looked toward the end of the table. Emma seemed to be staring at him expectantly, with a kind of mist in her eyes. What was she waiting for?

He remembered how his father had always asked a blessing before each meal. He'd tried it a few times himself, back before Lila left.

"Shall I say grace?" asked Josh, hoping he remembered how. In answer, they all bowed their heads, even Holly, but then he supposed she had learned about saying grace from the Mc-Dowells. Thinking of the McDowells didn't make it any easier. Josh cleared his throat and pronounced a short blessing. He hoped it was sufficient. Apparently so, because in the next moment everyone was chattering and passing the food.

"Ian and Dad are going to take you and Emma to a sing-sing," Matt told Angeline over a mouthful of potatoes. Josh observed Emma, gesturing with her head. Matt quickly swallowed, then continued. "Anyway, it should be exciting. You never know what might happen—especially if people get drunk, or there's a fight, or—"

"That's enough, Matt," said Josh in a stern voice. "Are you trying to scare Angeline?"

"So, Angeline," Emma was making an obvious attempt to change the subject, "how was your trip? What do you think of our mountains?" Josh smiled to himself. *Our* mountains? So now she was thinking of them as hers, too. Well, there were plenty to go around.

"I love it up here. Although I suppose it's a little isolated. Do you ever feel cut off from the world?"

Josh studied Emma's face as she shrugged and said, "Not really. The truth is, I was never much of a social butterfly. My life in Iowa was pretty much all work and no play. I guess I'm not used to much excitement."

"I noticed there's a TV. Do you get good reception way up here?"

Matt laughed. "I wish! We just use it to watch videos. And what we have, we've seen so many times we could probably act them out for you!"

"Now, that sounds like good entertainment," said Angeline. "How about the piano? Do you play, Josh?"

"No. It's Sara who has the talent. Mary McDowell gives her a lesson now and then."

"Well, I love to play," Angeline offered.

"Would you? Play for us after tea, I mean?" asked Sara hopefully.

"If no one objects."

"We'd love it," said Emma.

"Well, ladies," Josh pushed his chair back and stood when the meal was over. "Don't tell Tabo, but we didn't miss her at all. Tea was smashing!"

Emma and Sara excused themselves to help Mina in the kitchen. He didn't try to stop them, but he did wonder why Mina needed any help. It was her job, after all. He'd discuss it with Emma later.

In the living room, Angeline, flanked by Holly and Matt, had already seated herself at the piano. The sight of the three of them was disturbing. For some reason it reminded him of Lila and Skip. They'd enjoyed playing duets in the evenings. He knew he was being irrational, but he couldn't help it. He lingered for as long as he could stand it, then slipped out to the porch.

He sat down, staring out into the darkness. The nighttime sounds and smells were comforting, like sitting with an old friend, where conversation wasn't necessary. He wasn't sure how much time had passed when he heard the screen door open and quiet footsteps on the porch.

"Josh?" He liked the sound of his name when Emma said it. "Everything all right?"

"Sure. Everything's fine. I'm just enjoying the night. What about you? Have a good day?" It felt odd—making small talk like this. "Nobody got hurt or kidnapped or anything, did they?"

"No . . . nothing like that." She seemed a little hesitant, like she might have something on her mind. "I have to confess, though, I did get a little scared last night."

"Oh?" He sat up, peering through the darkness. "What happened?"

"Oh, nothing at all. I suppose it was having you gone. Made me feel a little edgy."

She made sense. Didn't rattle on all night. Josh realized why he preferred her to other women.

"I'd locked everything all up, but then I opened a window—just to get some air—and heard Ian playing his pipes. Somehow it was very comforting."

Oh. Ian again. Josh rolled his eyes, thankful that Emma couldn't see in the protective darkness. "Yeah. Nice of Ian to think of you like that."

"Oh, I don't think he was actually playing for me. . . ."

"Father! Emma!" called Holly. "Come hear the Angel play."

Emma laughed softly. "I guess we might as well forget about trying to correct her. You coming, Josh?"

Piano music floated out of the house and onto the porch, and Josh had to admit it did sound nice. But his earlier mood was spoiled. Ian McDowell indeed!

"I'm coming." He held the door for Emma and went inside.

Thirty-one

J osh sure doesn't hang around the house much," said Angeline on Saturday. "We didn't see him all day yesterday until dinner—or rather, tea—and I haven't seen him all morning. Wonder where he keeps himself."

"Oh, he stays pretty busy with the plantation." Emma loaded some food items into the picnic basket. But even as she answered her friend, she was thinking that Josh *had* made himself a little more scarce than usual lately. "He should be back any minute to take us over to the McDowells to drop off the children and pick up Ian."

"Hmm. Can't wait to meet this Ian. From your letters, he sounds like such a dreamboat."

Emma laughed. "I wouldn't exactly describe him that way. But he's a great guy. I think you'll like him."

"Oh-oh." Angeline frowned as she checked her bag. "I almost forgot my camera. I'd better go to the room and get it."

"On your way, could you tell the kids to load their things in the Jeep now?" said Emma. "It's getting late, and Josh ought to be ready to go soon."

"Will do."

Emma closed the basket and took one last glance around the kitchen. Tabo would be back this afternoon to put away some shopping produce, and Emma didn't want her to find anything out of place. The cook had been grumpier than usual in the past few days, and Emma wondered if this might have to do with their guest. But then again, Tabo didn't seem to need a reason to be grouchy.

"Can I help you with that?"

Emma turned to see Josh putting out a hand to hoist the basket. He'd put on a fresh shirt for the sing-sing, she noticed.

"Thanks. It *is* pretty heavy. We must have enough food in there for two days."

"Hopefully we won't need it, but it's best to go prepared."

She'd been joking, but he seemed to have taken her seriously. "What do you mean?"

"Well, one year several blokes got their tires punctured. And it's not easy finding new tires during a sing-sing. No businesses open."

Emma let out a sigh. "I suppose it's a good thing the children are spending the night with Mary." She cast him a skeptical look. "You sure it's safe for us to go?"

He shrugged. "Probably as safe as living around here right now."

"Have there been more problems?"

"No, but something is brewing. I'd bet on it. Fortunately, the local tribes are focusing on the sing-sing right now. But it will be important to stick together once we get there."

Josh slid the basket into the back of the Jeep, then turned to take the folded quilt Emma handed him. Their eyes met, locked, and she had to force herself to remember what they'd been talking about. "Right. I'll let Angeline know we need to stay together," she repeated, then recalled another detail she'd forgotten to mention. "Do you mind if Mina stays at the house while we're gone? She's still upset over Makiba's death and is afraid to walk home alone."

He arched one brow. "Was something going on between her and Makiba?"

Emma averted her gaze, remembering her promise to Mina. "I'm—not at liberty to say."

"I see. I guess that doesn't surprise me. Poor kids. Those two would have made a great match."

Emma looked up in pleased surprise. Now *this* was a change.

"All right, you guys!" called Angeline. "Looks like we're

ready to get this show on the road."

The children piled out of the house behind her. While they loaded their belongings, Emma dashed back into the house to look for Mina. She found the girl placing a stack of clean linens in Josh's bathroom.

"Mina, Mr. Daniels says it's fine for you to stay here tonight. And something else . . ."

Mina waited, her dark eyes haunted.

"He's very sorry about—you and Makiba."

"Truly?" She brightened.

Emma stepped forward to catch Mina's free hand in hers. "Be careful while we're gone, and remember to lock up after we leave."

"Yes. Have a good time."

By the time Emma got back to the Jeep, Holly and Sara were already in the backseat, and Matt was closing the front passenger door behind Angeline, then jumped into the back with the girls. As Josh slammed the tailgate, he eyed Emma dubiously. "With room for only two in the split front seat, it'll be a tight squeeze until we get to McDowells."

"Oh, I'll sit in back and hold Holly in my lap." Emma climbed in, made room for the child, then glanced toward the front. For some reason, it bothered her to see Angeline sitting next to Josh. She chided herself silently, then to occupy her mind, started up a chorus of "Waltzing Matilda" with the children. By the time they had run through all the verses and chorus twice, they were at Mary's place.

Ian met them in the driveway, and Emma and the children spilled out, while Josh unloaded their overnight things. Angeline didn't budge.

"Mary's out back, working on a special project," said Ian with a mischievous twinkle in his eye. "You kids had better go see what it is."

Quick farewells were exchanged, and Josh slid under the wheel again, leaving Ian to open the back door for Emma and go around to sit on the other side. Apparently Angeline believed in squatter's rights, Emma thought with more than a trace of irritation.

The minute Josh pulled out of the drive, Angeline turned around to bestow one of her sunniest smiles on Ian. "So nice to meet you at last. I've heard so much about you—from Emma."

"Aye, and I've heard about you. Emma has been looking forward to your visit."

The roll of his r's seemed to enchant Angeline. "I just love your accent. In fact, I've always been fond of anything having to do with Scotland."

"Now, is that the truth?" Ian chuckled. "And how about grown men who wear skirts and make raucous sounds with leather bags?"

Angeline laughed. "Kilts and bagpipes? Terrific!"

"Aye, you're right, Emma," Ian sighed. "Angeline is a bonny lass indeed!"

Josh seemed to be concentrating on his driving, saying very little. In fact, Angeline did most of the talking, with Ian putting in a few words now and then. But the conversation, like Angeline herself, was upbeat and cheerful, and Emma was sure no one noticed her own dreary state of mind. She stared out the window, alternately wishing she'd never invited Angeline for this visit and silently scolding herself for her wishing it.

The rare sound of Josh's laughter snapped Emma's attention back to the present. What had she missed? Something charming Angeline had said, no doubt. While they chortled, Emma pretended to be enjoying the joke, although she had no idea what it was all about, and no intention of asking for a replay.

"But seriously—" Angeline dabbed at her eyes, "that's when I knew I couldn't stay there another day. I thought making movies would be nice for a change, but I can't see making that kind of trash. And I didn't believe God had brought me all this way to be involved in something like that."

"And you were able to walk away from a promising career—just like that?" There was a teasing note in Josh's voice.

"It was easy. The great part my uncle had in mind was some ditzy bimbo who didn't wear enough clothes. No, thank you."

"Well, good for you, Angeline," said Ian. "Many women would have had their heads turned by that sort of offer."

At that moment Angeline turned to regard Emma with a

little frown. "Hey, you. We haven't heard a peep out of you. Are you taking a little snooze back there?"

Emma forced a smile. "I guess I was . . . spacing out."

"Spacing out?" Ian lifted one craggy brow.

Angeline didn't wait for Emma to translate. "You know, it's like daydreaming." She turned back to Josh, putting a hand on his shoulder in a proprietary manner that irked Emma. "Now, I want to hear all about this sing-sing business."

Josh obliged, explaining how the different tribes, dressed in their unique costumes, came together—an annual event that included native foods, music, and dancing. "The people travel from all over to compete for prizes. Some of these folks take it all very seriously," he concluded.

Then, glancing over at Angeline for the first time, he added, "You'd better wear a hat."

"A hat?" Angeline put her hands to her hair. "Does it look that bad?"

" 'Tis a bonny head of hair, Angeline," Ian put in quickly. "What Josh means is that lovely, long blond locks like yours are quite unusual around these parts. 'Tis best not to call attention to oneself in these unsettled times."

For a horrifying instant, Emma was reminded of the headhunter jokes Tim Miller had loved to tell aboard ship.

But Angeline seemed delighted. "Ah, an element of danger, too. Don't worry about me. I plan to stay *very* close, Josh. What a treat—having two big guys to protect us. Right, Emma?"

"Right." Feeling more miserable by the minute, Emma was relieved when Josh finally pulled to a stop near the grounds.

True to her word, Angeline stayed glued to Josh's side, and Emma was left with Ian. Not that she minded. He was a congenial companion, pointing out various tribes he recognized by their unusual dress. And soon Emma was so caught up in the panorama that she forgot to be jealous of Josh and Angeline. The sights were mind-blowing—glistening bodies decorated with colorful feathers, yards of beads, leaves sewn together, gourds, mud masks, and wild-looking face and body paint. Some had incorporated modern elements—bottle caps strung together, shredded T-shirts, and even some brightly colored underwear being worn as outerwear. Noses and ears were pierced with bones or tusks, and some of the warriors carried spears and shields. It was a fierce-looking sight, and Emma found herself sticking as closely to Ian as Angeline to Josh.

Finding a good spot to take in some of the competition, the four sat on the quilt Emma had brought along and watched as groups performed dances and acted out battle or hunting scenes. After a while, the foreign antics didn't seem so strange, and Emma began to enjoy herself. Too bad stuffy white people couldn't let their hair down like this more often. Glimpsing Angeline's hat covering her blond hair, Emma stifled an impulse to laugh at her own joke. On the other hand, she thought, recalling Ian's warning, letting down one's hair could be downright dangerous!

After a late picnic lunch, they walked around to stretch their legs, pausing to examine the displays of various vendors who had spread their goods out on mats on the ground. At one point, Angeline was haggling with a leathery old woman over the price of a pretty shell necklace when another woman walked up and bought it right out from under her nose.

"Rats! I really wanted that necklace."

"Too bad," Josh said, attempting to console her.

And Ian was quick to suggest, "Maybe we can find another." They began to look, moving from one vendor to another.

Emma, tired of searching for the necklace, paused to watch a particularly interesting-looking group of tribesmen rehearsing their act. She had heard they were from the Asaro tribe, and wore huge, round masks made of mud. The performers were almost comical-looking, but she could tell by their movements that they were intent on their preparation for the competition. It must have taken weeks to work out those steps, then learn to execute them with such precision.

When the rehearsal came to an end, Emma realized that she had lost sight of the others. She walked on a bit, scanning the vendors and their wares, looking for any sign of her friends. But they were nowhere in sight. In fact, there was not another white person around.

Fighting a wave of panic, Emma quickened her pace, trying to find the area where they had had their picnic. But the farther she walked, the less familiar the surroundings.

She turned and walked the other way, swallowed up by the crowd, praying they were heading for the parade grounds. For all she knew, some of these people could be going off to their own private sing-sing. She'd been told that some of the disgruntled tribesmen, having been unsuccessful in their attempts to win a trophy, would take off for their own brand of celebrating. She wasn't sure she wanted to know what that might be.

Truly frightened now, and claustrophobic at the closeness of all these unwashed bodies, Emma was desperate to get away. But she had no idea which way to turn. Where were her friends?

She glanced at her watch—nearly six. It would soon be dark. Others were beginning to eye her curiously, but she was too fearful to return their looks or to ask for help. Not that they would be able to understand her if she did. Best that no one suspect she was lost. Once again, she scanned the crowd, searching for a familiar face. Finding none, she prayed silently, fervently, that God would help her . . . somehow.

The sun disappeared suddenly, and torches were lit, illuminating the scene. The flickering light cast grotesque shadows, causing the masked warriors to appear even more ferocious and threatening. Seeing a group of women sitting on the ground to eat from their bilum bags, she moved as near as she dared, preferring their company to the fearsome men. She took off her sandals and rubbed her aching feet. No doubt her route had only taken her farther from the picnic grounds. It might be hours before she caught up with Josh and the others.

She tried to ignore the chattering women, some of them looking her way with undisguised interest. Finally one of them spoke to her in Pidgen. Emma's command of the language was still limited, but she pointed to herself and told the woman her name. Suddenly they all began speaking at once, and she held up her hand, explaining in her halting Pidgen that she did not understand.

"Do you speak English?" asked one of them, and Emma felt a wave of relief.

"Oh yes! Do you?"

The attractive dark woman nodded. "I learn in mission school."

Emma felt tears well in her eyes. *Thank You, Lord!* "I'm lost," she confessed.

The English-speaking woman translated this news to the other women before turning back to Emma. "I help you."

Emma felt as small and helpless as Holly, but she attempted to explain her dilemma and the place where she thought she had left her friends. The woman rose, motioned for her to follow, and led the way through the crowd.

Finally, they reached a lighted area that looked vaguely familiar.

"Emma!" She whirled at the sound of his voice and saw Josh running toward her. "Are you all right?"

She threw her arms around him and sobbed out her story. "I'm so sorry!" But it felt safe in his arms, his hand stroking her head as if she were one of the girls.

It was over much too soon. He pulled out a handkerchief and, feeling self-conscious now, she took it and stepped back to introduce the little group of women who were huddling around. He was thanking them in Pidgen just as Ian and Angeline joined them.

"What happened to you?" asked Angeline as she hugged Emma. "We've been worried sick!"

Emma felt like such a dunce. Cool, collected Angeline would never do anything so immature. "I was watching some performers while we were looking for your necklace, and the next thing I knew, you were gone. I looked everywhere. But by then, I was hopelessly lost." She shrugged, smiling sheepishly. "I'm so sorry to have caused all this trouble."

Ian put his arm around Emma's shoulder. "No, lassie, 'tis the lot of us who owe the apology. We all just walked off without you. But thank God you're fine. No harm done."

Emma wasn't so sure when she noticed the shell necklace Angeline was wearing. "Oh, you found your necklace, I see."

"Yes, Josh got it for me. We were probably closing the deal when we lost you, Emma."

Josh was standing next to Angeline now. And the stunning blonde laced her arm through his. "All's well that ends well," she said with a big sigh. With Ian's arm still around Emma's shoulder, Emma figured they must look like two happy couples out on a double date. In some subtle way, a line had been drawn tonight—Josh and Angeline, herself and Ian.

She studied Josh and Angeline standing side by side in the flickering torchlight. They made a striking couple—Josh, with his dark good looks; Angeline, hat in her hands, her blond hair flowing loosely over her shoulders.

It felt like a strange déjà vu as Emma suddenly recalled the first time she'd seen Angeline. She'd been sitting with Aaron in the jazz club on board the ship. But Angeline had quickly discarded Aaron, and foolish Emma had snatched him up. But this was different—Josh was not Aaron.

Thirty-two

*T*hey took time for a snack in the Jeep, then headed home. Angeline, as Emma had expected, hopped into the front seat next to Josh. He didn't seem to mind, either. In fact, he'd warmed up to Angeline considerably.

The return trip was more peaceful, but Angeline managed to keep up a cheerful flow of conversation, mostly with Ian. Even he seemed taken with her. Emma eventually tuned them both out. She was bone tired, more than ready for this day to end. Ready for Angeline to go back to San Francisco or Vancouver or wherever she had come from. Fat chance. Besides, Emma felt guilty for harboring such inhospitable thoughts.

"Why don't you stay for dinner . . . er . . . tea, Ian?" Angeline invited warmly, then gasped in mock dismay as she turned to Josh. "Oh, forgive me for playing hostess with your house. But I did notice a delicious-looking pie cooling this morning. Some kind of berries, I think."

Josh gave in without a struggle. "Good idea, Angeline. And I'm sure Ian would be interested in hearing you play the piano."

Ian was interested. Intrigued was more to the point. "You play?"

"Oh, not all that well, but I enjoy music."

"Nonsense, she plays beautifully," said Josh in a tone of voice that Emma had never heard before and couldn't quite read.

When Josh pulled up to the house, it was completely dark. No lights on, inside or out. "Looks like Mina may have decided to go home after all," he said as he climbed out from behind the wheel. "I'll go turn on the generator."

Not waiting for Ian to come around and open her door, Emma got out and headed for the porch, longing for some excuse to say good night and go to bed. She felt emotionally drained; partly from being lost today in what could have been a hostile environment. But there was another reason, of course. Angeline. She was ashamed of herself, but she was beginning to wish her friend had never come.

Emma trudged up the walk, carrying the quilt they had used as a ground cover. She had just reached the door when the porch lights came on.

"Emma!" It was Josh, calling from the back porch. "Come here!"

Emma dropped the quilt and hurried through the darkened house until she came to the enclosed laundry area where Josh was kneeling over a prone figure. Mina! She appeared to be either unconscious . . . or dead.

Josh felt for a pulse. "She's breathing."

"What's wrong?"

"I can't tell yet. There's no blood that I can see. It almost looks like she just collapsed here."

Emma knelt and cradled the young woman's head in her lap. "Mina? Can you hear me?" The girl's dark lashes fluttered briefly. It was enough to give Emma hope.

"What's going on—" Ian stopped mid-sentence when he stepped onto the porch. "Is she all right?"

"We don't know, Ian. Let's carry her into the living room so we can get a better look."

Ian and Josh lifted Mina easily and carried her through the kitchen where Angeline was filling the big teakettle.

"What on earth!" cried Angeline, dropping the kettle into the sink with a loud clang. "Is she dead?"

"No, she's not dead." Emma's patience was wearing thin. "But something is definitely very wrong."

The two men gently laid her on the couch and Mina's eyes opened, but the expression was blank and dull.

"Erratic pulse. Labored breathing—" Ian checked her eyes

with a penlight he pulled from his pocket. "Dilated pupils—"

Angeline slanted him a puzzled look. "You a doctor, too?"

"No, but I've had to be something of a vet, and people aren't all that different from animals when it comes to vital signs. I'd say she needs to go to hospital."

"Then I'll go with her," Emma announced, clasping one of Mina's lifeless hands between hers.

"Fine. I expect they'll keep the girl overnight for observation." Ian rose from the couch where he had been examining Mina and turned to Josh. "Since Emma wants to come, I suggest you and Angeline stay here so you can pick up your children in the morning. If it's all right, I'll borrow the Jeep to transport your girl to town."

"Sure." Josh dragged his hand through his hair and searched Emma's eyes. "You don't mind going?"

She lifted her chin. "Not at all. Mina is my friend. I'll do whatever I can to help." The defiant statement was made, she realized, almost as a challenge. Emma didn't care what he thought anymore. Angeline could have him—racial prejudice and all!

They bundled Mina in blankets and loaded her into the backseat. Not knowing whether Mina could hear or understand, Emma spoke soothingly while Ian drove, taking the curves as carefully as possible. And she did her share of praying, stroking the cropped curly hair.

The two-hour trip seemed to take a week. It was midnight before Mina was finally placed on a gurney and rolled into the small hospital admitting office. Ian and Emma waited in an adjoining room. There were only a few personnel, as far as she could see. Emma began to wonder if there would even be a doctor available in the desolate little hospital at this hour of the night.

Finally a gray-haired woman, wearing a white medical coat, came out to greet them. "I'm Dr. Moller. Are you the people who brought in the unconscious girl?" she asked with a heavy Scandinavian accent.

"Yes, we brought her in." Emma leaped up. "Is she going to be all right?"

The woman frowned slightly. "I don't know for sure. Perhaps we'll know more in the morning."

"Can we see her?

The doctor looked surprised but nodded. "She is still unconscious, but I suppose it won't hurt."

Dr. Moller led them to a small room with several neatly made beds—unoccupied, except for Mina's. To Emma's relief, a nurse was on duty, checking on an IV running into Mina's left arm.

She looked so small lying there, so helpless. Still, she appeared to be resting comfortably. Nevertheless, Emma was worried. What could possibly be wrong?

"Do you know of any place where we can stay?" asked Ian. "It's too late to make the trip back—"

"We have a guesthouse." The doctor made a notation on the chart and handed it to the nurse. "Come, I will show you. I am going there myself."

"Ian," whispered Emma, "can we pray before we leave her?"

Flanking Mina's bed, they prayed, each holding a dark hand. Emma was thankful for his earnest words.

"Thank you for your help, Doctor," Ian told her, turning to address Dr. Moller, who had stood back during the prayer.

She waved a hand in dismissal. "Ah, it is nothing. We help wherever we can. We, too, believe in the power of prayer. It is God who makes miracles."

They followed her outside and down a dark alleyway, then into a small office where the clerk behind the desk peered over her glasses.

"These people need a place to stay the night, Mrs. Stoltz," the doctor explained.

The woman handed Ian a key. "Four doors down the walk, to your left."

"Er . . ." Emma could see that Ian was embarrassed. "We'll be needing two rooms. We're not married, you see."

"I beg your pardon." Dr. Moller lost some of her clinical cool. "I could only assume . . ."

The woman behind the desk took down another key from a giant ring. "You room is right next door. Breakfast at eight."

Emma procceded to her assigned room, told Ian good night, and unlocked the door. The room was tiny and bare except for a single bed and a small chest. She flopped onto the bed gratefully, too exhausted to worry about tomorrow.

❧   ❧   ❧   ❧

Emma rose early and skipped breakfast to hurry back to the clinic. When she arrived, another nurse was on duty. But Emma was allowed to see Mina. What she found was encouraging. Mina was sitting up in bed, eyes open, though with a cloudy stare.

"Well, you're looking better this morning, I see." Emma touched her arm tentatively. "You had us worried "

Mina looked past Emma, as if she were not even present.

"Mina? Can you hear me? It's Emma."

Mina blinked. "Emma?" Her voice was raspy, her tongue thick.

"You're in the hospital. Ian and I brought you last night. Can you tell me what happened?"

The girl only shook her head and gazed down at her hands, folded limply in her lap. She looked dazed—or drugged.

Emma tried again. "Mina, can you tell me what's wrong?"

Mina's eyes filled with tears. "I . . . going to die."

"No, Mina. You aren't going to die. You're very sick, but you're not going to die."

She nodded solemnly. "Like Makiba."

"What made you say a thing like that?" Emma was horrified, imagining all kinds of eerie scenarios that might have taken place outside the kitchen.

"I will die." Mina was sobbing now. "Poison."

Emma gasped. Was it possible that Mina had become so depressed over Makiba's death that she'd actually tried to harm herself? Or—"Did someone poison you, Mina?"

Mina only shook her head, her shoulders heaving.

"Now, listen to me." Emma kept her voice firm. "You aren't going to die. You're here in the hospital where it's safe. Now just rest. I'll be back soon."

Emma glanced at her watch. If she was lucky, she could catch Dr. Moller at breakfast.

Emma found Ian seated in the small coffee room of the guesthouse when she arrived. The doctor had left to check on lab reports. It didn't take long to fill him in on her suspicions. "I just don't get it," she said. "How does this kind of poison work?"

"Let me try to explain." Ian poured her a cup of coffee and passed a plate of sausages. "Do you know anything about black magic?"

"Like witchcraft and voodoo?"

"Exactly. Here it's called 'poison.' And it's a lot more common than some would like to think."

"Are you saying that Mina practices some sort of black magic?"

"No, but I think she's trying to tell us that someone has worked poison on her." Ian rubbed his chin. "Considering her symptoms, I'd say it's highly likely. No visible sign of a health problem—yet she was deathly ill."

"Then she should be just fine," said Emma hopefully.

"Not necessarily. You see, there's no real way to treat this kind of poison, since it's not exactly a medical problem."

"Well, who would poison Mina? And why?"

Ian shrugged. "It's all very mysterious. I've heard of cases where strong men, on the way home from a hunt, have been accosted by some enemy who put them in a trance and inserted bamboo slivers in the bottoms of their feet."

She shuddered. "How painful! But can't they be removed? Surely it would be a simple matter for a doctor."

"The doctors can't remove them—" he gave her a long, meaningful look, as if trying to gauge her level of understanding—"because the slivers aren't there."

She felt a tingle of terror snake down her spine. "They aren't there?"

He shook his head. " 'Tis not a matter of flesh and blood, you see, Emma. The Bible says we battle against the invisible powers of darkness. So—if it's what I think it is—this kind of illness is beyond the realm of the physical."

Emma had never felt so helpless. Her faith was so new—not nearly strong enough to meet this challenge. Maybe it was a test. "So . . . what do we do?"

Ian drew his craggy brows together in a frown, his eyes piercing and warlike. "We pray."

At the clinic, they found Mina unconscious again, Dr. Moller off to learn the results of the latest lab tests. When the doctor stepped back into the room with the chart, her expression was grim. "Standard blood and urine tests are normal, but her vital signs are still extremely irregular. We'll continue the intravenous therapy, but in the meantime, I'll be in my study, doing some further research."

After she had left, Ian shook his head. "She won't find any answers in her medical textbooks. This is going to take another kind of medicine."

Following Ian's prescription, they spent the next moments in prayer, doing battle for the frail girl who hovered between life and death. Emma had never heard such praying as Ian invoked the Mighty God, Creator of all life, to bind the forces that were seeking to take Mina from them, and to bring her back to full health and wholeness. When he was done, Emma felt a sense of peace in the room. But there was no sign that Mina was aware of anything going on around her.

"Emma," Ian spoke under his breath, "this is all we can do for now. Under the circumstances—with the Osabe problems brewing—I'd best be getting back to check on Mary and the others. Will you be going with me?"

"Thanks, Ian, but I'd like to stay—at least until we see how Mina . . ."

He held her close and pressed a kiss on her forehead. "Pray, lassie. Stay by her bedside and pray."

"Yes. I will. Tell Josh—and the children. I'm so sorry I can't be with them."

"Aye. But just remember that Angeline is there. They're in excellent hands."

Emma groaned inwardly. That was all she needed right now—a reminder of her problems back at the plantation. She shook off the persistent ache in her heart and forced a smile. "Sure. They're in excellent hands."

With a quick squeeze of her shoulder, Ian was gone, leaving Emma to her own feeble attempts to ward off the evil that threatened to choke the life out of Mina and rob Emma of her own peace of mind. Ian was right. It was a battle—a battle with no physical dimension and no weapons, except prayer. And that she did—at least, as best she could, borrowing Ian's phraseology, punctuated by frequent childish cries of her own. "Help her, God! Please!"

Each time Mina regained consciousness, Emma was there to encourage her, holding her hand, trying to break through the fog of her confusion. But by evening, Emma was convinced that Mina had pronounced her own death sentence. If she didn't show some improvement soon, she might surely die.

Emma wouldn't give up, though. Never. And when Mina's long lashes fluttered open this time, Emma put her face close and spoke firmly, "Mina, you have to tell me. Do you have any idea who worked poison on you?"

Mina didn't answer. Instead, she turned away, compressing her lips tightly.

"Mina, talk to me. How will you get well if you keep this all inside?"

A silent stream of tears rained down the smooth cheeks. "I cannot tell. People get hurt if I tell. She work poison on them."

"Shh. Don't say that. God is in control, and His power is greater than poison. We have to trust Him." Not knowing what else to do, Emma laid her head against the bed and prayed quietly. If nothing else, the steady rhythm of her words was soothing to Mina, and the sick girl dropped off into a deep sleep, the furrows creasing her high forehead easing.

Leaving Mina's room, Emma left the hospital. It was tea time, but she had no interest in food. Instead, she took a walk around the grounds that surrounded the clinic and guesthouse, finally settling on a bench next to a huge hibiscus bush. She closed her eyes and leaned back. Only a week ago, life had seemed so simple, so blissful. Then Makiba had been killed. And Angeline had come, complicating things with Josh. And now this dreadful sickness . . .

Emma felt a twinge of guilt, lumping Angeline's visit in with the more serious matters at hand. Still, her presence here felt almost as devastating. Josh and Angeline together. What were they doing now? Sitting down to tea with the children? Who could resist those three, not to mention Josh?

Josh and Angeline. Emma shook her head, trying to erase the picture from her imagination, and released a deep sigh. "Dear God, my life is in your hands. You know what's best—*I* sure don't. If you have a plan for Josh and Angeline, then I'll step out of the way." Even as she spoke the words, she felt her heart breaking. How could she just walk away from that family? From Josh? "But if it *is* your plan, Lord—you'll have to give me the strength!"

♏ ♏ ♏ ♏

The next morning, Emma was in and out of Mina's room several times—feeding her some broth, quietly encouraging her to take frequent sips of water, helping her into a fresh gown, and silently praying for a breakthrough.

By mid-morning, Emma decided it was time. She knew only that a woman had worked poison on Mina, and Emma's suspicions were growing. "Mina," she began, phrasing her approach carefully, "the woman who worked poison on you has made you believe that other people will be hurt if you talk. But if we find out who has done this, we can stop her before she hurts anyone else. Don't you see?"

Mina cringed, her eyes filled with dread. Emma had seen that look before—when Tabo had been scolding her. "It's Tabo, isn't it?" Mina's small gasp told Emma all she needed to know. "Don't worry, Mina. We'll make sure that Tabo doesn't hurt anyone."

"My mama! Tabo will get my mama!"

"I will let Mr. Daniels know—"

"No! She get him! Osabe get him, the children—" Mina broke down, sobbing uncontrollably.

Even with Mina's hysterics, Emma was calm. "Hush now. God is with us. And He's with you—right now. I've asked Him to station big, strong angels all around your bed. No poison could possibly get through."

Still sobbing, Mina reached for Emma's hand.

She gave it a squeeze. "Now, you rest, Mina. I'll notify Mr. Daniels about Tabo. He'll know what to do."

On the way to the office of the guesthouse, Emma decided to send two messages—one to Josh and one to Ian, doubling her chances of reaching someone—soon.

The hours passed with no word from either Mary's place or the plantation. By near the end of the day, Emma felt alone and forgotten. Even God seemed far away.

Disheartened, Emma headed for Mina's room again, ready to call it a day. The girl had said no more since the revelation about Tabo. And Emma had little hope that she would hear anything new today.

But when she pulled up a chair near the bed, Mina was more talkative, and Emma listened, spellbound, as the girl unfolded an unbelievable tale.

"After you go to sing-sing, I help Tabo in kitchen. Tabo lean over the sink to wash pot, and I see string fall from her dress. When I look, I see ring tied on. It Mrs. Daniels's ring—the one she always wear." Mina held up her left hand. "She call it a wedding ring."

Emma was shocked. "How did Tabo get the ring?"

Mina's hands were shaking now. She took a deep breath to reply, then shuddered and fell back against the pillow, her head jerking from side to side and her eyes rolling back in her head so that only the whites showed.

"Mina! Talk to me!" Emma grabbed her hand and patted it, patted the now pale cheeks. But the young woman was too far gone, her body seizing violently.

Emma rang for a nurse, who called Dr. Moller in. The doctor administered a sedative, and Mina's contorted muscles relaxed at last.

"This happens sometimes. She'll sleep now." Dr. Moller placed a hand on Emma's shoulder. "Perhaps you should get some fresh air."

Checking with Mrs. Stolz, Emma discovered that there were still no messages. She would send another. This one to the children, asking them to pray for Mina. Sara would take on the assignment, she knew. Maybe even stubborn Matt. And little Holly's prayers would be sure to go straight to the heart of God. Thinking of the children brought a spasm of pain that was almost physical in its intensity, and she wondered if it were possible to die of a broken heart. But this was no time for selfish speculation. Mina's life was at stake.

Wandering back out to the garden bench, Emma sank down, her thoughts whirling. What did Mina's story mean? How had Tabo gotten Lila's wedding ring? Had Lila taken it off before she'd run away with Skip and left it lying where Tabo could find it and keep it for herself? If so, maybe that's why she had worked poison on Mina—so that Mina wouldn't betray her ugly secret.

A horrifying idea took root. If Tabo could do something like this to Mina, what might she do to the rest of them? To the children? To Josh? The very idea of losing them—even if they really weren't hers to lose—was torture.

Thirty-three

*E*mma!" She looked up to see Josh striding across the grounds toward her.

She stood and waved, every fiber in her wanting to run to meet him and fall into his arms. But she resisted the wild impulse, forcing a casual tone that would not betray her rioting emotions. This man was her *boss*, not her boyfriend, after all! "Hello, Josh. It's good to see you. How is . . . everything?"

"All is quiet at home. Angeline is a wonder—helping out with the meals, pitching in with the kids. What about you?"

Emma really didn't need this rave review of her friend right now. Not only that, but it tightened the screws on her own guilt. "Sorry I had to leave you in the lurch," she murmured. "But I was just so worried about Mina."

He frowned. "How is she? I got your message last night— too late to radio back. So I decided to come see for myself."

At his look of genuine concern, she launched into her story. "I have some startling news, Josh. But I didn't want to leave a message on the radio for fear Tabo might hear it."

"Tabo? What's she got to do with it?"

"She's the one who made Mina sick."

"What?"

"It's a long story." She sketched the details, observing his reaction carefully.

"Hmm. I had heard that she's the daughter of a spirit man and claims to have some powers, but I've never seen anything out of the ordinary."

"Until now."

His frown deepened. "We don't know that Tabo is responsible."

The man was so stubborn! "Why would Mina make this up? I had to pry it out of her, and when I did, she was scared to death—afraid that Tabo would hurt her mother or you and the children. She said something about the Osabe, too, but it didn't make sense. I think Tabo is in cahoots with them—and I think it has something to do with Makiba's death. I was worried about the children, and about you and Angeline, too, of course."

"Are you suggesting I dismiss Tabo? She's been a trusted employee for years."

"Well," Emma fought back feelings of frustration. "It's really none of my business. Maybe you should just talk to Mina when she wakes up." She felt like storming off, but there was nowhere else to go.

"You look beat." Was there a note of tenderness in his voice—or was it pity? "Let's go find something to eat. I know of a good Thai restaurant in town. How about it?"

"I guess so." She studied his expression. She didn't need his pity.

Emma had to admit it felt good to sit next to Josh in the old Jeep. Familiar and . . . right.

"The children miss you," Josh began when they were seated in the near-empty restaurant and he had placed their order.

"Really?" Was there too much hope in her voice? "I miss them, too."

"But they're glad you're taking care of Mina. They're quite fond of her." He narrowed his gaze in speculation, and Emma couldn't keep quiet.

"Josh, I wonder if you ever think of your workers as real people. People with feelings. Sometimes I think you consider them more like slaves!"

"That's not true!" He threw down his napkin, dark eyes flashing.

She kept her voice carefully lowered. "Well, my grandmother always says that actions speak louder than words."

Josh winced, looking subdued, and suddenly Emma felt bad. Who was she to judge him? He had, after all, given the indigenous good jobs and paid decent wages. "Sorry, Josh. I guess I'm a little stressed right now."

"It's all right, Emma. What you said just struck a nerve. I reckon I do forget they have feelings, though I wouldn't say it has anything to do with racial prejudice. Take Makiba—" He choked a little. "He was plenty sharp. I learned a lot from him . . . but I don't think I ever told him so. Now it's too late."

Emma blinked back tears. *But it's not too late for Mina*, she thought. She almost wished she were not seeing this side of Josh. It was too easy to love a man like that, and she was already in, head over heels.

The waiter set down a couple of dishes and a bowl of rice, and she watched numbly as Josh served careful portions and then handed the plate to her.

"Thanks," she said, waiting for him to serve himself.

To her surprise, he bowed his head and asked a short blessing. "I'm trying to get back into the habit," he confessed as he took a bite. "Angeline has been encouraging me. Says it's good for the children." He gave a wry smile that tugged at Emma's heartstrings. " Guess I haven't been much of a dad these past few years. You know, now that I think of it, I haven't treated my own children all that much differently from my employees. I haven't thought much about *their* feelings, either."

Emma nodded solemnly, feeling torn. Angeline again. Angeline, encouraging him to pray. Angeline, influencing him to be a better father. "I was way out of line with that slave business, Josh," Emma said, trying to shut out the notion. "Please forgive me. I know your life was turned upside down when Lila left."

He shrugged. "Maybe, but it's time to move on. Angeline agrees. She's been a real shot in the arm, Emma. I'm sure glad you asked her to come."

"Yeah." Emma sighed in defeat. "Angeline was a great encouragement to me coming over on the ship. Pulled me right up by the bootstraps."

"Hey, I thought you were hungry, Emma. You've hardly touched anything. Don't you like the food?"

She forced down a bite and smiled. "It's . . . delicious." To prove it, she took another. They ate in silence for a while, Emma feeling like her heart was in her throat. She washed down the sticky rice with sips of tea, longing for this meal to end.

"Ian wanted to come over today to check on you, but I told him I wanted to come."

Emma looked up with interest. Was there some hidden message she was supposed to pick up? "How are Ian and Mary?"

"Mary has been asking around about poison. But nobody's talking. Mina's mother has been praying night and day."

"Mina's mother? Is she a Christian?"

Josh nodded. "Along with most of the people in the village. That's what Mary has been up to for the past two decades. Just another reason for the Osabe to hate them. Come to think of it, that may be why they've had it in for me all these years. My mother was a strong Christian woman—always reaching out to the villagers. She took Tabo on, you know."

"Tabo. What are you going to do about her, Josh?"

"For starters, I'm going to take your advice and talk to Mina. It's not that I don't believe you, Emma, but this is a serious accusation."

She shrugged. "I understand. Maybe she'll feel up to seeing you this afternoon."

"Ian said—" Josh paused as if weighing his words—"that the only way to beat this kind of poison is through prayer."

"I've been praying with her, Josh."

"Right. But there's more. Ian says evil spirits are very strong and that we shouldn't take these things lightly. If Tabo has put a spell on Mina, she is under the influence of an evil spirit. But the Bible teaches that the Holy Spirit is greater than evil spirits, and that it's possible to cast them out."

"You mean like . . . an exorcism?"

"Something like that, I suppose." He frowned, his expression dead serious. "I don't think it's anything a weak Christian should try." He ducked his head in embarrassment. "I'm no prime example of a Christian—although that's going to change.

But I'm willing to pray for her, if you are."

Emma felt a warm rush of gratitude. "I'd do anything to help poor Mina."

When they reached the hospital, Mina was just waking up. She seemed surprised to see Josh standing over her bed.

"Don't worry," said Josh in a gentle voice. "I just came to see how you're feeling."

"Mina," Emma stepped nearer the bed. "Mr. Daniels knows about Tabo, and he wants to help you. You must tell him everything so he can make things better."

The girl moaned and covered her face with her hands, trembling all over.

"This is what happened last time," Emma told Josh. "It was almost as if she were having a seizure."

Josh stared down at the dark-skinned girl, contemplating. "I think we should ask God what to do, Emma."

She nodded and bowed her head, feeling the bed shaking violently.

Josh took a deep breath and began to pray. "Dear God, this young woman is your child. She believes in you. She doesn't deserve what's happening to her, and we're asking you to hear our prayer."

Emma dared to peek through slitted eyes. Josh was looking down at Mina with deep compassion as he continued. "We aren't strong enough to fight this evil, God. Only you can do that. Please, God, we ask that Mina be freed from whatever curse is poisoning her mind and her body. We pray this in Jesus' name."

Feeling another presence in the room, Emma glanced over to see Dr. Moller step up. "In Jesus' name," she echoed.

"In Jesus' name," Emma added.

"In Jesus' name. Amen."

They stepped back and watched. The dark lashes flickered ever so slightly. Then Mina opened her eyes, and for the first time in days, Emma saw the soft glow of rationality returning.

"How are you feeling?" Emma was almost afraid to ask.

Mina swallowed and nodded. "Better," she whispered.

"Let's see about that." Dr. Moller adjusted the blood pressure cuff around Mina's arm and listened through the stethoscope. When she looked up, she was smiling. "I think Mina will soon be ready to leave."

"Today?" Emma was hopeful.

"No. In a day or two. You forget that she has been very ill. We watch and see what God has done."

Dr. Moller left the room, cautioning them not to stay long, and Josh moved nearer the bed. "Mina, this may be hard for you, but I need to know the truth about Tabo."

She sighed, her forehead creasing as if trying to recall something unpleasant. And then she began to speak, her story confirming Emma's report.

"Do you know where Tabo got the ring?" he asked.

Mina nodded, then pressed her lips together. "It is very hard to say, Mr. Daniels."

"Don't be afraid, Mina. Whatever it is, I need to know. I only want the truth."

"When I see ring, I say, 'Tabo, that Mrs. Daniels' ring. How you get it?' Tabo say no. But I know that ring. I know it belong to Mrs. Daniels. I say, 'Tabo, I tell Mr. Daniels—' " Mina's eyes clouded over, and Emma feared a setback. She breathed a silent prayer. "Tabo scream at me. She say . . . Mrs. Daniels . . . dead."

Mina continued, tears rolling down her cheeks. "Tabo say if I tell, she see that all of you end up same way as Mrs. Daniels. She say . . . she kill me and my family. She say she work poison on me already and that why . . . Makiba die." Her voice rose to a wail.

"That's not true! It couldn't be!" exploded Josh. "Tabo lied! Poison had nothing to do with Makiba's death. She just wanted to frighten you! Tabo has gone way too far, and I've got to get to the bottom of this!" He gulped in a breath. "Did she tell you how Mrs. Daniels died—if it's really true?"

"I was scared. Tabo yell and speak village talk, and she hit me and hit me. When I wake up, I here with Miss Davis."

"It's not your fault, Mina." Trancelike, Josh spoke comfortingly, patting the girl's hand. "You were right to tell me the truth. I'll make sure Tabo doesn't hurt anyone again." He turned away, and Emma could see the awful suffering in his face.

"That's right, Mina," said Emma, patting her hand. "Mr. Daniels will take care of everything."

"There's something else, Mr. Daniels. Tabo say Osabe going to get you—get the children." Her eyes were wide, the whites exposed. "They have some sort of plan. Tabo say I keep quiet . . . but I *not* keep quiet." She lay back against the pillow, limp, damp with perspiration.

Josh ran his hand through his hair, and it was all Emma could do not to go to him. "You were very brave to come forward like this. I'm sorry, too—that I've been so blind to so many things. But I'll take care of it now. You have my word."

He tore out of the room as if all the demons in hell were on his coattail.

♪   ♪   ♪   ♪

Josh knew he was driving too fast. At least it wasn't raining. He had to get home. And he had to get there as quickly as possible. He didn't trust Tabo—not for another minute. What might she do to his children? What might she be doing while he was on his way to them! For all he knew, he had been harboring his own wife's murderer!

Lila . . . dead? He was ashamed to think of the many times he had wished it. How often he had thought it would be easier to be able to tell the children she had died. That she hadn't really meant to abandon them. A wave of overwhelming emotion— guilt, loss, grief, anger—assaulted him, and he veered toward the shoulder, wrestling with the wheel. But he didn't slow down.

Skip too. How could it be? Josh had actually prepared himself for the day he would confront the two of them as they bounced back into his life to collect Holly and be on their merry way. He knew now why he'd always kept his distance from the poor child.

He had actually looked forward to that visit. It would have given him a chance to speak his mind, maybe punch Skip in the nose. Or maybe he would have forgiven them and wished them good riddance. Now he would never know.

When the blinding tears came, he pulled off the road and parked. He climbed out, then turned and jammed the side of the Jeep with his fist. By the time his fury was spent, his knuckles were bruised and bleeding.

He leaned his head back and took a deep breath. "Help me, God! I was trying to get on with my life. Now this! Why, God? Why? I didn't really want them to die! I'm sorry . . . I'm sorry."

He sat down next to the road and buried his head in his hands. A verse his mother had quoted came to him: "Cast all your cares on God, for He cares for you."

The words tumbled around in his mind for a while. Then, spotting a rock, he picked it up and hurled it into the side of the mountain. "Here, God! I'm casting it on you. Here it is—the whole mess!" He picked up another rock and sent it sizzling through the air after the first. "Please, take it. Take my whole life back into your hands." Again and again he threw the rocks. "No matter how hard I try, I can't do it on my own. Please, help me. Show me."

He sighed and opened his eyes. There were the mountains in front of him. Strong and secure. But even the mountains could be shaken. He had felt them tremble with earthquakes in these parts.

Only God was mightier than the mountains. God was unshakable. He could handle anything Josh could throw at Him.

He rose to his feet with a new strength and peace. One he had never known before. He'd get through this somehow. He knew it.

Thirty-four

*E*mma checked Mina out of the hospital after breakfast, only to learn that Josh had taken care of all expenses in advance. Lately her respect for him had taken giant leaps. Too bad. That would only make it harder to let him go when the time came. Still, she hadn't heard a word from him since he'd left here two days ago.

Finding a bench in the courtyard, they sat down to wait for Ian. With Mina soaking up the sunshine after her long siege of darkness, Emma let her thoughts wander. She was thankful for the girl's recovery, of course. Josh might never fully understand—despite signs of growing awareness—but Mina was so much more than an employee. She'd been a friend to all of them—especially Josh.

She dared to dwell on him again, just for a moment. He must consider *her* only an employee, too. The kind of woman one hired to balance his books or care for his children, not the kind a man would want to marry.

Emma looked down and smoothed the lap of her wrinkled dress; she hadn't had time to pack properly when they'd rushed off to the clinic that night. No, Emma was not the kind of girl a man like Josh would want for a wife. Not with someone like Angeline waiting in the wings. And if it were true that Lila was dead, then Josh was free to marry again. She leaned over, holding her head in her hands.

"Are you all right, Miss Davis?"

Emma straightened and flashed a reassuring smile. "Fine,

Mina. Just a little tired. And please call me Emma." She sighed. "Yes, it will be nice to get home."

Home. Once again, she had thought of Josh's place as home. Well, she'd better get over it. She was due for a change of address any time now.

"Yes . . . Emma," said Mina with a faint smile. "Home feel so far, far away."

"Emma! Mina!" They looked up to see Ian approaching.

He easily lifted the weak woman in his arms while Emma ran ahead to make a nest of pillows and blankets in the backseat of the Land Rover. Then she ran around to climb into the passenger's seat up front.

With Mina soon drifting off to sleep, there was time to question Ian about the fiasco with Tabo. "Can you tell me what's going on at the plantation?"

Ian nodded. "Aye, 'tis all quite incredible, really. In fact, that's why Josh went me to fetch you. He's all tied up with legal matters." Ian paused to adjust the air conditioning, and Emma waited expectantly. At least Josh had been thinking about her.

"Well, now, where shall I begin?" Ian went on. "When Josh arrived day before yesterday, he stopped by the police station for help, and as soon as they reached the plantation, they confronted Tabo. Naturally, she denied everything—until Josh identified the ring. Then Tabo confessed. Josh says she even seemed a bit penitent, though that could easily have been another of her tricks."

He gripped the wheel as they approached a particularly difficult stretch of road. "Apparently, when Skip and Lila took off three years ago, they were driving too fast past Kirando Point just as a truckload of Osabe workers were coming home from the mine. There was a collision, and Lila's vehicle went off the road, tumbling straight down the ravine."

Emma shuddered, feeling a twinge of the old fear. "How horrible!"

"Aye, 'twas a terrible thing indeed. Tabo said that the Osabes were afraid that if anyone found out, there might be a payback. So they went down into the ravine and, after stealing anything of value, buried the car in brush and foliage. Since the location can't be seen from the road, nobody knew."

"Is Josh sure . . . that the body was Lila's, I mean?"

Ian's profile was grim. "Aye. He took some police officers with him to face down the men who had participated in the cover-up, and when they realized the police were involved, they decided to cooperate. They led him down to the site of the accident, and he identified the vehicle . . . and the remains."

He drew his brows together in a frown. " 'Tis sad. Here Josh was thinking all this time that his wife had run away with his best friend. And now he'll never know for sure."

Emma was silent, thinking of little Holly. Of Josh's suspicions about the father. "But where did Tabo get the ring?"

"She learned of the accident from her brother, who's an Osabe. Since the Osabe have never treated her well after her failed marriage, she threatened to tell Josh unless they paid her off. They gave her the ring to shut her up."

"So she's known all this time."

"Aye, and Josh was none too pleased. Needless to say, he let her go, and the police took her into custody."

"Poor Josh."

"All in all, the lad seems to be holding up fairly well—with Angeline's help. The woman is a godsend, Emma. She's just jumped right in, helping out wherever she can. I must say I admire a woman with spunk."

Emma nodded stiffly. "She is one in a million, all right." Emma shifted her thoughts to more neutral territory. "Do the children know . . . about their mother?"

"Josh broke the sad news, and of course, they were upset. 'Tis a funny thing about children—they never seem to give up hope. I'm sure they thought their mum would come home one day."

She was silent again, thinking of three little lives that would never be the same. Four, if she counted her own.

"With Josh taking care of some business down in Lae today—death certificates, the shipping of the remains, and whatnot—the children are with Mary. We'll go there first to pick them up."

"Why didn't Angeline stay with them?"

"She went to Lae with Josh." Ian sounded despondent.

"Oh." What else was there to say?

"Yes, Angeline is a very special lady," said Ian wistfully.

And suddenly Emma knew—the man was smitten! Well, why wouldn't he be? Angeline was a beautiful, charming, and intelligent Christian woman. Why wouldn't Ian fall in love with her? After all, hadn't Josh?

"Do you know why she went along?"

Ian shrugged. "To keep Josh company, most likely. He needed someone at a time like this. 'Twas very thoughtful of her. She's like that, you know."

"Yes, I know." Emma turned and pretended to look out the window at the passing scenery. There had been a time when she'd thought Ian cared for *her*. At the time, she'd had no interest in his attentions—all she could think of was Josh. Now it seemed they'd both fallen for Angeline's charms. It wasn't fair!

Emma was instantly contrite. Angeline couldn't help being attractive. Emma was only jealous. If there were no men involved, Angeline would still be her dearest friend. Or would she? If everything moved to its logical conclusion, if Emma lost both Josh and Ian, wouldn't she be losing Angeline, too?

She checked the backseat. Mina was still sleeping peacefully. It was likely she wouldn't be seeing Mina much longer, either. Or the children. That thought struck her with such force that she almost bent double.

Ian looked over, concern sketched on his face. "Are you all right?"

She took a deep breath. "I guess so. It's just all so overwhelming. Where do we all go from here?"

Ian shrugged. "I don't know for sure, Emma. As for me, I'll be returning to Scotland next week."

"Oh, Ian. I didn't know. I'll miss you." She was genuinely grieved.

"Aye, and I'll miss you, Emma. 'Tis been a fine pleasure getting to know you. But we'll be meeting again."

Emma blushed. "I know you'll be coming back to visit Mary . . . but I probably won't be here."

He glanced over with a fierce scowl. "And why is that?"

"Oh, I expect Josh won't be needing my help much longer."

"What makes you think so?"

"Well, now that he knows Lila is dead, I'm sure he'll re-marry, and he won't need me with the children."

Ian nodded sadly. "I s'pose it's quite likely. I must admit, I've wondered if he might be interested in Angeline. 'Tis a fine woman, that one."

Emma leaned her head back and closed her eyes. If only they could talk about something else, *anything*.

The children were beside themselves with joy when Emma and Ian pulled up at Mary's place, although Matt extended only a restrained handshake. "We missed you so much!" Sara was holding Emma's hand in a death grip, and Holly wrapped her arms around Emma's waist as if she were afraid to let go. "Yes, Emma, I thought you were never coming home!"

"Of course I was. But Mina needed me, too. You know she has been very sick."

"We know," Sara said solemnly. "Daddy told us to pray for her. And we did—every night."

"Well, God heard your prayers. She's much better, though she still needs rest and lots of care. So maybe we should let Ian take us home now."

"Here you are, dear." Mary bustled out of the kitchen with a box in her hand. "Thought you might welcome a little lunch, since you'll be shorthanded when you get back."

"Thanks, Mary. And will you tell Mina's mama that she's all right? Tell her, too, to keep praying."

"Yes, indeed. This kind of thing takes time, and a Power greater than our own. We must be sure to keep Mina covered. Now, girls," Mary clucked to the children, "see that Emma gets some rest. She's looking a little peaked herself."

After Mina was settled on the couch back at the plantation, Ian motioned to Emma to follow him to the front porch.

"Didn't want to speak in front of the children, but Mary warns me that there have been rumblings among the Osabe. They're angry that some of their men are being detained at the police station. They think it's Josh's fault."

"How unfair!"

"Fairness has nothing to do with it, lass. The old bitterness runs deep."

"I know. Josh has told me about the land dispute."

"Aye, and you must understand that the indigenous people dwell on something like that, blowing it all out of proportion to the truth."

"I'd think they'd be feeling a little ashamed for the way that they've hidden Lila and Skip's deaths all this time."

"Oh, they have their own way of looking at things."

Emma felt a tingle of alarm. "So what does this mean? Do you think we're in any real danger here?"

"No-o, but I must admit I'd feel better if Josh were back. I'll stay on awhile, if you like."

"Oh, I couldn't let you do that, Ian. These are your last few days with your sister. We have the radio, and we can call if there's a problem."

"Just make sure you do then. Night or day. I'll keep our receiver on."

With an eerie sense of abandonment, Emma watched the Land Rover pull out. But she busied herself the rest of the afternoon with odd chores that Angeline had left undone. Apparently, her friend didn't do laundry, for one.

After washing out some clothes, Emma hung them on the line to dry. As Emma pinned the last piece to the line, she noticed how quiet it seemed. Not even the usual insect chorus disturbed the stillness. The air felt different. Heavier. More ominous. She looked around but didn't see any of the workers. Maybe Josh had given them the day off.

Having reminded the children at lunch about their dad's rule, Emma suddenly realized that she had broken it herself. She picked up the laundry basket and hurried back inside, casting a furtive glance over her shoulder.

She wondered when Josh and Angeline would be coming

home. Ian hadn't mentioned it, but for some reason, she'd thought it would be this evening. Even though she was eager to see Josh, she wasn't looking forward to seeing the two of them together.

The afternoon dragged on. Everyone seemed bored and cranky. But by tea time, Mina was feeling well enough to sit in a kitchen chair and peel carrots. Emma and Sara prepared dinner while Matt entertained Holly.

"Are Father and Angeline going to be home in time for tea?" asked Sara as she set the carrots on the stove.

"I'm not sure. Ian didn't say. Did your dad mention anything to you?"

Sara pushed up her glasses and scooted the pot to the back of the stove. "No, just that he had to take care of—" Sara frowned up at Emma—"the remains."

"Oh," said Emma with a sigh. "How does that make you feel, Sara?"

Sara's face pinched up as if she were trying to think of the right answer to a quiz. "Well, I know it's true that Mummy is dead, and even though that makes me feel sad, it's like in my dream. I feel like I knew it already. Do you know what I mean, Emma?"

"Remember what I told you about my parents' death?" Emma put her arm around the slim shoulders. "It was very much the same."

Sara looked up with a sunny smile. "I knew you'd understand, Emma. You always do." She turned to give Emma an impulsive hug. "I just hope you never leave us again."

They waited until after seven before finally sitting down to tea. Emma said a blessing, and they ate with little conversation. After the dishes were cleaned up, Emma helped Holly into her pajamas.

"Dear God," said Holly as she finished her bedtime prayers,

"please don't let Emma go away ever again. Amen!" She opened her eyes and looked at Emma, as if expecting a confirmation.

"I don't want to go away, pudd'n," Emma said. "But sometimes things happen that we can't help." Holly's face collapsed into a frown. "But, Holly," whispered Emma, putting her nose close to the little girl's button nose, "it would take a herd of wild, purple elephants to drag me away from you right now." Holly burst into giggles and Emma kissed her good night.

Emma was about to sit down to write an overdue letter to her sister, when she remembered the laundry still out on the line. Rule or no rule, she couldn't leave it there overnight, and it seemed senseless to disturb Matt or Sara.

Emma slipped out the back door, felt her way to the line, and began unpinning the items. Out here, where the dim light from the house didn't penetrate, it was pitch black.

A rustling noise in the bushes almost stopped her heart, and she froze. "Who's there?" she called. No answer. Again, the rustling. "Is anyone there?"

Feeling a presence behind her, Emma dropped the basket. Whirling, she threw up her arms to defend herself. A hand gripped her arm.

"Emma?"

"Matt?"

"I saw you come out, but I wasn't sure where you went. So I came looking for you."

The breath she had been holding left her lungs in a whoosh. "Matt! You scared me half to death!"

"You shouldn't be out here, Emma. You broke Dad's rule."

"You broke it, too, young man. But let's don't stand here arguing. Let's get back to the house." She did not breathe easy until they were safe inside.

"I'll make sure everything else is locked up," said Matt with a stern expression that reminded her of his father.

"Thanks, Matt. I feel better knowing we have a man around to help out."

Matt set off on his mission without cracking a smile, and Emma turned off the light in the kitchen, peering into the back yard. Nothing. It was probably her imagination. Some animal, most likely.

"Emma?" said Sara, coming up beside her. "Why are you standing in here in the dark?"

"Just looking outside, honey."

"Emma?" The soft childish voice came to her in the darkness. "Do you think Father loves Angeline?"

Emma was thankful that the child couldn't see her startled expression. "I don't know, Sara. What do you think?"

"I think she's beautiful and nice, but she isn't always comfortable."

"Comfortable?"

"Yes. She talks all the time and, well, she's just not very comfortable. Not like you."

Emma chuckled. "Well, thanks, Sara. I'm glad I'm . . . comfortable. You are, too."

There was a small sigh. "We're just not like her, are we, Emma?"

Emma decided to turn off the generator early. Josh was accustomed to finding his way around in the dark. And Angeline, of course, would be fine—with Josh to take care of her.

Good nights were exchanged and they all headed for bed. Emma could hear Mina sleeping soundly in her room, but she could not make her mind stop spinning. First there was Josh's return to worry about. Then what would she do if he and Angeline had progressed in their relationship? It wouldn't be realistic for her to stay on with the children if Josh married Angeline. She could not for the life of her imagine watching Josh love someone else.

Thirty-five

$\mathcal{E}$mma awoke early after a sleepless night. She peered at herself in the bathroom mirror—dark circles under her eyes, skin too pale. Even her hair looked limp and lifeless. But what did it matter?

After a quick shower, she went out on the back porch to turn on the generator. From there, she thought she spotted someone moving through the shadows, but she couldn't be sure. Maybe it was her imgination. Today she would stick rigidly by Josh's rule. Everyone inside. And hopefully, he would be home before long.

In the kitchen, Emma put together a nice breakfast—hotcakes, canned ham, and fresh fruit—noting that they'd have to make a trip for more supplies soon. Tabo had always done the marketing. Well, they would just have to make do—or do without, at least until Josh was back. She reined her thoughts from further speculation. One day at a time. . . .

Mina insisted on cleaning up the kitchen while Emma supervised the children's lessons. Perhaps it was best to maintain a sense of order.

By mid-morning, the children were hard at work on their studies, and Emma had almost forgotten her troubles. Tabo's betrayal. Her terrible secret. Mina's near-fatal "poisoning." Angeline . . . Josh.

Lunch was a peanut butter sandwich prepared by Mina. Not as tasty as Tabo's, but at least they could eat it in peace.

"When's Father coming home?" Sara wanted to know.

"Maybe today." Emma avoided the child's gaze lest she give away the fact that she had no idea what Josh was up to. Maybe he had decided to deliver Lila's remains to Australia in person. But then wouldn't he have taken the children with him? Knowing he was with Angeline didn't help any. For all she knew, the two of them had eloped!

After lunch, with the girls absorbed in a video, Matt was bored. "I want to go outside."

"You know the rule, Matt."

"The rule just says we can't go out alone. You could go with me."

She grinned at him. "I thought we'd learned our lesson."

"Well, I don't see why we have the dumb rule. Nothing's going to happen."

"Probably not, Matt." She made eye contact. "But what if something did? Ian says there's trouble with the Osabe, and you know more about operating the radio than anyone. That's not the only reason I want you to be careful, though. I don't know what I'd do without you around here."

He brightened, straightening his shoulders. "Okay, Emma. You can count on me."

Around two, the sky darkened, mirroring Emma's growing unrest. Where was Josh anyway? What was going on? Why hadn't he radioed? They'd kept the shortwave radio on constantly, using the generator by day and hooking it up to a battery at night. But not a word.

Soon the rain started, driving against the metal roof with the force of a waterfall and cascading over the downspouts. Jagged lightning forked across the sky, and Emma knew that if Josh and Angeline were on their way, the bad weather would further hinder their return. The rain brought a small measure of comfort: If the Osabe were making any plans for a payback, this would surely put a damper on them. Emma wondered how long the police would keep the men in jail—or if there was really any evidence of foul play in Lila's death.

Afraid that Mina would overdo, Emma insisted she rest. And even though it was still early, she began making preparations for tea. It was cozy and pleasant in the kitchen, with the storm raging outside.

Sara wandered in and sat down on the kitchen stool. "Could we bake a cake? If Father and Angeline come home in time for tea, we'd have something special for dessert."

"Do you know how? I'm afraid it's been much too long since I tried."

"No, but I know where there are some recipe books. Tabo never used them. I think they may have belonged to Mummy."

Hearing the poignant note in the little girl's voice, Emma was quick to lighten the mood. "I think it would be great fun to bake a cake from scratch. Why don't you go find the cookbooks."

Sara bestowed one of her rare smiles. "Be right back." She returned, lugging a stack of books.

In the pantry, Emma found powdered eggs and baking powder and all the other ingredients for a cake, and together they stirred up a large bowl of batter, creating a mess that would have driven Tabo to distraction. That, in itself, brought some satisfaction. After pouring the batter into three round layer pans, Emma slipped it into the oven.

"Emma!" The piercing cry caught her off guard, and she leaped up and dashed into the living room, wishing she had grabbed a kitchen knife on her way.

"Matt won't let me watch my Barney video!"

Emma sighed and shook her head. "Is that all? Please don't scream like that again, honey." She eyed Matt, guilt written all over his face. "Matt?"

"She already watched one Barney video. I want to see something else."

"That seems fair. Holly, why don't you come and help us do some baking? Sara and I just put a cake in the oven. And now we're getting ready to make some cookies . . . biscuits to you."

Holly dropped the remote and skipped into the kitchen.

"Can I help, too?" asked Matt somewhat sheepishly.

"Of course, but you'll have to wash your hands first."

With the children busy mixing and rolling out dough, the minutes flew, and Emma lost track of the time until Mina came in from her nap, rubbing her eyes. She looked around the kitchen in disbelief. "Tabo—she *kill* you if she see this!"

There was a moment of silence, with only the sound of the rain drumming on the rooftop, as they considered what Mina had just said. Then, the tension broken, Emma and Matt burst into laughter, with the girls joining in the hilarity.

It didn't seem likely that Josh and Angeline would make it by tea time—if ever. With a mental shake, Emma put a halt to her negative thinking. A little voice within said, *Pray for them. Don't judge.*

They sat down to eat, the children more talkative than usual. What if this were her life? What if she were the only adult caregiver they had left? What if Josh were not in the picture? Would she want a ready-made family? She didn't have to give it a second thought.

As she was serving the cake, the lights went off, and the house was plunged into pitch darkness. Holly let out one of her blood-curdling screams.

"It's all right, Holly," said Emma soothingly, keeping her voice calm. "It's probably the generator. Just the same, I want everyone to stay right here until we know what's going on." Emma's heart was racing. She shot up a silent prayer for wisdom.

"I can go check the generator." Matt's voice didn't match his brave words.

"Thanks, Matt." Emma sent him a grateful smile though he couldn't see it in the dark. "But let's just wait a minute and see if we hear anything." The rain had let up in the last few minutes, and now there was an ominous silence. "I'm sure it's nothing, but you know what Ian said."

Emma could hear Mina's harsh breathing, and she knew the girl was frightened. "Mina, can you find your way to my room and bring back my lantern? But don't light it yet. And while you're in there, please lock the windows, pull down the shades, and bolt the doors. In fact, why don't you do the same in the schoolroom and Mr. Daniels's room."

"Yes," whispered Mina.

"Matt and Sara, check your rooms. I'll keep Holly with me, and we'll lock all the other doors. Now, don't be afraid. Let's just pretend we're playing a game, okay? When we're through, we'll meet back in the hallway."

Gamely they set out, Holly's tight hold on Emma's hand almost cutting off the circulation. They took care of the living room, then made their way to the kitchen, ducking low as they passed the windows. This might all be unnecessary precaution, but she was in charge now, and the children were her responsibility.

Warning Holly to stay down, Emma peeked through the window above the sink. Silent shadows moved across the yard. Her heart was pounding now. She grabbed Holly up, streaked across the kitchen, and slammed the bolt on the door shut.

Returning to the hallway, she found Sara and Matt waiting. Mina was on her way, judging from the quiet thuds of bare feet. They lit the lamp, keeping it turned low, then huddled together.

"What's going on, Emma?" asked Matt suspiciously as the soft glow of the lamplight illuminated their faces, casting weird shadows on the wall behind.

"Let's sit down here for a minute." Emma was doing her best to control the quaver in her voice. "It may be nothing. But I thought I saw someone in the woods at the back of the house."

Mina gasped.

"Who is it?" Sara's eyes were huge behind her glasses. "What do they want?"

"Probably nothing, but we need to be careful. Remember, it's like we're playing a game. But just the same, let's pray." Emma felt the children pressing closer, their little circle growing tighter. "Dear God," she began, "we don't know who's out there, but you do. We're a little scared right now, so please protect us. I know you're holding us in your hands. Please keep us safe. . . ." Emma paused, not sure what to say next.

"Please send angels, dear God," Sara added in a small voice. "Mary says that you send angels to protect your children. Please send angels to watch over us."

"Yes, Lord," Emma echoed, "please send angels." She turned to Matt. "Can you slip into the schoolroom, Matt, and hook up the radio to the battery? We need to reach Mary and Ian if possible."

"Sure, Emma." Matt, rising to his manly assignment, sounded a little braver now.

"But, Matt, you'll have to do it in the dark," she warned. "We can't let any light shine through the windows. And if you get Ian, you'll need to talk quietly and quickly. Can you do that?"

Matt nodded grimly, then crawled down the hallway toward the schoolroom.

"I'm going to take another look. Mina, you stay here with the girls. Don't move."

"Yes, Emma." Mina's eyes were round with fright, but she held to both girls' hands and pulled them closer to her.

When Emma reached her vantage point, the sight that met her eyes brought a gasp. Off in the distance, she could see flaming lights moving in and out through the trees and brush at the back of the house. The lights seemed to be rising and falling rhythmically. Torches! Osabe torchbearers advancing toward the plantation? The thought of what they might be planning was chilling.

If the Osabe intended to burn the plantation, there was one hopeful note. Fortunately, the trees and vegetation were still soggy from the rain. Still, that wouldn't protect the buildings for long.

Emma crouched down and hurried back to the hallway, praying as she went. Matt wasn't back yet, and she decided to check on him.

When she reached the schoolroom, she could hear Matt's urgent whisper. "Mr. McDowell? Come in, McDowells. Come in, come in. This is Daniels. We have an emergency. Come in, please, somebody—" His voice faded with his hope.

"You're doing fine, Matt," Emma encouraged through the darkness. "Don't give up." She waited for several more minutes, listening to Matt plead for Ian and Mary to answer.

Finally, the radio crackled to life, and the familiar Scottish burr came on the air. "This is Ian. That you, Matt?"

"Yes, sir." Emma could feel the boy's relief. "We have an emergency here. The generator is out, and we think someone may be outside—maybe a lot of 'em."

For a long, heart-stopping moment, the radio sputtered, only the sound of static on the line.

"Matt, let me try." She reached for the microphone. "Ian? Emma. Can you hear me? Come in, come in."

"What's . . . lass?"

She'd have to talk fast. With the radio breaking up, she might not get her message through. "I see a line of people advancing toward the house, and they're carrying torches. And I don't mean flashlights—I mean fire! I'm worried. Could you make it over here, and bring some of the village men with you?"

"Matt, go and get your dad's shotgun. Emma, we're on our way, but the roads'll be bad. It'll take more than an hour. Just hang on!"

Emma's spirits sank. The radio fizzled and died, leaving them both stunned.

"Do you think he heard us?" Matt's voice was a hoarse whisper.

"We can only hope and pray." Emma pondered, trying to sort it all out.

"Should I get Dad's gun?"

"Maybe we ought to get it, Matt—just to be on the safe side. Can you find it in the dark?"

"Sure, Emma. Follow me." Matt's confidence was back.

Emma stuck close behind the boy as he led the way to Josh's room, then rummaged in the closet. It was too dark to see when he finally emerged.

"I got it!" There was a note of triumph in his voice. "It's probably loaded, too. Dad uses it to scare away the birds in the garden."

Emma cringed. "Just be very careful, Matt. Keep it pointed up."

"Where were you for so long, Emma? We were worried about you." Sara's voice was plaintive when they returned to the hallway.

Emma gave them a report on the call to Ian, assuring them that he would surely be arriving any time now with armed warriors from Mina's village. What she *didn't* tell them was that she had not the faintest idea whether or not he'd heard most of her message. Nor did she tell them about the men outside, slowly creeping toward the house. If Ian didn't make it in time, they'd find out soon enough. . . .

"Mina, why don't you get some pillows and blankets, and we'll try to make ourselves more comfortable."

"Why do we have to stay in here, Emma?" Holly whined. "It's too tight, and I'm tired."

Emma wasn't sure how to answer her. "I think this is where God wants us to be right now, honey. But it's cozy, and we're all together."

"Yeah, Holly," Matt put in, going along with the game. "It's like a camp-out—except it's inside." Emma noticed that he was carefully keeping the shotgun out of sight. *Bless you, Matt! Your father would be proud.*

When Mina returned with the bedding, Emma helped her fluff the pillows and spread blankets. "Now it's even cozier. Why don't we make it a real party?" Emma added, thinking fast. If the girls heard sounds from outside, they might panic. "How about those biscuits we baked?"

A quiet cheer went up, and Emma welcomed the chance to see what was happening outside. This time when she looked, she counted twenty bare-chested men, their oiled skin gleaming in the torchlight. There could be that many more still making their way through the brush. "Oh, Josh, where are you?" she whispered aloud. "Please help us, God."

She felt along the counter until she found the plate of cookies. Then crouching below the windows, she hurried back to the hall where the others were waiting. "Here you are, Holly," she whispered. "Your Barney biscuit." Sure enough, one cookie was shaped like a fat little dinosaur.

Emma glanced at her watch, trying to read the numerals in the dim light. It seemed that the hands—like the generator—had stopped. Only the sound of the munching of cookies could be heard now that the rain had stopped altogether. That—and the sounds of an eerie silence outside the walls of this house.

Anything might break loose any moment. She couldn't wait for Ian. Besides, there was no guarantee that he'd even gotten her message. "Want to come with me, Matt?" she asked, nodding toward the gun propped in the shadows against the wall.

Matt, bringing the shotgun, followed her as she crept into the kitchen. This time there was no need to peer through the window. She could plainly see the light from the torches glowing in the yard and all around the house.

"Dear God!" she gasped, feeling Matt's body pressed close to hers. No doubt he was as frightened as she. "Pray, Matt," she whispered. "Only God can help us now."

Thirty-six

The tribesmen had moved past the line of trees and now ringed the house, still standing at a distance, their features fiercely distorted. Even from here, Emma could see their face paint—like death masks—causing them to resemble aliens. They were clearly not here on a peaceful mission.

"Wow!" Matt let out a low whistle. "I think we're in big trouble." He grasped the shotgun in both hands.

A distant drumming broke the silence, and one of the men took a step toward the house, signaling the others to fall in behind him. They halted at the sound of a vehicle turning into the lane.

"It's your dad," she told Matt, and he popped up to look for himself. Josh and Angeline leaped out of the Jeep and raced to the house.

"What's going on here?" Josh demanded the minute he was inside. His eyes traveled over Emma and Matt, then roamed the room. "Is everyone all right?"

"We're fine. But are we glad to see *you*!" Emma said. "Mina and the girls are in the hall."

"Thanks, son, but we won't be needing that." Josh grabbed the shotgun from Matt and leaned it against the wall. "The Os-abes are on the warpath tonight, and seeing that gun might set them off. Besides, I have something to say to them. Tell Mina and the girls to stay put." He set his jaw, then put his hand on the doorknob. "I'll be back."

"Josh, please don't go back out there—not without some

help or at least the gun!'' Emma was horrified. ''We tried to get a message through to Ian, and he should be here any minute.'' She *hoped*.

''Even more reason for me to get out there now.'' Josh's expression, in the glow of the torchlight, was baffling. He was gazing at her with tenderness. Or was it Angeline, standing behind her, he was communicating with so wordlessly? ''If I don't try to talk some sense into them, it could get very ugly.''

''But what could you say that would make any difference?'' She wanted to grab him, beg him not to leave them. The children needed him . . . Angeline needed him. Instead, she stared at his face, taking in every detail, memorizing it in case she never saw it again.

''All I know is I have to try.'' And with that, he was out the door.

They could hear him shouting in Pidgen from the porch, but Emma could only make out a few words. She glanced at Angeline. Poor thing—her face was as pale as a ghost. She must be suffering. Emma reached over and hugged her, thinking how strange it felt to be the strong one.

''Oh, Emma, Josh is so brave.'' Angeline was trembling. ''What do you think will happen?''

They could hear Josh yelling again, apparently calling the tribal leaders over to hear what he had to say. But he was outnumbered. And unarmed—except . . . Something Ian had told Josh came to her now. *The only way to beat this kind of poison is through prayer*. Well, she had been praying almost constantly since this whole mess started. But there was something else . . . What was it?

''Oh, Emma, he's such a good man,'' Angeline was persistent, Emma would have to say that for her. ''If you only knew—''

Still trying to hear what was happening outside, Emma put her finger to her lips. She didn't need a reminder of Josh's fine qualities. She knew only too well—now that it was too late.

''Oh, Em, how could you be so blind?''

''Angeline,'' said Emma in exasperation, ''this is no time for games. We need—''

''Josh is in love with you!''

Josh . . . loved *her*? Emma wasn't sure she had heard correctly.

She peered out the window again. Josh was still standing on the porch, calling once again to the torchbearers who were edging ever nearer the porch. Would they attack? And if—as Angeline claimed—he truly *did* love her, would he live to tell her?

"You were all he talked about on the trip back, Em. Of course, I helped to pry it out of him."

A rush of joy flooded her. "I'm going out there, Angeline. He needs me." Giving her friend a quick hug, Emma opened the door, slipped out onto the porch, and stood behind Josh.

"What're *you* doing out here?" Josh barked hoarsely, speaking to her out of the side of his mouth.

"I thought it might help if you had some light of your own." She handed him a lantern.

"Thanks," he mumbled. "Now get back inside."

But Emma didn't budge. She desperately wanted to ask Josh if what Angeline had said was true. But the timing was all wrong. She felt the tears sliding down her cheeks as she watched the men come closer, their evil faces leering out of the darkness.

"Josh," she whispered, "we're praying for you." She crept back into the house and rejoined the little group huddled in the hallway. They could hear Josh again, speaking to the men in Pidgen, not in anger, but earnestly and sincerely.

As he spoke, Mina translated for Emma and Angeline. " 'Come, hear me,' he say. 'I not be good neighbor to you. I not be good friend. But you not be my neighbor, my friend. You not tell me about accident that killed my wife. For three year, I not know what happen. For three year, my children not know if their mama coming home. Now they know she never coming home. But you not tell me this sad news. Now you only want war and hate?'

" 'My father buy land you think belong to you. I want to give it back. I hoped you be my friends. I hoped you make peace. Maybe you want police to lock you up in calaboose. Maybe I talking to the moon.' " Mina giggled slightly at this.

When Josh finally ended his speech, there was a deadly quiet. Emma held her breath. After an interminable wait, the door swung open, and she saw Josh coming inside, his head low. Her heart sank. How could those people be so hardhearted?

A man called out from the gathering outside. Emma recognized enough Pidgen to know that he was calling for Josh. She moved quietly to the living room and peeked out the window as Josh resumed his position on the front porch. At that moment several older Osabe men dropped their bows and arrows and approached him. Those few might be unarmed, but there were at least twenty more with weapons poised!

Josh didn't flinch. "If you will let me," she heard him say, "I want to introduce you to my Friend. His name is Jesus."

"Yes, Lord, please protect him," Emma prayed.

It was all over in a flash. The head man threw down his shield and stepped forward to clasp Josh's forearm in a salute just as a screaming siren announced the arrival of the police, led by Ian in the Land Rover. "I got here as fast as I could, mon," said Ian, his brogue thick tonight.

But Josh waved the officers away. "You won't be needed. The matter has been settled by a higher Authority." He glanced toward heaven as if he couldn't quite believe what had just taken place.

For several minutes the men—Osabes and whites alike—milled about in the yard, laughing and talking congenially. Some of the braves hung back, then skulked into the underbrush and melted into the dense foliage.

The electricity was turned back on, and Emma began to shuttle the children to bed.

Angeline shooed her off. "I can take care of this." She took Holly and Sara by the hand and gave Emma a nudge toward the front porch. "I think there's a certain someone out there who wants to talk to you."

Emma smiled her thanks.

She slipped out to the porch and sat down in the darkness. One by one, the Osabes left, as well as Ian and most of the policemen. Only one remained on duty until daybreak to make sure there was no reccurrence of the incident.

Emma sat and watched as Josh walked up the steps, unaware

that she was sitting there in the darkness. "Nice night," she said as he reached the top step.

Josh turned and looked out at the sky where the yellow moon was peeking between some clouds. "Not bad, after all. Mind if I join you?"

"Not at all."

"Thanks for all your help tonight, Emma." He set his lantern down on the porch, its golden aura illuminating his face.

"Anytime." She smiled to herself.

"Anytime?" he repeated with a teasing note to his voice. He moved to the front of her chair, placing his hands on the arm rests, as if to trap her.

"Sure." She looked up at him, their faces only inches from each other.

"I've been meaning to tell you something, Miss Davis."

"And what would that be, *Mr. Daniels*?"

He reached down for her hand and pulled her to her feet. "That . . . I love you."

"You've been pretty busy lately. . . ." She wondered if he could feel her heart pounding.

"But I'm not busy now." Although he was smiling, there was a look of uncertainty in his eyes. "So how about it, Emma? What do you think?"

"I think I should tell you that I love you, too." She threw her arms around his neck, and when he returned the embrace she knew for certain she could remain in his arms forever.

"I don't know how you found me, Emma Davis, but I thank God that you did."

Suddenly Emma remembered the globe in the travel office, spinning around, just waiting for her finger to pick a spot. "Only God could have brought us together, Josh," said Emma. "And believe me, it was no easy task!"

Then Josh drew her face to his and their lips met in a long, lingering kiss. Never in her life had Emma been kissed so lovingly. As they both pulled away, she looked up at Josh with wonder, and he smiled warmly.

Epilogue

Six months later

Emma watched the waves rolling in gracefully, as if they too had all the time in the world. She curled her toes into the warm, white sand and studied the palm trees silhouetted against the sky. Remembering the travel poster at Linda's office back in Iowa, she laughed. Better be careful, or she'd be looking like the woman in the poster—magenta!

She leaned back and stretched. *Perfect*. Well almost perfect, anyway. If only the children could have come along. But then they were down under enjoying a holiday with Nana Daniels. Besides, you didn't usually take one's children on your honeymoon.

She glanced over at Josh, sleeping peacefully in the sun next to her, and smiled. It was probably time for him to have some sun protection, too. She gently rubbed some cool lotion on his back, and he mumbled his gratitude. As she massaged the cream into his skin, the diamond on her finger glinted brightly in the sunshine, and she smiled as she remembered Josh slipping it on her finger.

Grandma and Fran had been shocked when she told them of her marriage plans. Emma was sorry they couldn't come for the occasion but understood it was quite a trip. Josh had offered to take her and the children to Iowa someday, but she was in no hurry.

The Osabe had come to terms with Josh, once he had followed through on his promise to deed them back the land his father had purchased so many years ago. And now some of them were even beginning to attend church in Mary's village. Another miracle.

Ian had returned to Scotland, and Angeline had gone back to Canada with the understanding that she would visit him after the new year. Emma had a suspicion that that little travel package would turn out to be more than a visit. She recapped the lotion and leaned back on the towel.

"Everything all right?" asked Josh sleepily.

"Perfect."

"You sure are." Josh rolled over and looked into her eyes. "I've gotta be the luckiest bloke on the planet."

Emma laughed and used her best Aussie accent. "Then I reckon that'd make me the happiest sheila!"

Bethany House Publishers
Books by Melody Carlson

——————— ෪ ———————

THE ALLISON CHRONICLES

1. *On Hope's Wings*
2. *Cherished Wish*
3. *Autumn Secrets*

෪   ෪   ෪

Awakening Heart
Jessica